I0598125

Pride Publishing books by S. J. Coles

Blood and Bonds

HUNT IN THE NIGHT

S.J. COLES

Hunt in the Night
ISBN # 978-1-80250-742-3
©Copyright S.J. Coles 2024
Cover Art by Kelly Martin ©Copyright August 2024
Interior text design by Claire Siemaszkiewicz
Pride Publishing

HUNT IN THE NIGHT

Dedication

For all my fellow shadow-dwellers.

Chapter One

Mason knew it was over when Amelia got out of bed and started dressing in silence. Rain lashed the bedroom windows. Thunder rolled and cracked in the night beyond the half-drawn blinds. The storm had been a long time coming and was a blissful relief from the heatwave that had been choking the city of York for weeks. But all Mason could focus on was the stiffness in Amelia's movements as she buttoned her blouse.

She never stayed the night. By mutual agreement this — whatever *this* was — was just about what time they could snatch around their cases. But she usually stayed for a while after the sex...to talk. She liked to talk. Mason had come to like it, too.

But now she stared fixedly ahead as she dressed, and the silence was heavy between them.

"Everything okay?"

She sighed. "I think it's time."

He knew what was coming but, somehow, Mason just felt...blank. "Time for what?"

Amelia sat on the edge of the bed to pull her heels on. "Come on, Mason. We both know this has run its course."

Mason searched for the right reaction. "I thought we were having fun."

"We were. We did. But there's something missing, isn't there?"

He didn't meet her eye.

"Mason, if you can't be honest with me, at least be honest with yourself."

"Honest about what?"

"You need...more. I don't know what, but you're not getting it from me."

"That's not true."

"It is," she said with a frank look. "I'm okay with that. But I'm not okay with sex that isn't blowing both our minds. Life's too short."

He blinked. "You've never complained."

"It's not a complaint," she said and retrieved her earrings from the dressing table, "or a comment on your performance." The smile she gave herself in the mirror eased his wounded pride. "But I know you're not getting everything *you* want."

"I like you, Amelia. I thought you liked me."

"I do. And this has been good. But it's time to end it."

"Is this because of that email from HR? About relationships at work?"

"This isn't a relationship," she said, patting his leg. "We both agreed on that from the start. And, yes, technically, I am your boss—"

"Boss's boss," he said with the lopsided smile that usually brought an answering smile from her.

But her lips remained a flat line. "Do yourself a favor, Mason. Open yourself up. You don't limit yourself at work. Don't do it in your personal life."

"I wasn't aware I was."

She looked at him hard. "It's time for something new...for both of us. That's it." She kissed him softly and straightened. "You understand, right?"

Mason opened his mouth to answer before he knew what the answer would be. His phone started buzzing on the bedside table. Amelia's rang half a heartbeat later.

"It's the station," Amelia said as she frowned at her phone screen.

"Me, too," Mason said. "That can't be good."

* * * *

Mason crawled along the country roads, hardly able to see ten feet in front of the rain-pelted windscreen.

He cursed under his breath the whole, fraught journey then out loud as he climbed out into a lay-by crowded with police cars and SOCO vans. A uniformed constable appeared with an umbrella, which promptly turned inside out, dousing them both with spray.

"Don't bother," Mason said, raising his voice over the wind. "Where is he?"

"This way, DI Walker."

Mason bent his head to follow the constable's bright yellow rain poncho through an open gate. They battled uphill through the wind with his shoes sinking into four inches of mud.

Finally they came under the relative shelter of some close-growing trees. Mason stepped, blinking, into the brightly lit interior of a forensic tent.

"Lovely night for a murder." A petite woman with close-cropped orange hair appeared at his side in a white forensic bodysuit. She was bearing a cup of take-out coffee and a grim expression.

"You're telling me," Mason muttered, sipping the coffee and examining the organized chaos around him. "So, Vickers, who found him?"

"A uniform did, out here doing a routine sweep. The victim's partner rang the station a few hours ago. He's been gone less than twenty-four hours, but the partner was pretty insistent."

"Has next of kin been informed?"

"Not yet. He fits the description of the missing person all right, but there's no ID."

"And just how much evidence have we lost?" Mason said as the wind renewed its efforts to tear the tent from the ground.

Vickers winced. "They won't know for sure until they get him back to the lab," she said, heading to the plastic curtain that protected the crime scene. "But doc says there's unlikely to be any fingerprints or DNA."

Mason swallowed a curse. "And how long does she reckon he's been out here?"

"She's not sure about that, either."

Mason frowned as a scene tech took his barely touched coffee and handed him his own suit and gloves. "I've never known Kumar to not have an estimated Time of Death."

"Yeah, well, this is kinda beyond her expertise. Didn't they tell you on the phone?"

Mason's heart sank. "Tell me what?"

"The victim's a haemophile."

His stomach dipped. "Who?"

"We think…Darragh Kelly."

Mason stared at his DC for a long moment then took a breath, pulled on his mask and stepped through the curtain.

Mason had seen many bodies over the course of his career. He remembered his first murder victim like it was yesterday. He'd been a drug dealer, beaten to death by a rival while they'd both been high. They'd caught the perpetrator within twenty-four hours. He'd walked into an A&E with two broken hands and blood on his clothes that wasn't his. It was an open and shut case, and neither of the men had been good people. But seeing the victim's body in the dumpster, thrown away like trash, had been a shard of ice driven into the pit of Mason's stomach.

He'd had that same feeling to a greater or lesser extent with every body he'd examined since.

But this was different. The feeling was deeper. Colder. More like fear.

The haemophile lay in a shallow, muddy hole between the roots of a tree. One leg was bent under him. His arms were splayed. The techs had removed as much soil as possible, but the dirt clung to his fine suit and the luminous blue of his disarranged tie. His shirt had probably been a very crisp white. Now it was filthy and clung to the pale skin like cling film. The eyes were open and hooded. Even from where he stood, Mason could see they were green, like ivy or bottle glass — and eerily bright, even in death. He made himself step closer.

The victim's hair was red — not the bright red-orange of Vickers' natural ginger, but blood-red. Not dyed, but not human, either.

Mason examined the single, neat hole in the center of the forehead with an uncomfortable feeling.

"I tell you what, Walker," Dr. Kumar said, standing from her kneeling position next to the body. Her face was obscured by a mask, but her eyes behind her goggles were dark with mixed feelings. "Haemophile forensics are baffling. I'm not sure I can face the amount of stuff I'm going to have to un-learn to be able to deal with this."

"I hear you, doc. Just give me what you do have."

The doctor gazed down at the body with an expression that was part-regretful, part-bemused. "I'm guessing gunshot to the head as cause of death. It looks like it was pretty close range. But their bones don't break the same way ours do, so I can't be sure."

"Any bullet?"

"There's an exit wound," Kumar said, nodding to the head. "But the techs haven't found anything."

"So probably killed elsewhere."

Kumar shrugged again, unwilling to commit.

"Anything else?"

"Time of death…I don't know. I'll have to do some reading on decomp and body temp statistics in haemophiles — if there's even any reading to be found. Oh…and I think both arms are broken," she said, pointing. "The humerus on both left and right appear misaligned. I'll know more once I've done X-rays."

"That must have taken a hell of a lot of strength," Vickers murmured. "Their bones are like iron, aren't they?"

Kumar nodded. "That much I do know. But that's about it. No ID on the body, either, so we can't even be sure—"

"It's Darragh Kelly, all right," Mason said. "I met him once."

"Shit," Vickers muttered. "As if we didn't have enough mess with the whole Lucien-escape thing. Oh," she winced. "Sorry, boss."

Mason shook his head. "No, you're right. That is very much my personal mess. But let's just deal with one earth-shatteringly unorthodox crime at a time."

"Seconded," Kumar said, shaking her head.

"He was dumped," Mason murmured, pacing around the scene. "In a shallow grave. Hasty. Undignified. Not meant to be found?"

"There's no regret here," Vickers mused. "But no passion, either. The execution-style killing, the impersonal dump site… It's almost…"

"Routine," Mason finished for her.

"Right," Vickers nodded. "Even though there's absolutely nothing else routine about it."

"Also right," Mason said. "Okay," he said, finally looking away. "I want a full work-up—forensics and autopsy, everything you have on the scene and the body. Whatever there is, I want it."

"You'll have it," Kumar said levelly. "If it's here, you'll have it."

Mason nodded. "Vickers, you're with me."

She nodded and followed him back through the curtain. "Next of kin?"

"I'm afraid so."

Vickers sighed as they stripped out of the white suits. "This part never gets any easier. Aw *crap*," she added as she checked her phone.

"What?"

She held out the phone. "This has already hit the internet."

Mason swore. "How?"

"The partner, Tom Addams? He posted online trying to find Kelly. The news sites have taken a wild guess and run with it. The story's everywhere. And this time the bastards are actually right."

"This does not help us...or Addams," Mason muttered as he stepped into the howling rain.

"I doubt he's thinking straight, boss," Vickers muttered. "Poor guy's been in limbo all day."

Mason suppressed a surge of guilt. "Well, let's go put him out of his misery."

"And into a worse one," Vickers murmured with a solemn expression.

* * * *

Apart from some rather sinister scarring on his neck that Mason had a hard time not staring at, Tom Addams was a pleasant-faced young man. He was classically handsome with a chiseled jaw, tanned skin and chestnut curls that seemed to effortlessly fall into place. Mason spent a full fifteen minutes in the bathroom mirror every morning attempting to tame his unruly ash-brown waves with product and, even given the circumstances, he knew a small stab of jealousy. But he did not envy the way his news leached the color from the man's face.

"I'm so sorry," Mason said softly, knowing how inadequate the words were, but knowing there was nothing else he could do except say them.

Addams sank into a chair and put his head in his hands. Vickers went to see if she could find some water.

They were in one of the many private sitting-rooms in Oswald House, Baron Emory Von Magnusson's luxurious mansion. The furniture and décor were minimal but opulent, and the soundproof glass reduced the clamor of the weather to a dim rumble. The air was laced with the scent of the flowers on the coffee table but was thick with the intensity of the security engineer's sorrow.

Vickers returned with a glass of water. Addams took it with a shaking hand but didn't drink.

"Mr. Addams, I'm sorry. I know this is a terrible time, but would you be up to answering a few questions?"

Addams continued to stare into space, ashen faced.

"We can come back tomorrow," Vickers started, but Addams shook his head.

"No," he said, gulping water. He coughed and set the water aside. "No, I want this over with. I want whoever did this to be found." He raised his eyes to Mason. They were dry but red and deep as wells. "Whatever you need. Ask me."

Mason took a seat. Vickers remained standing and withdrew a notepad and pen from her pocket.

"First, I have to ask if Mr. Kelly had any enemies?"

Addams's mouth turned down at the corners. "Enemies? Darragh? How long a list do you want?"

Mason winced internally. "He was involved in some…controversial politics?"

"Putting it mildly," Addams said bitterly. "Arranging the first legal adoption of a human child by a haemophile? Fire-fighting Lucien's vigilante attacks? Not to mention his work on the haemo-human marriage bill…" Addams swallowed and went silent.

"Was there anyone in particular that objected?"

"People have protested at the gates, thrown stones, vandalized the place. They picketed the courthouse on the night of the Baron's hearing…"

Mason nodded. "I remember. That must have been hard."

A shaky smile warmed Addams' face. "But it was all for love, DI Walker. Everything Darragh did..." He took a shaking breath. "He wasn't an easy person to get close to. People who knew him, even other haemophiles, thought him cold...stiff. He gave the impression that the law was his life, his only passion. But he knew love. He knew it deeply." He took a shaking breath. "He didn't deserve this."

"Mr. Addams."

"Tom," the young man interrupted, closing his eyes. "Please. Call me Tom."

"Of course," Mason said, "Tom, you are right. Darragh did not deserve this. But you are also right in that not everyone saw his work the way you do. I know it's hard, but are there any individuals that you know of that were more...persistent than the others? Anyone who threatened him directly?"

Tom picked at his fingernails. He had stopped shaking, but the color still hadn't returned to his face. Mason wondered if it ever would. "The hate mail has increased a lot recently. The marriage legislation is being finalized as we speak." He raised his eyes. A sad smile turned up his mouth. "Emory and Jesse's wedding is booked for October Thirty-First. Halloween night. Some people are saying it's inappropriate... We're all trying so hard to move away from the concept of vampires. But Darragh insisted that getting married the very day the law becomes live sends a strong message." Tom sighed noisily. "To answer your question, DI Walker — "

"Mason," Mason said with a half-smile.

He was rewarded with a weak one in return. "Mason," Tom said softly. "To answer your question...no. There are so many people out there that hate us...that hate *him*...I couldn't pick any one of them that hates more than the others."

Mason exchanged glances with Vickers. Her face reflected the grimness he felt inside.

"Let's focus on his most recent movements, then. When was the last time you spoke to him?"

"Last night," Tom said. "He was in London this past week, working with Honor Ford-Byerson."

"She's Ivor Novák legal assistant, isn't she?"

Tom nodded. "Novák is the official parliamentary representative for Haemophile Affairs, the public face and voice of the movement. But Honor is the one who's been doing all the legwork, with the legal stuff, anyway." Another shaky smile. "I must confess, I'm only a security engineer. I don't understand a whole lot about Darragh's legal world."

"I'm willing to bet you understand more than you think you do," Mason said softly. "So, he was in London?"

Tom nodded. "He was traveling back last night. He rang me from the car, told me to go to bed and he'd see me tonight." He gave an awkward shrug. "Dating a haemophile is sort of a nocturnal activity. So yeah, I took the chance to get some sleep. But when I woke up, there was this text from his number on my phone. I knew straight away something was wrong."

His hands were shaking again as he pulled out his phone and tapped the screen. He held it out.

The text message had been sent at four-sixteen that morning.

Sorry, dearest. Something's come up. Urgent. Will be unreachable for a few nights, but don't worry. I'll be back soon. Love you.

"Was this unusual for him?" Mason said, watching Tom's face carefully.

Tom shook his head. "No. His schedule's pretty hectic. And when we're apart, our sleeping patterns are all over the place. We don't often get a chance even for phone calls."

"So what made you think something was wrong?"

"He doesn't call me 'dearest'…ever." Tom's face was hard. "He calls me *acushla*. It's Gaelic for —"

"Darling," Vickers put in with a crooked smile. "My Nanna's from Cork. She used to call me that when I was small."

Tom nodded, his eyes bright with unshed tears. "Literally it means 'pulse' or 'vein'…something from the heart. From a haemophile, it had even more meaning." He closed his eyes.

"Tom, if you want —"

Tom shook his head, sipped the water again and set it aside, slowly and deliberately. "No. No, I want to continue." Tom met Mason's eyes then Vickers'. "Darragh did not send me that text. Or if he did, he was telling me something was wrong."

"Sixteen minutes past four…" Mason looked at Vickers. "That's before sunrise."

Vickers nodded.

"What happened to him?" Tom asked shakily. "Am I allowed to know?"

Mason tapped his fingertips together but didn't break eye contact. "If you think it would help?"

18

Tom bit his lip. "During Blood Winter, another haemophile was killed. Terje Kristiansen. Died of blood loss after being shot."

Mason nodded, keeping his face blank. "I remember."

"I know Terje," Tom said. "He visits Oswald House. After he died…he came back." Tom gripped the arms of his chair. "Unless you tell me how Darragh died, I don't think I'll be able to believe it."

Mason remembered the broken body, filthy and cold — the staring eyes, the unnatural stillness.

"He was also shot, Tom," Mason said softly. "But in the head."

Tom's eyes darkened. "So he's dead. Really dead."

Mason felt Vickers' eyes on him. He opened his mouth to speak when the door opened.

"Tom?" A young man stood in the doorway. Dark, uneven hair fell in his face. He had facial piercings and tattoos on his arms. His striking face was a mask of horror as he took in Mason and Vickers, then it clouded with anger.

"Tom, my God." He hurried forward and sat next to him. "They shouldn't be talking to you *now*." He put his arms around Tom. "Oh God. Oh God, Tom. I'm sorry. I'm *so* sorry."

Tom held on tight, so tight his grip must have been hurting, but the two men just held each other and rocked as silent sobs shook Tom's body.

"Jesse," he sobbed. "He's gone. He's really gone."

The newcomer directed a glare at Mason. "What the fuck do you think you're doing, huh? Interrogating him when he's just found out his partner's been murdered?"

"Mr. Truelove?" Mason guessed.

"It doesn't matter who I am," Jesse Truelove retorted. "Get out...*now*."

"No," Tom choked, straightened and rubbing at his blotchy face. "No, Jesse. I want to talk to them. I have to feel like I'm doing something."

"You've done enough for tonight, mate," Truelove replied. "You need to rest. Cry. Scream. Anything. But being rational and answering questions?" He shook his head. "There's time for that tomorrow."

"Actually," Mason said, "I think we have all we need for now. Vickers?"

Vickers nodded and made for the door. Mason paused before leaving.

"Mr. Truelove?"

"What?" Jesse's face was pale with emotion.

"Look after him, will you?" Mason said quietly. "It's only just sinking in."

Truelove's face softened, and he nodded. "I will. And anything else you need, you call me. Got it?"

Mason nodded. "Got it."

Mason shut the door behind him. Vickers was standing in the lobby, rigid and staring at a figure approaching across the marble floor. Mason's stomach dropped as Baron Emory Von Magnusson joined them.

Mason had seen news footage of the Baron. He'd studied everything to do with him during the endless briefings on his custody case and protests, as well as Lucien's attacks earlier in the summer.

But he hadn't yet met him.

He was larger than Mason could even have imagined. Mason was tall, pushing six-four, and went to the gym whenever his schedule would allow it. He was far from being a reed, but Magnusson dwarfed him. He had to look up to meet his eyes and the suit he wore had to have been custom made to contain those broad, sloping shoulders.

"DI Walker, I believe?" His voice was low and deep as the thunder outside and was weighted with about the same amount of danger.

"Yes, sir," Mason said, dredging some dignity from somewhere. "And this is DC Phoebe Vickers. I'm afraid we have some bad news about Darragh Kelly."

For less than a second, emotion tightened the Baron's passive face. Mason had a hard time maintaining eye contact. But it was gone as quickly as it had come.

"Yes, Jesse told me. The police station just rang the house."

"I'm sorry you had to find out that way. Some of this has appeared to have leaked online, and the legal team will be getting ahead…"

"I'd rather know sooner than later." Magnusson glanced at the door. "Jesse's in with Tom?"

Vickers nodded. "He's looking after him. I think he needs it."

Magnusson looked at Mason. "Do you have any idea who has done this dreadful thing?"

"Do you have any suspicions?" Mason asked.

"Tom didn't?" Magnusson said carefully.

"He says there's been widespread hate in response to a lot of Mr. Kelly's work," Mason said in a measured tone. "He wasn't aware of anything more…personal."

"Was this personal?"

Mason weighed his words before speaking. "I don't know yet. Possibly not. But choosing to end someone's life has personal implications, even if they're not conscious."

Magnusson sighed deeply, his large chest swelling.

"I'm afraid I'm no wiser than Tom is. I can tell you about all the targeted attacks we've been subject to, though we have already reported everything."

"Yes and we have those records, thank you," Mason said. "I'll be working my way through those as a first order of priority. But, Baron, just one thing...."

"Yes?"

Mason hesitated. "Could this have been Lucien?"

"Absolutely not."

"You seem very sure of that."

Magnusson was silent for a moment. "Darragh has been managing the fallout from Lucien's behavior for decades. He's very skilled at it. Lucien knows that. They were far from close, but they were not enemies. And Lucien has never once killed without justification."

"Justification alters rapidly, depending on your point of view."

"I understand you have to ask these questions," the Baron eventually replied. "And all I can do is give my word that Lucien did not do this. For one thing, there really was no motive, no matter what you think. For another, I can tell you that Lucien was still incarcerated in London until sunset tonight. I believe Tom was convinced something was wrong from the early hours of this morning."

"Forgive me, Baron, but Lucien got out tonight. He could have got out last night."

Magnusson tilted his head. "How much do you know about haemophiles, DI Walker?"

"A lot more than I did before Lucien blew into town."

Magnusson studied him. Mason realized with a start that he didn't seem to blink. "Then perhaps you've come across the fact that a haemophile can sense their maker—roughly where they are, what they're feeling, however far apart they might be?"

Mason glanced at Vickers, who nodded. "It's true, boss. There are studies being done on it."

"Okay," Mason said carefully. "And Lucien is your maker, so you know where he was last night. How about now?"

A tilting smile curved the Baron's lips. "Nice try, DI Walker. All I can tell you is that he has left the country."

Mason schooled his face. "You just said you could 'sense' him, wherever he was."

"I can. Though the details become harder the greater the distance. I can tell you that he was in London, in his cell, last night and all of today. After sunset, he came to York. Now, he's gone."

Mason started. "He came to York? Why?"

"I'm assuming to fetch Mr. Lomax."

Mason swore under his breath. "So *both* Lucien and Tyler Lomax are gone?"

"I believe so."

Mason ran a hand through his hair, then took a breath. "Thank you, Baron. I apologize for having to ask all this. But there's a lot of unprecedented violence happened in my city, and I can't help but wonder if it's all linked."

"That's because you're good at your job," the Baron. "And I am guessing that Darragh's work will be at the root of all this. But all I can tell you for sure is that Lucien didn't kill him. Now, if you'll excuse me," he stepped to the side. "My family needs me."

Chapter Two

"What was all that about, boss?" Vickers asked, shaking rain from her hair as they climbed into Mason's car. "You don't really think Lucien shot Kelly and dumped him in a shallow grave? It's not exactly his MO."

"No, I don't," Mason admitted, starting the car. "Just checking every angle. And Lucien's still a thorn in my side."

"He was convicted and awaiting sentencing," Vickers pointed out. "You did your job."

"But tonight he escaped. A known killer. And even Magnusson admitted he was in the area."

"The timing doesn't line up. And Lucien's not killed anyone in a long time," Vickers replied as they passed through the gates.

"That we know of."

He sensed Vickers giving him a sideways look. "You don't really think Lucien's the bad guy. Not anymore. Lomax, either."

Mason gave her a look then focused back on the road. "Still got to do the job."

She sighed. "So where are we heading now?"

"Tyler Lomax's place," he said. "Let's see if he really has skipped town."

* * * *

The door to Lomax's flat was open. The lights were on, but the place was empty. Lomax's phone was on the sofa. The bedsheets were rumpled. A wardrobe was open, and a few hangers were scattered around the floor.

"The Baron was right," Vickers said, looking around with a solemn expression. "On the run after committing murder?"

Mason sighed and shook his head. "No, I think you're right. That just doesn't add up. Shit." He rubbed his face.

"What is it, boss?"

"I shouldn't have..." He looked at Vickers then away. "I shouldn't have taken that break tonight. I heard about Lucien escaping just before I left the station. I should have stayed."

Mason wondered if Vickers' gaze was knowing before she looked away. "You're not in charge of the London Haemo jail, boss. Not your fault he escaped. And we all know there's no point in looking for a haemo that don't want to be found. Going home and...having a break." She shrugged without making eye contact. "I'd say that was the healthy thing to do."

Mason hoped nothing showed on his face. "But now we have a dead haemophile lawyer and *two* violent criminals missing."

"It must have been another haemo though, right?" Vickers said dourly, examining Lomax's collection of action movies. "No human could be strong or quick enough to murder Kelly."

"Why would a haemophile use a gun?"

Vickers sighed. "Look at it this way, boss. Lucien and Lomax have done us a favor by running away. Not sure I can handle more than one of these batshit cases at a time."

"Except that Lomax is our best link to the hate groups," Mason said. "And I really thought he'd start talking after he'd simmered down."

"So the current theory is the conspiracy nuts?"

Mason stared at Lomax's abandoned phone, pulled out an evidence bag and sealed it in. "It's the most obvious explanation."

"You taught me obvious is convenient, not factual."

"I know," Mason said. "But we gotta start somewhere."

"Then what about that Damon creep?"

"Heard anything to indicate he's gonna start talking?"

Vickers shook her head. "No. I've not checked in with his security detail today, mind. Who knows? Maybe he's had a change of heart?"

"Who knows," Mason said. "Why don't we go find out?"

Vickers looked at her watch. "It's almost two a.m., boss. Don't you think we should…you know, sleep?"

"Crime doesn't sleep, Vickers. I'll get the coffee this time."

Vickers rang the hospital as Mason drove. She frowned, swore and hung up. "They're still not picking up."

"It's a hospital," Mason said, smothering a yawn and willing his coffee to cool faster. "Have you ever known them to pick up the phone?"

"But Alonso's not answering, either." Her face was drawn as she tried again.

Mason frowned. "They put PC Alonso on babysitting duty?"

"Everyone else was assigned. I've tried him twice, boss. Nothing."

"Ring the station," Mason said, turning left to take a faster road to the hospital.

Vickers put the phone to her ear. "Val? It's Phoebe. Yes. Look... Has anyone talked to Alonso today?"

Vickers looked over at Mason. The look on her face made his heart sink. "Well, what about the security checks? Val, I know we're short staffed but... No one? Are you kidding me?"

"What? What is it?"

Vickers hung up with an inpatient noise. "No one's checked in with Alonso all day. They've all been out double-shifting the door-to-doors."

"He's probably just forgotten to report in," Mason said after a heartbeat.

"Yeah," Vickers said uneasily as they pulled into the hospital car park. "Sure that's all it is."

The thin hope evaporated the minute Mason stepped into the chaos on the Intensive Care Unit. A nurse was on the phone, talking hurriedly, while three other phones rang around her. All the other staff were rushing or gathered in huddles, stabbing at iPads with furrowed brows. The bedridden patients were peering around with bleary, frightened eyes.

A security guard came straight over to them as they entered, raising a hand to block their way.

"Closed ward, mate."

Mason drew out his warrant card. "DI Walker, here to speak to PC Alonso and the secure patient." The security man paled. "What's going on here?"

The man drew them aside and lowered his voice. "They're gone."

Mason blanched. "Who's gone?"

"Both of them. The prisoner. Your man. Gone."

"Start explaining, pal," Vickers demanded, but Mason was already moving to the secure room. He flung the door open.

The bed was empty. The blankets were rumpled and stained with blood. An IV and blood bag dripped onto the floor. The window was wide open, the curtain flapping in the wind. Rain soaked the floor and the bed.

He was dimly aware of the security man yammering behind him.

He turned. "Stop talking," he said, quietly but firmly. The round-faced man clamped his mouth shut. "Okay. Now tell me what happened. In order. Quietly."

"The ward manager just called me ten minutes ago, mate. I had no idea about any of this until then. The door was locked all day. Your guy was watching him."

"When did someone notice they were gone?"

"Like I said, about ten minutes ago. I was just calling your lot when you showed up."

"When was the last time someone checked in on them?" Vickers asked.

"Ward manager isn't sure. Patient's on strict bed rest. And like I say, your guy was supposed to be watching him."

"The bed and floor are soaked," Mason muttered. "That window's been open a long time."

The man shrugged helplessly.

"What about security cameras? CCTV?"

"They only cover the halls, and I monitor them myself. They didn't go that way. They musta gone out through the window."

"Secure this room," Mason ordered. "And the rest of the hospital. No one goes in or out until we've confirmed they're not still on the premises." The security man nodded and started barking orders. Mason strode off the ward, and Vickers followed.

"They won't still be in the hospital, boss," Vickers said. "They're long bloody gone."

"I know. Still, I want a forensic team going over every inch of that room."

"What are they looking for?"

"Damon was badly injured. There's no way he escaped on his own."

Vickers hesitated. "Alonso?"

"He either helped Damon escape—"

"He wouldn't," Vickers protested.

"—or he's been taken, too."

Vickers shook her head. "If they really don't know how long they've been gone..."

"Then Damon could have been loose this morning when Kelly went missing. Yes. The thought had also crossed my mind."

"Could they really have been missing from here *all* day with no one noticing?" Vickers frowned. "Damon was in a bad way. Shouldn't they have been checking on him?"

"Busy hospital. Unpleasant patient. I guess mistakes happen."

Vickers snorted. "And now look at the mess we're in."

"So let's now waste any more time. Call the station. We need people on this...*now*."

Despite the hour, the office was abuzz when they reached Fulford Road Police Station.

"Any sightings?" Mason demanded as he made for his office.

"Nothing yet, guv," came the answer.

"Keep looking."

He stripped off his wet coat but then someone called his name. He turned. Amelia stood in the door to her own office, grim-faced. Mason drew a breath, threw his coat on a chair and went to her. She ushered him inside and shut the door behind him.

Mason froze. The haemophile sitting on Amelia's sofa was even larger than the Baron. Even seated he was massive, looking too big for the room. His skin was bone-white, his hair even whiter. His eyes were the deep, dark black of a winter night. His fingernails, like claws, caught the light as he pressed his fingertips together and surveyed Walker with his blank, shark-like gaze.

"DI Mason Walker, allow me to introduce Dragomir Soroka." If Mason didn't know Amelia, he would have no idea just how unsettled she was. But the stiff way she drew out her chair and sat on the very edge of it told him, if anything, she was more nervous than he was. "I'm sure you've heard of him?"

"Of course." Mason inclined his head. "Haemophile rights campaigner. I've read a lot of your work."

"I'm flattered," Soroka said in a voice like ice sheets shifting on the sea. "Though I have to say I'm a little surprised. Humans aren't often interested in the things I have to say."

Mason glanced at Amelia then back. "I believe in poking my nose everywhere, sir."

"A good trait in a detective. And that is why I'm here." He turned his large head to survey Amelia. "I'm here to ascertain that everything possible is being done to get to the bottom of this diabolical hate crime."

"Let me assure you, again, Mr. Soroka, that that is entirely the case. Detective Inspector Walker is our best."

"I'm glad to hear it," Soroka said and stood. Mason fought the urge to back away as he moved past. He paused by Mason and looked at him. "It's not just me counting on you, DI Walker. It's my entire kind. We will be watching this...just so you are aware."

When he left, it was like he took all the air in the room with him. Mason melted bonelessly against the wall, and Amelia let out a shuddering breath.

"Well," Mason said, "he's quite something."

"I don't mind admitting he scares the living crap out of me, Mason," Amelia said. "You know he didn't even come through reception. He just *appeared*, right at my office door."

"What? How?"

"I don't bloody know, but I don't bloody like it. He even gives other haemophiles the willies."

"Really?"

Amelia nodded. "The Baron rang me to warn me he was coming. I've never heard Magnusson sound edgy, but there was definitely something in his voice."

"How does the Baron know him?"

"Apparently they go way back. And Soroka's now up here demanding some sort of meeting with all the haemophiles that live around York."

"Why?"

"Getting every last one of them in line on this murder. Getting their eyes, and whatever weird extra senses they have, trained on us."

Mason frowned. "Again, *why*?"

"They're making sure we give this just as much juice as we would a human murder."

"Why wouldn't we?"

"Because they think — or some of them think — that we wouldn't take this as seriously as a human murder. Christ, Mason. Tell me you're on top of this."

"I'm on top of it, Amelia…as much as I can be. Everything so far is a mess."

"So it's true?" Amelia said. "About Damon?"

"Both he and PC Alonso are missing."

Amelia swore under her breath. "Do we know how long they've been gone?"

"No. Alonso hasn't checked in all day, and the hospital staff can't tell us when the patient was last seen. Oh, and it appears Tyler Lomax has skipped town…with Lucien."

Amelia studied him. "Let me get this straight… A prominent haemophile lawyer has been murdered, and all our key suspects and witnesses are currently MIA, along with one of our own?"

Mason took a breath. "That's about the shape of it."

"Christ," Amelia said again.

"Vickers has already sent the search parties out," Mason stated. "And we've got a tech team on their way to the hospital. Everyone has orders to feed me findings as soon as they come in."

"I want all the ward staff who were on duty today and last night interviewed," Amelia said. "Someone must know something."

Mason nodded. "I'll get right on that."

"Not you," Amelia said firmly. "You go home. You were already hanging by a thread when I came over, Mason."

He looked at her. "Is that why you broke up with me?"

Her face softened. "You know it isn't. But I know you. And you're no use to me burnt out."

"Boss—"

Amelia opened the door. "Go. The crime will still be waiting tomorrow. And maybe, just maybe, we'll start to get some answers."

Mason hovered in the hall. A wave of exhaustion threatened to pull him down. He returned to his own office to get his coat, knowing Amelia was right. Dawn was brightening the windows. He shrugged on his still-damp coat and was turning to leave when Kumar video-called him.

Her face was impassive, but her eyes were shadowed. "Walker, I had a feeling you'd still be up."

Mason managed a smile. "You're burning the candle at both ends, too, I see."

Kumar's lips twitched. "I can't leave this alone any more than you can. I've done the autopsy, such as it is."

"What did you find?"

Kumar eyebrows drew together. "Not nearly as much as I would have liked. Not to go into too much detail, but let's just say I had to send out for some more hardcore equipment to get into him. And I don't know enough about their anatomy to draw any solid conclusions." Mason winced but Kumar continued. "Having said that, cause of death was most likely the gunshot, as we thought. And initial toxicology has come back clean. If he was given anything, I can find it."

"You thought he might have been drugged?"

She shrugged. "I couldn't see how anyone could get close enough to shoot him point-blank like this. They're strong…and fast. So, yes, I wondered if he'd been drugged. But I can't see that that's the case. The X-rays have confirmed both his arms are broken, though. Badly." She stepped to one side and turned the phone camera around. Mason could see a sheet-draped figure on a metal table. Kumar lifted the sheet to expose one arm. The pale flesh was blotched and angry. Purple, red and brown marks stood out livid in a ring around the bicep.

"He was restrained?" Mason guessed.

"Yes. And he struggled."

"So he was secured, made to send a text to his boyfriend to throw us off the scent, then shot in cold blood."

Kumar nodded. "That would appear to be the case, yes."

"But he was able to let Tom know something wasn't right or we may not have looked for him for days." Mason shook his head. "Thank God for doting partners. Can you tell me anything else?"

"The bullet was likely a 9mm, looking at the wound. But ballistics still haven't found anything in the woods and, like I say, their bones don't break in the same way ours do, so I can't state much with as much certainty as I'd like."

"But likely a handgun."

"You'll probably want to confirm with ballistics, but that would be my guess, yes."

"I trust your guesses more than most people's facts, Kumar," Mason said, trying for another smile.

She didn't smile back. "I appreciate it Mason. But I mean it when I say I'm not happy about any of this. I'm trying to round up some specialists, but so far I haven't found any. We've got a hell of a lot to learn about haemophiles — and we need to be learning quicker than we are."

"I agree," Mason said softly, then an email notification slid in at the top of his screen.

"I have to go. The security footage from the hospital just arrived, and I need to chase ballistics and forensics."

Kumar examined him. "I think you should go rest first, Walker. You look half-dead. And you can consider that an official diagnosis."

He smiled. "I will if you will."

Kumar visibly stifled a yawn then nodded. "Deal. I'll check in with you tomorrow. Today. Whatever."

She hung up.

Mason pocketed his phone and rubbed his aching eyes. He knew that email was waiting…but his head was fuzzy, and his mouth tasted foul.

A couple of hours, he thought. *Just a couple.*

* * * *

When he woke, he was stiff, groggy and felt like he hadn't slept at all. He'd dreamt of being tied down while someone held a gun to his head. He'd dreamt of black eyes and hard hands. He shook the dream away and pushed back the covers.

Splashing his face with cold water and changing into a clean shirt and suit helped. By the time he was back in the office, the sun was creeping toward the horizon again, but he definitely felt more human, though the sight of his inbox made him want to return home and crawl back into bed.

He shook himself and loaded the hospital's security footage. He watched it sped up, sipping coffee with mounting frustration when the security man's statement was confirmed and nothing of interest had happened. He began making calls. Ballistics confirmed a 9mm handgun, but nothing more. Forensics had nothing on Kelly beyond what they'd expect to find on a body buried in the woods. They were still working on the hospital room.

He swallowed his now-cold coffee with frustration and re-read the written autopsy report, even though by this point he basically knew Kumar's words by heart.

Inconclusive.

Inconclusive.

Inconclusive.

When Vickers tapped on his doorframe, the sun was fully set, his head was aching and his stomach was a hard knot in his gut. She held up a brown paper bag.

"Burritos, sir," she said, taking foil-wrapped burritos and cans of pop from the bag. "From that place you like."

Mason's stomach growled as the smell reached him. "Vickers, you're not my minder."

"Like Mum always said, eat a good meal, solve half a bad problem. You gotta eat, sir," she said, sitting and peeling the foil off her own dinner. "And so do I." She took a wolfish bite and began to chew.

"Please tell me you have something for me," he said, unwrapping his own and taking a bite. It was spicy and rich and full of flavor, and his stomach sang out with joy, even though he couldn't help but hit 'refresh' on his email as he chewed.

Vickers took a swig of her can to clear her throat. "We've interviewed the hospital staff. The last person to see Damon and Alonso was a nurse on the night shift who changed his dressings the night before last."

"The night Kelly was driving to York from London?"

Vickers nodded. "They admitted staff shortages meant he wasn't checked on as regularly as he should have been, just like you said." She shrugged. "He was in no immediate danger, and Alonso was with him. They thought he would alert them if anything changed."

Mason stared at his food. "So, Damon could have been missing for anything up to twenty-four hours before anyone even knew?"

"And Alonso with him."

"And that's on us. We should have been checking in with him." Mason put down the burrito and wiped his hands on a napkin. "Anything at Alonso's place?"

Vickers shook her head. "He lives alone, sir. And it didn't look like he'd been home."

"Not good."

"Alonso's not exactly the married-to-the-job type, sir," Vickers said, pulling a ring of chili pepper from her food. "But there's no way he'd help a criminal escape custody."

Mason made himself take another bite of his own dinner, even though his appetite had gone. "We have to assume someone's taken them both."

Vickers ate the chili while staring into space. "What the hell's going on here, sir? Do you think Damon killed Kelly? The timings are tight, but it's possible."

Mason stared at the wall. "Damon wasn't in any fit state to climb out of a window, let alone restrain and murder a haemophile."

"So, he had help."

"But who?"

"He had connections, sir, to who knows how many nut bags."

"Nut bags who know a lot more about haemophiles than we do," Mason said quietly.

"Enough to know how to hunt them. Kill them."

Mason nodded. "Maybe Soroka is right to be worried."

Something went through Vickers' eyes. "Soroka?"

"He was here. Came to see the DCI."

Vickers raised her eyebrows. "Wow. Fletcher musta loved that."

"I must have loved *what*?" Amelia stood in the doorway.

Vickers jumped. Mason stood. "Ma'am."

Vickers also stood, wiping sour cream from her face hurriedly with the back of her hand. "Ma'am."

She gave Vickers a level look then folded her arms. "Any progress?"

Mason winced. "Largely inconclusive autopsy. Ballistics have confirmed the type of weapon, but without a bullet, there's no way to match it. Forensics are a bust so far."

"Great."

"We'll get there, ma'am," Vickers said. "We just need time."

"You need help."

"Ma'am?" Mason said carefully.

"That wasn't a criticism," Amelia said. "We all need help. *Specialist* help."

Vickers frowned. "What sort of specialist, ma'am?"

Amelia stepped back out of the door. "Walker, if you wouldn't mind coming with me."

Uneasiness snaked around his insides as Amelia took him to her office and held the door open to let him in first.

A young man turned from the window. He wasn't as tall as Mason but was so lithe he gave the impression of being much taller than he was. He wore a steel-blue suit with a gray shirt but no tie. The top buttons were undone. Mason found his eyes drawn to the hollow of his collarbone. He realized what he was doing and hurriedly raised his eyes but then his throat closed over. The man was uncommonly, unnervingly attractive. The angles of his jaw were sharp. His cheekbones, too. His skin was like sun-warmed ivory and seemed to glow from inside. His hair was the color of a cool morning's sunrise, parted at one side and styled neatly back from his face.

But it was his eyes that stopped the breath in Mason's throat. They were the bluest of all blues he'd ever seen. Bluer than the sky. Bluer than the ocean on a tropical shore of white sand.

It stirred something in him that was all at once deeply, personally familiar and utterly alien.

The knowing flicker that went through those eyes seemingly in response to Mason's examination only fanned the sudden, disconcerting flames that had started in his chest.

If they'd been alone, the knowing half-smile the man then gave would have probably had Mason fleeing the room. But, thankfully, Amelia started speaking.

"Detective Inspector Mason Walker, I'd like you to meet Specialist Officer Cai Bracken."

"Pleased to meet you, DI Walker," the young man said, his lips tilting to reveal a glimpse of a sharp canine as he held out his hand.

Mason, still stunned, shook the offered hand. It was cool and strong. He pulled his hand away the second he felt he could do so without being impolite.

"Specialist Officer?" Mason finally said, surprised his voice was steady. "I've never heard of that—"

"Don't worry," Bracken said. "No one has."

Mason looked at Amelia.

"SO Cai Bracken was a detective with the Met," Amelia said, closing the door.

"*Was*?" Mason asked, very carefully.

A shadow passed over Bracken's face. "When I was human."

Mason stood still, words alluding him. He sensed Amelia glancing between them but couldn't bring himself to look away from Bracken's penetrating stare.

"Bracken reached the rank of DS before he was turned into a haemophile," Amelia stated levelly, stepping into Mason's eye line. "He has worked closely with the Metropolitan Police ever since, off the books."

"Off the books?"

"Unfortunately, the Home Office does not allow non-humans to work for the police force." Bracken's smile was still stunning but now also a little hard.

"Nonetheless, his unique skills and perspective have been invaluable in solving a number of crimes," Amelia continued. "Especially ones that involve haemophiles."

"Don't get me wrong. There's still a lot of mystery," Bracken said. "And I've not been...non-human, long. But I'm learning more every day."

Mason continued to stare. He searched for a response, anything, but words still wouldn't form.

"I understand this is a lot to take in," Amelia said, studying Mason closely. "SO Bracken, perhaps you should go and start familiarizing yourself with the case files?"

Bracken nodded and moved to go.

Mason shook himself. "So...I'm off the case?"

"No," Amelia said. "But you need help, Mason."

"Help from a"—he swallowed—"an outsider, ma'am?"

Amelia gave Bracken an apologetic look and opened the door.

"Ma'am." Bracken inclined his head and left.

"Mason," Amelia started as she closed the door, but Mason cut her off.

"What is this, Amelia? You don't think I can handle this?"

"This isn't about just you," she replied levelly. "The whole department is in over its head. I know the Assistant Commissioner at the Met. I'd heard rumors. I reached out." She spread her hands. "They sent me Bracken."

"But he's... He's..."

"He's a haemophile, yes," Amelia said, weighing her words. "Is that a problem for you?"

"No," Mason said quickly, stung. "Of course not. But he's not a commissioned officer? He's what, a freelancer? A consultant?"

"It's a gray area. Had he stayed human, he'd be a DI by now, like you. But like I said, the Home Office is behind the times with their recruitment policy. However, for all intents and purposes, he's a rank-holding detective with the experience and qualifications that go with it. They just can't have him on the official payroll."

Mason sank into a chair. "I don't understand any of this."

"Cai Bracken is the specialist we need," Amelia said, taking the seat next to him, sitting close but not touching. "He can answer any questions we have about haemophiles, and he can communicate with and explain them better than we can. He has superhuman senses on top of everything. We need him, Mason. *You* need him."

Mason stared at the door, cold and warmth mixing in his insides.

"Mason, what is it? Talk to me."

"I don't know," Mason murmured. "I'm just not sure I like it, Amelia. Can a haemophile really be objective in this?"

"I think we'll only know that if we give him a shot."

Mason continued to stare at the door. Amelia retrieved a file from her desk. "Here."

"What's this?"

"Probably not something you should have. But it might help."

Mason opened it and blinked. "Bracken's personnel file?"

"If you're going to trust him, I think it's important you know as much as possible."

Mason blinked as he read. "He's only been a haemophile for ten years?"

Amelia nodded. "Turned against his will, for the record." Mason raised his eyes to hers, his body going cold. Amelia nodded. "Not all of this is in the file. And you didn't hear it from me. Understand?"

Mason nodded stiffly. Amelia resumed her seat and examined her hands.

"He was on the trail of a child kidnapper. A girl had vanished from a play park in London. It was winter, so it got dark early, but it was well-lit, and there were other families around. Cara Sullivan was on holiday there with her family. Her parents were both social workers from Belfast. They'd gone to the Christmas markets then the playground. Both her parents were right there. One minute she was there, the next she wasn't. It was like she'd vanished into thin hair." Amelia stared at the file in Mason's lap. "Bracken was the DS on the case. They were getting nowhere. Then one night, he, too, vanished."

Mason blinked. "What happened?"

"He went out to follow a lead and didn't come back. Weeks later, he turned up at a hospital's emergency department, weak and starving, a newborn haemophile, crying for blood."

A chill went over Mason's skin. "Where had he been?"

"He doesn't remember."

"He doesn't *remember*?"

"Apparently it's not uncommon," Amelia said, taking the file and turning to a crime report. There were photos of Bracken, looking drawn and pale, cut and bloodied. There were closeups of his wrists, bruised and red-raw. "We're not officially allowed to know the process of turning a human into a haemophile. But by all accounts it can be…traumatic."

"Jesus," Mason breathed.

Amelia nodded, closed the file and handed it back to him. "As soon as he was well enough, he went straight to the commissioner and begged to keep his job. He had a case to close, he said."

"Did he ever find who did it?"

Amelia shook his head. "Didn't find his attacker. Didn't find the girl." Amelia looked at him hard. "You can see why he's determined to do anything and everything to help in cases like ours."

Mason stared at the file.

"Cai Bracken is a registered haemophile," Amelia said quietly. "He is listed as a resident in a commune near London. He has a Kill List of zero. He's lived off donations his entire haemophile life." Mason met her gaze. It was earnest, but kind. "He's trustworthy. He's skilled. He's the asset we need right now. Use him…please."

Mason didn't dare examine the emotions simmering just under his skin. Bracken's blue eyes and his reaction to them were still hot in his mind. But he thought of Kelly, tossed aside like rubbish, staring at him with his dead eyes. He remembered Tom Addams' raw grief burning in his.

Mason nodded. "Yes, boss. Anything to get this done."

Amelia smiled. "Good."

Chapter Three

By the time Mason got into bed again he was so exhausted he didn't think he would stay conscious long enough to pull the covers up. But ten minutes later he was still awake, staring at the wall and thinking about Bracken.

He couldn't shake the image from his head—the blue eyes, the sculpted jaw, the smooth sweep of his collarbone at the neck of his shirt. He started to grow hard and rushed to the bathroom. He splashed cold water on his face.

What the hell is going on?

He'd never even glanced at another guy, not even at uni, when everyone he knew was experimenting. He'd even tried kissing his roommate once, after a few beers, just to see. But it had ended in giggles, and they had both agreed that no, they were definitely into girls.

Bracken wasn't human, and, yeah, Mason had to admit he was objectively attractive. But he was still male. Definitely male.

Mason stared at himself in the mirror, at the hollow look in his hazel eyes, and told himself to get a grip. He shook his head, returned to bed and reached for Bracken's file.

If he wasn't going to sleep, he might as well do something useful. And there was more going on here than just confused arousal, he was sure.

The picture on the first page was from when the guy had been human. The lines of his face were softer. His skin was warmer. His eyes were still a startling shade of blue, but again, warmer — the natural blue of a summer sky, not the unearthly brilliance that had burned in the man's eyes earlier that night. Mason stared at the picture, ignoring the other feelings that curled along his spine, and he made himself focus. There was *something* about that face... Something...familiar?

He thought hard. Nothing came.

He shook his head and turned to Bracken's service record — an exemplary officer, by all accounts, who'd disappeared on the trail of a kidnapper a decade before. He was thirty-five years old at the time. Mason frowned at the thought. That meant he was forty-five now, more than a decade older than Mason, and yet he had looked years younger — younger than thirty-five, even.

Mason returned to the crime report. Bracken had been missing for almost four weeks. The medical report from the hospital was there. Bruising. Blood loss. Fractures in his wrists. Positive results for the presence of haemophile Blood in his system. Evidence of sustained abuse and the use of restraints on his body, though it was already disappearing by the time he had been examined.

Mason shuddered and turned the page.

Next were summaries of all the cases he'd helped solve under his new position of 'Specialist Officer'.

A human attack on a haemophile that had ended with both parties in hospital. Arson on a haemophile compound. Several attacks and murders that had been unsolved for years until Bracken had come in and discovered the culprits were haemophiles.

Dozens of arrests of perpetrators from both species.

Mason raised his eyebrows at that.

He turned back to the picture of Bracken's human face, trying to pin down the feeling he was having, but still he had no luck.

He let out a sigh and loaded his emails to see if any of the outstanding reports had come back.

He awoke hours later with a crick in his neck, his phone in his hand and Bracken's file still open in his lap. The sun was shining through a gap under his blinds. He blinked and peered at his phone.

It was almost midday.

He swore and scrambled out of bed, dressed and hurried out of the house.

He skimmed his messages while he waited for his drive-through coffee. The full forensic reports on both the dump site and the hospital room were back and revealed...nothing.

He bit down curses as he accepted his coffee and sped all the way back to the station.

"Afternoon, sir," Vickers said brightly as he hung his coat in his office. "You look better. Got a bit more sleep, I hope?"

"Too much, if anything," he said, sipping his coffee and pulling out his chair. "Did you see the reports?"

She scowled and sat. "I saw they had nothing in them, if that's what you mean."

"Not what we wanted. But the lack of evidence does tell us something in itself."

"That whoever did this was too good to leave evidence?"

"Exactly."

"A pro?" Vickers said dubiously. "Wouldn't have thought Damon would have the kind of funds to hire a pro."

"Damon *is* a pro," Mason reminded her. "Remember that compound where he held Lucien? The security? The equipment? He and a lot of people like him seem to be well-funded and well-trained."

"So we're back to another conspiracy-nut accomplice?"

"Until we have anything else, yes. So we need to round up all his known associates…every last one."

"We've quizzed them all once already," Vickers reminded him. "When we arrested Lomax—"

"We're doing it again," he said firmly. "And again, until we get something. *Someone* knows where Damon's gone."

"Find Damon, find the murderer?"

"Especially if Damon's the murderer himself, which I'm still not ruling out."

"That's great, boss," Vickers said, dropping her feet to the floor. "Apart from one thing."

"What thing?"

"Fletcher says we're to wait until nightfall."

Mason paused. "Wait for Specialist Officer Bracken, she means."

Vickers shrugged. "She thinks we should follow his lead."

Mason made an impatient noise. "Sunset is hours away."

"I know," Vickers said, leaning her elbows on her knees. "I wanna be out there doing stuff, too. But right now, we have a big fat load of nothing, right?" She spread her hands. "Can't hurt to see what he has to say, right?"

Mason rolled his eyes to the ceiling. "Yes. Fine. But I'm not sitting round here twiddling my thumbs, no matter what Fletcher says. Get that list of associates. We can at least be going through the background checks in the meantime."

"Is everything okay, boss?" Vickers said after a pause. "You know, between you and Fletcher?"

Mason schooled his face. "What do you mean?"

Vickers scrutinized him. "You can talk to me if you want. You know that, right?"

"The background checks, DC Vickers," Mason said firmly. "Please," he added in a softer tone.

Vickers sighed and stood. "Whatever you say."

Mason spent the rest of the afternoon buried in checks and reports and resisting the urge to glance out through his window to see if the sun was any closer to setting.

He'd succeeded in finally losing himself so well that when SO Bracken appeared — literally appeared — in his office, he jerked and banged his knees on the desk.

"Sorry," Bracken said with another slanting smile. "I don't try to make people jump. It just seems to happen." His voice was smooth and low, like a warm drink laced with honey. Mason swallowed and pushed aside his reactions with an effort.

Bracken held out a takeaway coffee cup.

Mason eyed the cup then took it. "You didn't need to."

"Unfortunately, it's practical. Working with me means mostly working at night."

Mason pursed his lips. "I find people are less likely to cooperate in an investigation if you have to wake them up to ask questions."

Bracken's pleasant expression didn't waver. "We'd better find a way. We need to find this killer."

Mason turned his attention back to his laptop. "I guess so."

"May I?" Bracken was gesturing at the seat next to Mason. Mason hesitated and nodded. Bracken took the seat, his movements fluid as a dancer's, and sipped from his own cup. Mason tried not to stare. Bracken glanced at him and chuckled softly. "It's only coffee."

Mason raised his eyebrows. "You need coffee?"

"No. But I like the taste. And don't worry. I feed immediately after sunset, in private. You'll never see me drink… You know."

Mason typed distractedly on his keyboard. "You can drink what you want," he said. "Just so long as it's legal."

"It's always legal." Bracken's face had hardened. "It's very important you understand that, Walker. I didn't choose any of this. But I choose to use it. Work with it. Try to make sure some good comes out of the whole thing."

Mason nodded. "Of course. I'm sorry."

"No need to be sorry. This is new…for both of us. You can ask questions if you want. But you have to trust me, or this won't work."

"I agree," Mason said simply. "So, where do we start?"

"Where you've already started…with motive."

"The most likely motive for Kelly's murder is his work on haemophile rights," Mason said, "which definitely puts Damon in the picture. He was an active member of a hate group."

"But there's one problem with that," Bracken said.

"His body wasn't displayed," Mason agreed. "I don't think we were meant to find it. I think he was just meant to vanish."

"It's not a statement murder," Bracken said. "It's a practical maneuver. The confusion while we looked for him would have disrupted his work more than his murder inquiry would. If he were just missing, everything would be on hold, waiting for an outcome. Now it's known he's not coming back, other people will be scrambling to keep the work moving."

"I agree," Mason said after a moment. "And if that's really the motive...any other person who has been working on Kelly's cases could be next."

"We need to move quickly."

"You know about Damon?"

Bracken's expression darkened. "I know about Damon."

"Well, he vanished from his hospital room, potentially about the same time Kelly went missing."

"So he's still our most likely suspect," Bracken said, sipping his coffee. The muscles in his throat moved as he swallowed, and Mason looked away.

"I would expect a more flamboyant body dump from him, to be honest. But he's the best lead we've got. I want to start by rounding up all his known associates—"

"I would like to see Kelly's body."

"Why? There's an autopsy report."

"There may be more I can get than the human doctor," he said, then apparently seeing Mason's expression, raised his hand. "I'm sure she's competent, but I'm guessing this is her first haemophile victim?"

"And you have a medical degree, do you?" Mason said, not completely unable to withhold the snideness from his voice.

"You know I don't," he said. "You have my file." Mason colored as Bracken studied him. "As far as I know, there *are* no medical degrees in haemophile physiology yet. But I know my own body. And I can sense things that chemical tests can't pick up." Mason wondered if the look in his eyes had changed. Mason suddenly had the unnerving sensation Bracken was looking right into his head. But then he lowered his eyes, and the impression was gone. "Let me see the body."

"Fine," he said, standing and grabbing his coat. "But Vickers is going to start on Damon's goons while we're gone."

Bracken stood back to let Mason leave the room first.

The drive to the hospital was silent. Mason snuck the occasional glance at his passenger. Bracken gazed ahead, his expression mild but unreadable, his blue eyes fixed on the road. Again something tickled at the back of Mason's mind, something that made an unfamiliar sensation rush over his skin. He clamped down on it and told himself to concentrate.

To his surprise, Kumar was waiting in the morgue.

"It's late," Mason said as Bracken approached the shrouded corpse. "You could have just sent an assistant."

"I'm not used to knowing so little," the doctor said, watching Bracken as he lifted the sheet from Kelly's face. "Anything he can tell me, I want to know."

They watched in silence as Bracken studied Kelly's face. The victim's skin was the same shade of gray as when they'd lifted him from the ground. At this point, Mason would have expected more discoloration, drooping muscles, pooling blood making bruise-like markings on the skin. Whatever TV might show to the contrary, the dead were unmistakably dead.

Kelly looked like he could sit up and walk out at any moment.

Thankfully, someone had managed to close his eyes.

Bracken bent close, examining the face and bullet hole intently. Then he folded the sheet back to his waist and studied his neck, his chest, his arms. His gaze was focused. He inhaled deeply as he moved, like he was smelling him.

Mason suppressed a shiver.

"Is he...?" Kumar asked hesitantly.

Bracken nodded. "He's dead. Definitely."

Kumar exhaled sharply.

"We weren't sure?" Mason asked, incredulous.

Kumar spread her hands. "I heard about Terje Kristiansen after Blood Winter. He lay in the morgue for days, his chest and abdomen shot to pulp. No pulse. No brain waves. Then one day" — Kumar met his eyes, her own haunted — "he blinked."

Mason bit the inside of his cheek.

"I know the attendant who was on duty," she continued, her voice gravelly. "Poor sod needed counseling."

"Think I'd need more than counseling," Mason muttered.

"Even my kind don't know a lot about how we work," Bracken said. "But there's one key difference between Kristiansen's shooting and this one." Bracken pointed at the bullet hole in Kelly's forehead. "This is point blank in the brain. It would kill anything."

Kumar nodded. "Okay...noted. But can I ask how you can be certain? Since all the usual markers don't necessarily count?"

Bracken's eyes flickered to Mason then back to the doctor. "I can tell his Blood is dead."

Kumar frowned. "His blood?"

"Blood with a capital 'B'. Haemophile Blood is different to yours. It keeps us alive indefinitely. Stops us aging or catching diseases. But Kelly's is dead. I can't really explain how I know. It's just something I sense. Though, if you want, I can show you how you can test it?"

Kumar nodded eagerly.

"Got a microscope?"

Kumar indicated the bench along the wall.

"We'll need a sample from Kelly and" —he rolled up his sleeve—"one from me."

Mason hung back as Kumar collected microscope slides and produced two syringes. Watching how much effort it took for the doctor to puncture Kelly's skin made Mason very uncomfortable. But finally she drew a sample of dark, almost black, Blood from the corpse's arm then repeated the process with Bracken.

The haemophile stood patiently as she struggled to push the needle in. When she managed to break the skin, a heady scent wafted in the air, making Mason's own blood stir. Bracken stood at Kumar's elbow as she put the slides under the microscope.

"I can't see anything," she said after a moment.

"There should be a dark ring on the outside of Kelly's red cells? It'll be missing from mine. It's subtle, but it's there."

"My God," Kumar said, "you're right."

"The dark ring is the beginning of decay. It means the Blood is dead. I can just sense it, like I said. But this is a test humans can do to get the same result."

Kumar switched between samples again. "Well, I'll be damned. How did you find out about this?"

"I was allowed access to a study that's just been done at the King's College Forensics Department."

Kumar straightened. "I didn't hear about that."

"The findings are restricted...for now." He nodded at the microscope. "But I think this will be useful for you to know."

Kumar looked between them with a bleak expression. "You think this'll happen again?"

Mason looked at Bracken then away. "All right. It's always good to know that a murder victim is actually dead. But is there anything else you can tell us? Like who did it?"

Bracken gave a wry smile. "No such luck, I'm afraid. I can tell he was in close contact with someone human, but he's been cleaned. There aren't enough cells left to give me an idea of who that might be."

"I found bleach on his skin," Kumar said. "And his clothes had been sprayed with something antibacterial. We struggled to pull any fingerprints or DNA. It was in the report."

"Yes, I remember," Mason said quietly. He shook his head. "Everything about this is so practical. So methodical."

"The lack of emotion is telling," Bracken said.

"A human definitely touched him?"

Bracken nodded.

"You can, what...*smell* that?"

Bracken gave a half shrug. "Sort of. Taste and smell combined, really."

"Even though he's been sterilized?"

"Humans shed a lot of matter. And we're auto-tuned to detect it. Historically, you were our..."

"Prey?"

Cai returned Mason's wary look with a frank one of his own. "Well...yes. We're hard-wired to hunt you.

We don't do it any more...or we shouldn't." Mason wondered if his eyes had darkened or if it was just a trick of the light. "But it's what our biology is designed for."

"And how do you know you're not just sensing the tech team that handled him?"

"Because I can tell you all apart. And there's the age of the traces, too."

Kumar stared. "You're like a human mass spectrometer."

Something flashed through Cai's eyes. "Not human...sadly."

Kumar looked awkward. "Right. Sorry."

"My DC doesn't think a human would be strong enough to do this," Mason said, indicating Kelly's mangled arms.

"A haemophile wouldn't need a gun. They..." Bracken frowned. "*We* are more than capable of killing each other without weapons."

"Messy, though."

Bracken shrugged. "We don't care about being messy. And we wouldn't care about the body being found."

"You're untouchable. Is that it?"

Bracken's smile became edged. "We think we are...or some of us do." He looked at the body and a line appeared between his fair eyebrows.

"What?" Mason said. "What is it?"

Bracken hesitated then shook his head. "No. He's definitely dead. And it was most likely a human that did this. That's all I can tell. I hoped there would be more."

"'Most likely' a human?" Mason kept his voice neutral.

"We need more evidence," Bracken said. "But I can tell you that a human put that bullet in his head. And a human dumped him in that hole."

Mason examined his face. "There's really nothing else?"

Bracken's hesitation was so brief Mason again wasn't sure if he imagined it. "No. Nothing."

"So we're back to Damon," Mason said as they left the morgue. "Except…"

"Except Damon was wounded," Bracken said softly, "and had no reason to hide his handiwork."

They walked in silence, Mason's mind racing, then Bracken stopped. "He was being held here, yes? In this hospital?"

"That's right. Why?"

"And I heard one of your own disappeared with him?"

"PC Horatio Alonso," Walker said with a tight voice. "He was on security detail."

"Can I see the room?"

Mason's skin tingled at the keen look on the haemophile's face. "This way."

Mason took them to the ICU. It was quiet. The lights were low. The only sound was from the machines. They were allowed access to the taped-off room after Mason showed his badge.

Bracken stood in the middle of the stark, clinical space with a far-away look on his face. He was breathing, slowly and deeply like he was…

"Are you *smelling* something?"

"Like I said, it's not really smell," Bracken said distractedly. "But yes, I can feel the people who have been in this room." He frowned and moved to the window. "Two of them went out this way. That must be your suspect and your PC."

"Can you tell where they went?"

Bracken opened the window. The cool breeze whipped in, scattering rain drops in his hair and onto his shoulders. He was silent for a long time. "Yes. I can." He looked back over his shoulder. "Keep an eye on your phone."

Bracken was gone.

Mason started. He leaned out of the window. Nothing. He called Bracken's name. Again, nothing.

He ran back to his car, turned the key in the ignition, muttering curses. He'd almost reached the station again when his phone rang from an unknown number.

"Walker."

"It's me."

"Bracken?" Mason swore again. "What the hell? Where did you go?"

"I've found PC Alonso."

The tone of the other detective's voice had Mason's stomach dropping into his boots. "Is he okay?" he asked, already knowing the answer.

"No. He's not. I'm sorry."

Mason's grip tightened on the wheel. "Where are you?"

"I'll ping you the location. Bring forensics."

* * * *

Mason had only really known Alonso by sight. He'd always seemed to have some sort of protein shake on the go, and Mason knew for a fact he googled workout routines on work time. But he'd been generally hard-working and quick with a smile or dietary advice.

Seeing him now, staring blankly from dead eyes from the bottom of a dried-up storm drain in an overgrown coppice, Mason wished he'd gotten to know him better.

Vickers was hollow-eyed as she supervised the securing of the scene. Bracken stood by, out of the light, watching everything unfold with unreadable eyes. His shoulders were hunched.

Mason went over to him. "What is it?"

It was a second before Cai tore his eyes from the crime scene. "What?"

"Is there something going on with you?"

"I don't like seeing a dead cop, same as you."

They walked back to Mason's car in silence.

"I'm sorry," Cai said in a softer voice as Mason started the car.

"Did you get anything from him? From the area?"

"He's been cleaned, too," Bracken said, his voice and face neutral. "But the same human that handled Kelly was in close proximity to him when he died."

"Damon."

"That would be my suspicion."

"So we're back to him and an associate."

"You've been re-interviewing them?"

"The ones we know about, yeah. And they've been as forthcoming as you'd imagine."

"I think we should get some statements out about these people," Bracken said after a thoughtful pause. "About what they do and think."

Mason slammed on the turn signal with more force than was necessary. "We don't want to give them that kind of validation."

"Their anti-haemophile ethos has existed in a vacuum all this time. Let it out into the light of day, and let the public respond. Let's burst their bubble. Maybe one or two of them will be more inclined to talk."

"Maybe." Mason was doubtful.

"And while that's playing out, let's try to cut down the suspect pool. What does your gut tell you?"

"My gut?"

"You're a cop, Walker," Bracken said after a moment of silence. "You know this city...this case. Of all of Damon's friends, who do you think would be most likely to talk?"

Mason clenched his teeth. It had started to rain again. He switched on the wipers. "His accomplice in Lucien's kidnapping, Tyler Lomax."

"And what was different about him?"

"Well, he ended up banging Lucien, for one," Mason said. Then he grimaced. "More than that. He fell for him...big time."

"Lomax fell for his own victim?"

"I think he'd fallen for him already," Mason muttered. "He was just so messed up he didn't know how to handle it."

Bracken was quiet for a moment. "Well, if he switched sides, surely he'll rat on Damon."

"I think he would have. But he's gone."

"Gone?"

"Skipped town...with Lucien."

Bracken was silent again. "I heard Lucien had escaped. Didn't know he'd taken someone with him."

"Yeah, it's a romantic fairytale. Run off into the sunset together. Left all their troubles behind."

Another pause. "You don't believe in happy endings?"

"Not when you leave murders in your wake."

"I'm guessing Emory Von Magnusson didn't tell you where he went?"

"All he said was that Lucien had left the country. Said he was so far gone he couldn't even sense where or whatever." Mason snuck another glance at Bracken.

"Is all that true? Can he really sense that Lucien's gone? And yet not be able to give us even a ballpark as to where?"

Bracken's lips had paled, and his eyes were hard. "I don't know much about the maker-victim bond, but I know it's not like a Find My iPhone app. Nothing so useful."

Mason cursed inwardly. "Sorry. I didn't think."

"It's fine," Bracken said, not looking at him. "I'll find my own maker one day, whoever they are."

The silence that filled the car was heavy.

"So Lucien has vanished. He's the oldest haemophile alive, and he's more than capable of that. But Lomax is human." Bracken looked over at him. "Humans aren't as careful."

"There was nothing at his place to indicate where he'd gone. And he hasn't flagged at any travel security stations."

"Has he left any friends behind? Relatives?"

Mason raised his eyebrows. "There's always the Lord Mayor of York."

"The Mayor?"

"Tyler's sister. Emerald Lomax."

"Well-connected young man."

"That's why his arrest record is as long as my arm, but his conviction count is a big fat zero."

"Sounds personal."

"We go back a way, Lomax and I," Walker said grimly. "I was in charge of trying to track down Lucien after he assaulted Lomax during the Oswald House riots, apart from anything else. Don't ask," he added when Bracken looked at him sideways. "But yeah, I know him well enough to think he might have eventually talked to me. But he's gone."

"So we ask his sister," Bracken said.

"It's after eleven."

"Politicians don't sleep."

"She won't help us," he said. "The Lomax family has been a thorn in our side for decades. Racketeering. Fraud. All sorts of things. They basically own the city. They're used to giving cops the runaround."

"We have to start somewhere," Bracken said.

Mason opened his mouth to argue further when his phone started to ring in its holder. Amelia's name displayed on the screen. He answered with the car's Bluetooth.

"DCI Fletcher," he said carefully. "It's late."

"You're not asleep, so why should I be?"

"What's wrong?" he said, noting the strained note in her voice.

"It's Honor Ford-Byerson."

"Kelly's colleague?" Mason asked, stomach sinking.

"She's missing."

"DCI Fletcher, it's SO Bracken, here. When did this happen?"

"Reported a few hours ago by her wife. She vanished from their apartment."

"I'm sure she's had a busy day," Mason ventured, "dealing with the fallout of Kelly's death. Maybe she went out for a drink? Didn't tell the wife?"

"You don't understand, Mason. She *literally* vanished." Amelia was quiet a moment. "They were in bed together. Then she was gone. Windows and doors were all locked. Sadie, the wife, has had to be sedated."

"A human couldn't have done that," Bracken muttered quietly.

"What the hell is going on?" Amelia demanded.

"I don't know," Mason said. "But we're going to find out."

"Where are you going?"

Mason turned left, heading into the city center. "To see Emerald Lomax."

Chapter Four

Emerald Lomax lived in a Georgian town house near the York Minster. The limestone facade of the minster dwarfed the three-story building that sat comfortably on half an acre of private walled garden.

There was no answer when Mason pushed the gate buzzer, but he could see lights between the drapes on the ground floor.

Mason pushed the buzzer again. Still nothing.

He muttered and went to push it a third time when Bracken put his hand on his arm.

"She's coming."

Mason's arm tingled even after Bracken had let him go.

"Yes?" snapped the voice over the intercom. "Who is it?"

"Detective Inspector Walker, ma'am. Remember me?"

There was a pause of several moments before the gate buzzed and swung open.

Emerald Lomax met them at the front door. She still wore her jewelry and makeup from the day but was dressed in floor-length satin dressing gown and tartan pajamas. Her expression, however, was anything but casual.

"Do you have any idea what time it is, Detective Inspector?"

"Almost midnight, ma'am," Mason said levelly. "I apologize. But our inquiries are…time sensitive. This is Special Officer Cai Bracken from the Met Police."

Lomax's eyes moved to Bracken and widened. Bracken returned the look with a banal smile.

"Yes, ma'am," he said levelly. "I am what you think."

"The Met has a haemophile cop?" she said after a pause. "I hadn't heard that."

"I'm sort of freelance," Bracken clarified, "but I'm currently helping DI Walker. May we come in?"

Lomax looked between them both. Her eyes were hard and her jaw clenched. She looked so similar to her brother it was like Walker was back in an interview room with Tyler Lomax, his gaze defiant, his jaw set, but with that flicker of vulnerability so deeply buried in his eyes that you could mistake for a trick of the light.

Finally she stepped back and held the door open.

"I assume you don't actually need to be invited in?" she muttered as Bracken followed Mason into a richly furnished sitting room.

"No, ma'am," said Bracken with enviable good humor. "That's just a myth."

"Hard to tell between myth and truth these days," she muttered in reply, moving over to a walnut bar and pouring herself a generous measure of vodka. "I'm assuming you gentlemen are on duty?"

"We are," Walker said, casting an eye on the luxury décor and watching Bracken do the same. "Regrettably."

"Don't tell me someone else is dead," she said, sitting on the sofa and sipping her drink with a sullen expression.

"Like whom, ma'am?"

She barked a laugh and unfastened one of her earrings. The emerald caught the light as she dropped it into a decorative bowl on the coffee table containing some rings and what looked like a diamond bracelet. "Where do I start?" she said, removing the other earring then her gold necklace. "All those stiffs Lucien dumped on your police station steps were at death's door the last time I checked." She raised her glass again. "Now someone's murdered a bloody haemophile lawyer *and* a cop. The phone hasn't stopped."

"Actually, we're here about your brother," Bracken said.

She looked up. "Tyler? What about him? Is he hurt?"

Mason noted the panic in her expression with interest. "Not as far as we know," he replied. "But we're very keen to get in touch with him."

Her expression closed. "I assume you have his contact details, Inspector."

"We found his phone in his flat. He, however, was not there," Mason returned, "as I'm sure you know."

Lomax swirled her drink in her glass.

"Do you know where Tyler is, ma'am?" Mason said, more gently, sitting on the edge of a cushion-loaded armchair. "He's not in trouble…this time." She gave him a narrow look. He spread his hands. "We just want to talk to him."

The Mayor shook her head. "I don't know where he is. He ran off with Lucien, of all the bloody insane things to do. He was so obsessed with him. I should have seen where it was going." She shook her head again, slower. "He called me. He said goodbye. That's all I know."

"We know you picked him up from the station the day Lucien was arrested," Walker said. "We know the state he was in. Did he say anything to you? About anything?"

She stared into her glass. Mason made himself wait. Bracken stood at his elbow, stiller than a statue.

"Someone else has gone missing," Bracken eventually said, his voice cool and quiet. Lomax looked up. Bracken nodded. "Honor Ford-Byerson."

Lomax frowned. "She worked with Ivor Novák. And—"

"And Darragh Kelly," Mason confirmed. "Yes."

Lomax's face hardened. "You need to find Damon."

Mason exchanged a look with Bracken. "What did Tyler tell you about Damon?"

"I already knew about Damon. Heard he was dangerous. I tried to warn Tyler off before all this happened. He didn't listen. Little bugger never listened to me."

"Damon's escaped custody," Mason said after a seconds' consideration.

Lomax stared, her eyes were dark with anger. "He murdered Kelly? Right?"

Mason glanced at Bracken. "We don't know."

"You let him escape. Now you think he's taken Honor, too?"

Bracken's face remained impassive. "Anything you could tell us would be helpful."

"I know Damon's part of something big," she said, standing and refilling her glass. "Don't ask me for details. The way I hear things means you won't be able to use them in court" — she gave them a look over the rim of her glass — "so you know better than to ask. But yes. He's got connections. Resources. You found his little hidey-hole out in the woods?"

Mason nodded. "We did."

"Well, that was just the beginning. Did Tyler tell you about the Fort?"

Mason frowned. "The *what*?"

Lomax downed her drink in one and coughed, then poured another. "It's somewhere off the A19. Middle of nowhere." She sat down again. "Some sort of fortified bunker where Damon and others like him hunker down to plan their sick little missions. I was going to send my own people out there, but they're too busy firefighting everything else that's been going on around here." She looked at them. "Find the Fort, and maybe you'll find Damon."

"Thank you, Lord Mayor," Mason said, resisting the urge to rush out through the door and leap into the car. "That will be very helpful."

"One other thing," Lomax called as they made for the door. Mason paused "Find this sicko, you hear me? He tried to kill my brother. Now he's killing haemophiles?" Her expression darkened. "The man is dangerous. I want him the hell away from my city."

"We'll find Damon," Bracken replied. "You have my word."

Lomax examined Bracken for a long moment, intrigue obvious in her face.

"I didn't think anyone could make good on that promise. Certainly none of my own people have." She tilted her chin and studied them both. "But you and Walker? Maybe you actually stand a snowball's chance in hell."

"Thank you for the vote of confidence," Mason said levelly.

"I don't give them lightly, Inspector," she said. "Don't let me down."

"One bit of advice, ma'am," Mason said with his hand on the door handle. "Lock those away," he said, nodding toward the bowl of jewels. "We can't spare the resources to handle a burglary right now."

She clenched her jaw, but they left before she could answer.

"Nice lady," Bracken said wryly as they returned to the car.

"Corrupt as they come," Mason muttered, fastening his seatbelt. "But she's usually right."

He turned on the engine and backed out onto the main road and turned right.

"Where are we going?" Bracken said.

"To find the Fort."

"Now?"

"Yes, now," Mason said, turning right again, heading north.

"If Damon just swiped Honor from her bedroom in London, he's not going to be there."

"Only a haemophile could make someone vanish like that."

"So, are these cases linked or not?"

Mason didn't answer. He was too busy trying to decide that for himself.

"We only have this report third-hand right now," Bracken continued. "And even if we didn't, all we know about the Fort is that it's *'somewhere off the A19'*. I'm not from around here, but I know that's somewhere in the North York Moors."

"That means the sooner we start looking, the better."

"I know you're invested in this, Walker," Bracken said after another heavy pause. "And believe me, so am I. But driving wildly about the countryside will take too much time."

"What's going on, Bracken?" Mason demanded. "It feels like you're stalling. Holding out on me."

"I'm doing neither. I just think you've forgotten that I need to be inside before dawn."

Mason cursed under his breath. "So, tell me where to drop you off."

"You need to sleep sometime, too. I can tell how tired you are."

"Can you also tell how pissed off I am that we've wasted so much time already?"

Bracken didn't react. "We got a lot done tonight. Go home. Get some rest."

"If we'd had this sooner, we could have pressed Damon's goons about the Fort. We could already have the location."

"I can carry on for a couple of hours, Walker. And I can probably get more done in that time than you could. Drop me at the station. Then go home."

The exhaustion he'd been refusing to acknowledge began to wash over him in waves.

"What are you going to do?"

"I'm going to find out who Damon really is…a proper, working profile. That might lead us to the Fort. At the moment we're just guessing. We need something solid."

"You don't think we've tried to find out who he is? I've looked. The guy's a ghost."

"I've got a few more tricks up my sleeve," Bracken murmured in that voice that inexplicably had Mason's skin rippling with goosebumps. "You should call it a day. Tomorrow night, we'll start again."

Mason swallowed. "What about Honor?"

"Leave that to the Met," he said, with a curious weight in his voice. "They know what they're doing. And we've got enough to handle up here."

"You're right," Mason said grudgingly after a moment. "I'm sorry. I'm used to Vickers calling me out when it's needed. Not anyone else."

"I'll do whatever you need me to, Walker. You just need to be honest with me."

Mason refused to look at him, wary of what he might read in those enigmatic eyes.

* * * *

It was late by the time Mason woke up the next day. He lay in a stupor, blinking at the stripes of sunlight on the ceiling and groped for his phone.

There was a message from Bracken.

Have Damon's identity. Meet me at the station at sunset.

Bracken's image rose in Mason's mind. The jewel-bright eyes. The breath-stealing smile. The masked intensity he sensed was lurking just beneath the surface. The look in his eyes that seemed to be responding to Mason's reactions without words but with full understanding...and returned interest.

Mason blinked. He remembered he'd dreamt of Bracken. Then he started to remember the dream.

His cock twitched. He dug his thumbs into his eyes.

"Stop it," he muttered through clenched teeth. "You're *straight*."

But the dream stirred again. They'd been somewhere dark, but Mason had been able to see clearly. There were desks around them, a whiteboard on the wall. Bracken was close. Mason could smell his hair and feel his breath on his face. Every inch of his body was on fire with the need to touch him — a need so strong it was unlike anything he'd felt before. And yet...

He shoved the covers aside and went to his laptop. He opened a search engine and logged into the police database, too.

He typed *Cai Bracken* then clicked *Search*.

* * * *

"Afternoon, boss." Vickers frowned at him as he passed her desk. "You look like hell. What's up?"

"Are the interviews with Damon's cronies done?" he said as he made for the coffee machine.

Vickers watched him with a concerned expression as he filled the machine. "The reports are in your inbox."

Mason watched the dark liquid trickle into his mug. "Anything of interest?"

"What do you think?" she said and followed him to his office. "They're far from bright sparks, but they're all sewn up tighter than a pair of skinny jeans. No one's talking."

"No mention of something called 'The Fort'?"

"The what?"

"Figures," Mason said, though was unable to deny the slump of disappointment. He sat and booted up his computer. He took a sip of his coffee, glanced at Vickers then away again. "I'll explain later. Did you hear that Bracken identified Damon?"

"Shit, really? Who is he?"

"I don't know," Mason said, scrolling through his dozens of unread messages. "And the guy apparently doesn't know how to email."

"He probably wants to tell you in person."

"Yes, but then we have to wait until bloody sunset, don't we?"

"Boss, are you okay?" Vickers asked again, closing his door. "I know this is an intense case. And working with Bracken must be—"

"It's not..." He made an impatient noise. "I just don't know what to make of the guy. It feels like he's holding back...all the time."

Vickers perched on the edge of the desk. "He probably is. Must be bloody scary, being forced into being one of them, not having a clue what's happening to your body or why."

Shame was bitter on Mason's tongue.

"Is that really what's bothering you?" she asked quietly. "Wouldn't have pegged you to be spooked out by a weird partner."

"He's not my partner," Mason said quickly. "*You're* my partner."

She grinned. "I'm flattered, boss. But you know I'm spoken for, right? Currently, anyway."

Mason gave her a hard look. Realization dawned in her eyes, and he hurriedly dropped his gaze.

"Boss...is *that* it? Do you—?"

"The future of your career depends on you not finishing that sentence, Vickers," he muttered, swigging coffee. The coffee went down the wrong way, and he coughed. "In fact," he spluttered, his eyes watering, "don't even have it in your head. Banish it. *Now*."

"Yes, sir," she said, her face mock-serious. "Consider it banished."

"I mean it, Vickers."

"I know you do," she went on, her face softening. "But, seriously. You know it's not the end of the world if you fancy the guy, right? I'm pretty sure they're all pansexual for a start. And let's not forget he's fucking hot—"

"*Vickers*."

She shut her mouth and made the zip-up motion over it.

"Thank you. Now, how long until sunset?"

She glanced at her watch. "Five hours maybe?"

"Christ." He rubbed his face. "You know how much we could get done in five hours if we knew Damon's identity?"

"Well, let's do what we can," she said. "Where do you want me to start?"

"Can you get me an update on the Ford-Byerson case?"

"They haven't found her."

"I don't care. Just get me the most up-to-date report. Please," he added, making his voice kinder. "And find some maps. Not internet maps. Real maps."

"Maps?"

"Yes. Ordnance Survey. Any that cover the North York Moors National Park."

Vickers' face changed. "What am I looking for?"

"This 'Fort'. Sounds like Damon and his creepy colleagues had some sort of bunker where they all hung out. Sounds like the sort of place he might bolt if he were in trouble. Tyler Lomax told his sister that it's *'somewhere off the A19'.*" Vickers grimaced but he held up a hand. "Please. Just start looking."

"Okay boss…but if it's a secret bunker, it's not on any map."

"Vickers…*please*. Just see if there's somewhere likely. At this point, we just need a starting point. Literally anything will help."

"Fine, yes, sure, I'll see what I can see. What are you going to do?"

"I'm going to go over everything again. Just get me that Met update as soon as you have it."

"Yes, boss."

* * * *

The tension in Mason's body had reached breaking point by the time Bracken appeared in his office.

Literally appeared…again. One second he was alone. The next, Bracken was there holding a computer tablet.

Mason swore and began mopping his spilled coffee with some tissues.

"Sorry."

"You could give someone a heart attack doing that, you know."

"Sorry," Bracken repeated. "I just know we're on the clock. Here." He held out the tablet. He frowned. "What is it?"

Mason dropped his gaze and took the tablet, aware he was staring…again. He willed his mind to focus. To not get distracted again. To not stare at Bracken and remember…

He shook himself and began to read. "Michael Heron?"

"Damon's real name. Born in Galway, Ireland."

Mason blinked. "Kelly was Irish."

"Originally," Bracken said after a considered pause. "Don't think he's lived there for at least a century."

"Still… It's a weird coincidence. Bracken?" Bracken blinked. He had been staring at the wall. "What is it?"

"Nothing."

Mason studied him closely. "Your missing person case. The girl. Cara Sullivan. She was Irish, too. Her family were only on holiday in London."

Bracken's face was blank, apart from his eyes, which looked darker than usual. "They were from Belfast. Northern Ireland. And that has nothing to do with this."

"Are you sure?"

"How can it?" Something had changed in Bracken's voice, too. Mason wasn't sure he liked it. "That happened ten years ago."

Mason looked away. "You're probably right. It just seems…odd."

"Ireland's a big country, Walker."

"I'm aware. Okay, Heron. Go."

Bracken turned his attention to the tablet. "Heron's parents were both professors of history and folklore at the local university. Divorced when he was eleven. Apparently it hit him hard. He dropped out of school. There are some sealed juvenile records, then a conviction for assault at age nineteen." Bracken leaned over and swiped the screen. "He attacked a gay man at a nightclub."

"A hate crime?" Mason frowned. "But Damon and Lomax had a sexual relationship."

Bracken raised his eyebrows. "Does everyone sleep with everyone else around here?"

Mason hoped his face wasn't betraying his thoughts. "My point is, why would Damon do this? Even as a kid?"

"Maybe it was nothing to do with sex," Bracken said. "Or maybe Damon...Heron...just never learned to handle his impulses."

"And now he has a political ax to grind."

"And access to weapons and torture bunkers."

"We have to find this guy."

"Well, now we can." Bracken swiped the screen again. "Fingerprints. DNA. Known aliases. I've even found a few unknown ones. One is a fictional contractor called Harold Merlin." He tapped the scanned document on the screen. "Someone called Harold Merlin bought this transit van around six months ago. The same van was towed for parking violations recently. Guess where from?"

Mason swiped to the next report and his grip on the tablet tightened. "Illington?"

"That's where you picked up Damon and Tyler Lomax, right?"

Mason nodded.

"This is Damon's van. And it was top of the line. All mod-cons, including sat nav."

Mason's pulse quickened. "That may have logged all his previous locations."

Bracken smiled. "Believe I can do the job now?"

Mason's face warmed again. "I never believed you couldn't."

"Just not with you?"

Mason grabbed his coat. "We need the keys from evidence."

"I already have the keys," Bracken said, stepping back and opening the door. "And I've called impound. They're waiting for us."

Mason couldn't figure out if the drive was comfortable or not. They were both silent, but whenever he snuck a glance at Bracken his face was calm, almost serene. It made Mason's own uncertainty all the more keen.

"You want to say something."

Mason blinked and looked away, suddenly aware he'd been staring. "Sorry?"

"You want to say something to me. Something important."

"So, what? You're telepathic now as well?"

"You don't have to be telepathic to see something's bothering you. What is it?"

"Nothing."

Bracken ran a hand through his hair. "I've already said, Walker. This partnership would work a lot better if you were honest with me."

Mason tightened his grip on the wheel. The words were like a bubble growing in his chest. He opened his mouth to voice another denial, but instead it burst.

"Something about you has been nagging at me. I couldn't figure out what it was. But I got there last night." He slowed the car to turn left, using it as an excuse to work up the nerve to go on. "We've met before."

Bracken raised his eyebrows. "We have?"

"You came to my college careers day."

Bracken stared ahead. "I don't remember. I'm sorry." He fell silent. Mason felt his gaze on him. Felt it linger. "Is that what's bothering you?"

Mason forced himself to ease his grip on the wheel. "Nothing's bothering me. It's just you look the same as you did when I was sixteen. Younger, even. It's... unsettling. That's all."

Bracken's expression was guarded. "I can imagine."

"You really don't remember?" Mason forced himself to keep his voice level, telling himself he wasn't hurt. "We talked...a lot. You told me about the police training program. The shifts. The exams."

"It's not personal, Mason," he replied quietly. "My human life? It's" — he frowned — "It's fading. I've lost a lot of my memories from before I was turned. Eventually, I'll lose all of it."

Something cold and dark uncurled in Mason's chest. "Wow. That really happens?"

"It really happens."

Mason took a moment to find his voice. "I'm sorry."

"Don't be sorry. I just didn't want you to think I'd forgotten you on purpose."

Was there something in his tone? Heat crawled into Mason's face. He stared fixedly ahead for the rest of the drive.

The night porter let them into the impound lot after checking their IDs. He took them over to a white van at the back then left them.

The vehicle was large and new, not a scratch on it. Mason peered through the driver's window and smiled with satisfaction. The sat nav on the dashboard was brand new. He climbed in and turned the key in the ignition to activate the electronics. Bracken got into the passenger seat as Mason clicked through the sat nav's settings.

"There," he said, pointing at a location logged in the GPS list. "This is somewhere he's been almost as much as his compound in the woods—off the A19 in the middle of the national park, just like we thought. This is the Fort." His elation dimmed at the look on Bracken's face. "What is it?"

"Nothing," he said quietly, opening the door. "I just need some air."

"What's wrong?"

But Bracken was already gone. Mason got out and called after him. "Bracken? What is it?"

Bracken was several meters away, standing still and breathing deeply. "There was something in that van. It makes me feel ill being near it."

"Like what?" Mason said, retrieving the keys.

Bracken didn't answer. He kept his back turned as Mason opened the back doors. Mason stared at the rows of guns, knives, weapons, rope and other unspeakable things neatly hung on hooks or stowed in boxes.

"Jesus Christ."

Bracken looked over his shoulder then away. "Yeah…nice guy, this Michael Heron."

"You sensed weapons?"

"Not the weapons. Blood. Dead haemophile Blood." His shoulders were tense. "Like I could feel it in Kelly…but a lot more of it."

"I can't see anything," Mason said, flashing his phone torch around the interior of the van.

"It's been cleaned up. But it still makes me…" He shuddered. "I don't know. I just have to get away from here."

"Wait, Bracken."

But Mason was alone. He muttered under his breath, locked the van and returned to the car. Bracken wasn't there. He turned around in time to spot a dim figure stepping out of the streetlight into a park.

Mason followed with his phone torch. He found Bracken on a bench next to some play equipment. The shadows were dark around them. He was as motionless as marble. Mason stepped closer.

"Sorry," Bracken said in a thick voice. "You have no idea..." He stopped, raised his head and smiled a thin smile. "It's been ten years. But I'm still not used to being...this."

Silence hung between them for a long time. Then Mason heard himself ask, "What's it like?"

The shadows on Bracken's face shifted. "I can't even explain. Everything's just very...intense."

Mason perched on the end of the bench. He could hear Bracken breathing. He remembered his dream and hurriedly pushed the thoughts away before the heat rose in his body again.

"I'll organize a raid on the Fort."

"You mean you don't want to breach it yourself tonight, guns blazing?" Bracken's tone was amused but still strained.

"I'm aware I may have been hard to work with," Mason admitted in a soft voice. "It's like Dr. Kumar said. We're not used to not-knowing what to do next."

Bracken looked at him. Mason sensed his gaze even in the dark. "You know what to do," he said quietly. "You're a good cop."

"You hardly know me."

His smile glinted in the dark. "Humans give a lot away without realizing."

Mason went cold and hot all at once. "Like what?"

A pause.

"A raid sounds good," Bracken said. "How long will it take to organize?"

"Can probably have a team ready to go by dawn."

"But I need to be there."

"Why?"

"It's my case, too."

Mason examined what he could see of the other detective in silence. "You make it sound like there's something personal going on."

"This is a direct outcome of everything that's going on between our species over the last few years. It *is* personal. It affects who I am...who I might be." He took a breath and appeared calm. "I don't know what's going to happen, but I want to be a part of it."

"I get that," Mason said after a moment. "But you can trust me. I'm not going to let Damon slip away again."

Bracken was quiet for a long time. "I'd really prefer to be there."

"We have to move as soon as possible," Mason reasoned. "We've already lost too much time."

Bracken sighed and leaned back, staring at the sky. The starlight caught in his hair and eyelashes like gems. It bathed his pale face with its cool glow. The sadness that weighed his eyes made them shine like sapphires. He was so beautiful Mason could barely breathe. He just prayed the darkness hid his body's reactions.

"You're right," Bracken said "I know you're right. God, I hate this."

"Hate what?" Mason managed.

Bracken gestured wearily. "Only being able to work at night, all that fuckery."

"I can't imagine what it's like," Mason said quietly. "Having to compromise like that, especially with your record."

"You flatter me, DI Walker."

"You were the one that made me want to be a detective in the first place," he admitted.

His voice was low. Intimate. The look on Bracken's face seemed to free him, stripping away all the walls that had been keeping the revelations inside.

"Before that careers day, I was going to be an engineer. You made me see who I really was. The sort of man I could be." He swallowed. "You woke something in me I didn't even know was part of who I was…then and now."

Silence surrounded them for a long time. Mason drank in the sensation of Bracken's eyes on his, of the hot blue going right through his body. Even in the dark he could sense it, as strong as a flame against his skin.

Mason slid along the bench before he'd even decided to move. Their elbows brushed. Bracken's lips parted. Mason heard him inhale. Sparks danced along his nerves. Their faces were so close. All Mason had to do to find out if Bracken's lips tasted as good as they looked was lean in. One tiny movement.

He leaned forward. Bracken backed away.

Embarrassment wrapped around Mason's limbs like barbed wire.

"Mason…"

"I gotta get back," Mason said, standing and stepping away. "Start prepping for the raid."

"Mason, wait."

"You want a lift or what?"

Bracken hadn't moved. "I'll make my own way back."

Mason's heart slumped behind his ribs. "Fine."

He left the bench behind, making himself not run. He got to the car, slammed the door and put his face in his hands. What was going on with him? There wasn't a single thing about what he'd just done that made any sense.

But he had been so certain. The look in Bracken's eyes… The intensity of the sensations in his body… The force drawing them closer… It had been so…undeniable.

And yet Bracken had moved away.

Mason lowered his hands with a rich expletive and started the car. He checked his mirrors as he passed the park. The bench was empty.

Chapter Five

Mason was grateful for the controlled chaos that was the organizing of a raid. He and Vickers scrambled to alert the firearms unit and brief the raid team on the details of the job. Thankfully there wasn't a quiet moment that would allow him to think back to the encounter on the bench the night before.

Dawn found him in the back of a van in riot gear, clutching his weapon and unable to meet Vickers in the eye. His DC couldn't seem to stop looking at him with that concerned crease between her eyebrows, but, thankfully, she never said anything.

By the time they were surrounding a bleak, windowless structure surrounded by a tall wall and taller trees, his nerves were strung tighter than bow strings. He focused on keeping his position and listened to the crackled commands in his earpiece as the frontline officers approached the door.

The order was given, the door was breached and the team surged in.

Mason knew when they cleared the building in record time that it was bad news.

"Empty, guv," the firearms sergeant said, pushing back the visor of his helmet. "Empty and scrubbed. Not even a piss stain in the bathroom."

Mason's heart sank. He holstered his weapon and stepped into the building, Vickers at his shoulder. The concrete structure was deserted. No people. No furniture. There wasn't even any dust.

"This is more than clean," Mason said.

"More like sterilized," Vickers said, staring around.

Mason went through every single room, cupboard and closet anyway, but by the time he was back out in the warm morning air, the despair was like concrete in his gut.

"Someone musta warned them," the firearms sergeant muttered.

"Heron," Mason replied. "He knew we'd find the van and the sat nav. He warned them to clear out and leave no trace."

"I'll get the tech team out here," Vickers said, pulling out her mobile. "You never know."

Mason nodded because he knew it was all they could do, and he returned to the van.

* * * *

"We'll get him, boss." Vickers set another cup of coffee on Mason's desk. Night was falling. The raid report form sat incomplete on his computer, but he'd been staring out through the window for the last hour.

"What?" he said when Vickers repeated herself.

Vickers dropped herself in the chair with a sigh. "Wherever the bastard is, we'll find him... Heron."

Mason reached for the coffee. It was hot and rich. But it made his stomach growl.

"Have you eaten today, boss?"

"I haven't really felt like it."

"Come on," Vickers said, throwing Mason's coat at him.

"What's happening?"

"Remember what my mum said about good food and bad problems? I'm taking you to dinner."

"Vickers—"

"*Walker*," she cut him off. "I know you're my boss, but it seems I'm the one in charge of keeping you upright. We're going."

Mason followed her out of the station to a little cafe he'd only ever been into for takeaway drinks. The air was rich with a variety of savory smells, and his stomach clenched demandingly. But when the bowl of sweet potato soup was set in front of him, he struggled to lift the spoon.

"So are you gonna tell me what went on with Bracken last night?"

Mason blinked. "What?"

"You look like a kicked dog. No offense, boss…but really."

"We've been over this—"

"Cards on the table time. You've worked with all sorts before," she went on, dunking her crusty roll into her own soup. "Bigoted, stuck up, ignorant or just plain useless. I know Bracken is none of those things. And I know this is not how you act when you're struggling to work with someone for professional reasons."

Mason looked over her shoulder out of the window. It was dark, but there was no one there. He checked his phone. No messages.

He managed a mouthful of soup. "You're gonna be a DCI one day, aren't you?"

"If the shoe fits," she said around her large mouthful. She swallowed, set the roll down and planted her elbows on the table. "Come on, boss. I swear it'll be a hundred times better if you talk to someone. And you know I ain't gonna judge you."

Mason didn't lift his eyes from the bowl. "I just don't understand any of this. I'm straight. I've never even thought about another guy before, let alone…" He stopped, heat flooding into his face.

Vickers was silent for a moment. Then she shrugged. "Everyone's on the sliding scale somewhere, sir." She smiled an impish smile. "Maybe Bracken's your slide."

"He's a colleague."

"Doesn't stop the rest of us. Or, with respect, you, previously, sir."

He looked at her. "Look…me and Fletcher—"

"None of my business," Vickers held up her hand. "You're both adults as far as I'm concerned. And if the rules really are your problem, well, Bracken works for a different force. Technically, that's not against the rules."

Mason pushed the soup around his bowl. "He's not even human."

"Maybe that's what you want."

Mason raised his eyes. She was still smiling, but the look in her eyes was frank.

"So," she said, dunking her bread again. "Does he feel the same way?"

Mason spooned another mouthful, his eyes still fixed on his phone. He took his time swallowing to give himself time to think. "I thought so. But now I don't know."

"Have you asked him?"

"Vickers, this is all highly irregular."

"We're not at work right now," she reasoned, chewing the last of her bread. "Just two mates, chatting about our sex lives…or lack of."

"I know for a fact yours isn't lacking."

She grinned again. "Let's stay on you. Everyone needs something, now and again. And everything you've had before hasn't been enough to make you go the distance."

"Sometimes I think you watch me too closely, Vickers."

"You need something different, clearly," Vickers went on, spooning the remnants of her soup. "Something maybe you've never tried before. Something more…fulfilling."

"My job fulfills me."

She turned her head and gave him a sideways glance. "The badge is not much cop in bed though, is it?"

"Okay, that's enough," he said, pushing his food away. "We've got work to do. Bracken is here to help me do it. I need to focus, that's all."

"When was the last time you did anything just for yourself, boss?" she said quietly. "When was the last time you…I don't know, went to the pub? Went on holiday? Read a book, played a board game, anything?"

"I am grateful you care, Vickers. But I am a grown up. I can look after myself."

"Could have fooled me," she said, raising an eyebrow. "You're in before everyone else. You stay after we've all gone. You never have a tan, and you never share any pictures of anything you've been up to. Walker, really… Don't you have anything in your life that's just about you?"

He wanted to be angry but instead just felt...gray. Hollow. "If you don't know this about the job yet, you soon will. It doesn't allow for much of a personal life. Other people depend on you. That means sacrifice."

"Is it worth it?"

Mason thought he had an answer, but he opened his mouth, and nothing came out. He drew breath, but Vickers was gazing over his shoulder. He turned.

Bracken was in the doorway. His expression was guarded, but there was a question in his eyes as he approached.

"Am I interrupting?"

"Nope," Vickers declared, smiling. "What can we do for you?"

"I heard about the Fort."

"Another bust," Mason said, staring at the table.

"Not completely," Bracken said. "The tech team found one stray fingerprint."

"They did?"

"They did. And they've got a match. They're bringing the guy in now."

"Fuck yeah," Vickers said, pulling Mason's half-finished soup toward herself. "Off you go, boss. I'll take care of this." She began eating and gestured at the door. "You go take care of everything else."

Mason ignored the pointed look on her face and hurried out of the cafe. He shoved his hands deep into his pockets as they made for the station.

"It's cooler tonight," Bracken observed.

"Autumn's on the way," Mason replied.

"Magnusson and Truelove's wedding will be here before anyone knows it."

"I wonder if it's wise, with everything that's going on."

"No one should have to hide how they feel because of fear."

Mason glanced at him then away. "That's rich, after last night."

Bracken stopped walking. "Walker."

"Don't," Mason cut him off. Then, seeing the look on Bracken's face, sighed. "I'm sorry. That was out of line. We don't need to talk about it."

"I think we do."

Mason increased his pace and was grateful to get back into the artificial light of the police station.

"Where is he?" Mason asked the duty sergeant.

"Interview Two, guv."

"Thanks. Bracken, wait here."

Bracken looked stricken. "Walker—"

"He's a haemo-hater. You being there will just complicate things."

Mason didn't look back as he left the lobby.

The man sitting at the table in Interview Room Two was overweight, bald and glowering fit to kill with his look alone. His Legal Aid solicitor sat a noticeable distance from him, as if silently trying to communicate that it might be her job to defend him, but it wasn't a personal choice.

"We found your fingerprints at a location known as 'The Fort', Mr. Hill." Mason used his practiced, neutral tone that he started all interviews with, the one that allowed interviewees to interpret his meaning however they wanted, which allowed them to react, consciously or not, and show him what they were thinking. "We know you were there recently. I need you to tell me what the place is."

"I don't need to tell you nothing, pretty boy," the man drawled, pulling his lips back from yellowing teeth.

"It would be better for you if you did."

He snorted. "You think your laws are still worth anything? Take a long look out of the window, buddy—preferably at night."

"What do you mean by that?"

"Wakey wakey, copper. There's a war goin' on. And you ain't the one fighting it."

"I'm afraid the Home Office has failed to inform us of any war. I'd appreciate it if you'd enlighten me."

The man leaned forward, glowering from under heavy eyebrows. "The human race is under threat, and you ain't lifting a finger, so we have to." He straightened. "That's all I'm saying about that."

"Tell me about Michael Heron."

"Who?"

"You may know him as Damon."

The man's eyes flickered but he didn't speak.

"When we find him, he's going away for a long, long time, as will anyone who is tied to him, even by so much as a fingerprint." The man's jaw worked. Mason slid a glance at the solicitor, but she was focused on her notes. "Anyone who helps us find him, though, well…" Mason spread his hands. "Those people may have options."

"You won't find Damon."

"We will, Mr. Hill…eventually. But you could save everyone some time by pointing us in the right direction. Then I can tell the Prosecution Service how helpful you've been."

"Blow me, copper."

Mason sighed and sat back in his chair. He put on his most reasonable face. "We'll be releasing a statement about the Fort and about your arrest. We're also telling everyone about these interviews we're having with you and all your friends." Mason laid his hand on the table. "The world knows your part in this is over. They know you've already lost. Why not do yourself a favor and try to save what little future you have by doing the right thing now?"

Hill's smile was like a knife slash in raw bread dough. "You don't get it. You'll never get it. We *want* the word out there. We *want* you telling everyone what's goin' on." He *thunked* his fat elbows on the table. "We ain't lost nothin', copper. It's all part of a plan, see?"

Mason weighed him up in silence. "I hate to tell you this, Mr. Hill, but the public response to the statements we've released so far only varies between disgust and apathy. Your imagined support? It's not there. People don't think what you believe is right."

His face twitched. "You're so wrong you can't even see."

"I think you have mistaken my colleague's implication," came a voice from the corner of the room.

Everyone in the room, including Mason, started. The solicitor tightened her grip on her pen. Hill's mouth dropped open.

Bracken smiled, pulled out the chair at Mason's side and sat.

"Where the fuck did he come from?" Hill flushed to his receding hairline.

"What Detective Inspector Walker is trying to explain," Bracken went on, as calmly as if Hill hadn't spoken at all, "is that there is no war. What you are doing isn't clever…or noble. You are criminals, and you are in a very precarious position. Walker is trying to help you, but he can't do that unless you help him."

"I ain't helping anyone, especially not the likes of you."

"How much do you know about your boss?" Bracken tilted his head. Mason kept his mouth shut with an effort. "You didn't even know his real name. Got to make you wonder what else he didn't tell you. Odd, to be fighting a so-called war for a man you know nothing about."

Hill lurched to his feet, pointing a quivering finger at Bracken. "Get this thing out of the room," he bellowed. "I will *not* be in the same room as one of them. Get him out...*now*."

"Special Officer Bracken is working with me on this case," Mason said, keeping his eyes forward and his tone flat. "He has just as much right to be here as I do."

"Bullshit. He's a vamp. A bloodsucker. A monster and a murderer. They have no rights. They should be exterminated, every last one."

"Mr. Hill—" Mason tried, but the man raised his voice.

"I *won't* be in here with *him*," he yelled at his solicitor, quivering with both rage and fear. "I got rights. Get 'im out. Get 'im out *now*."

"Mr. Hill," she said, holding up her hand. "I suggest you calm down."

"Fuck calming down. Get that thing" — he jabbed his finger at Bracken again — "out of here this second, or get me out. This is against my human rights. I'll sue!"

The solicitor stood with a weary expression. "Gentlemen, if I could have a moment alone with my client?"

Mason's pulse pounded in his temples as they stepped outside. Bracken took one look at his face, took him by the elbow and steered him toward his office.

Mason was able to contain himself until Bracken shut the door, then he swore, richly and at length.

"I told you to stay out of there."

Bracken just looked at him. "Come on, Walker. It's not me your mad at, and you know it."

Mason let out a frustrated nose. "What a five-star asshole."

"Not going to argue with you there."

"How are you not kicking furniture?"

"That's what we wanted."

"Come again?"

"It's no use telling these people they're wrong. You have to show them."

"And how's that working so far?"

Bracken sighed. "He's confirmed the level of hatred these sorts of groups have for my kind. That's something."

"We already knew that. And I could have got more out of him if you hadn't done your little appearing act and scared the living shit out of him."

Bracken's face clouded. "He wasn't going to say anything, anyway. You knew that. But what I would have said, if you hadn't stormed off, is that if I'm in the room, he doesn't need to speak."

Mason ceased his restless pacing. "You got something?"

Bracken nodded. "He doesn't know anything useful about Heron. That's a fact. It's not just that he didn't know his real name. The feelings he has for the man are groundless, completely fabricated. Heron shared nothing with these people apart from his manifesto. So if he's working with someone…none of his goons are even aware of their existence."

"Why hide them?" Mason mused. "If he really has a partner in all this, someone working toward the same things as the rest of them, why hide their identity?"

"A question I'd very much like to ask Mr. Heron myself," Bracken said.

"And still no word on Ford-Byerson?"

Bracken shook his head.

Mason made a frustrated noise. "This is all so fucked. And it's going to get worse before it gets better."

"It's okay, Walker."

'It's not okay." Mason rounded on Bracken. "I had to run the briefings after Blood Winter. We had the pictures, the eyewitness reports. We got the reports of the aftermath, too. Waves of violence on both sides that spread all over the country. All over the world." He slumped against the desk. "And now it's happening again. On my watch."

Bracken took a step closer. "Change is never easy. But you've got this. I know you do."

Their toes were almost touching. Mason looked up. Bracken's face was so perfect in the middle of all this ugliness. He was so still it looked painful. But something in his eyes was blazing and unrestrained.

Mason reached up. Bracken's eyes widened but he didn't pull away. Mason wove his fingers into the fine, soft hair and pulled Bracken's face to his own. He crushed his mouth to his, panting against his perfect lips. Bracken shivered and opened his mouth. Mason's blood surged and he plunged his tongue in, swallowing, tasting and tightening his grip on the back of Bracken's head.

His body melted into Mason's. Mason thought he might expire with the intensity of the sensation. His frame was firm and fit against Mason's like it was made to. His skin was cool and smelled like winter breeze and spiced pine. His mouth tasted like the richest of red wines Mason had ever tasted. Even the unfamiliar feeling of sharp teeth against his tongue only heightened the pleasure.

Bracken grasped his arms with a grip so strong it hovered on the edge of pain.

He was sliding his other hand up Bracken's back when he broke away, shaking.

"Mason, I can't."

"No." Mason shook his head, reaching for him. "Please..."

But Bracken had gone. Mason was alone in the office with a racing heart, a swollen erection and a deep pit of darkness in his gut.

* * * *

"My Christ," Vickers said by way of a greeting the following morning. "What the hell's happened now?"

"Nothing," Mason said, putting aside his phone after checking for the hundredth time that Bracken hadn't rung him back, aware of his rumpled clothing, disheveled hair and unshaved stubble.

"Walker—"

"We kissed," he blurted, fisting his hands in his hair. "Me and Bracken. We kissed."

Vickers blinked then grinned. "And that's bad because?"

"He broke it off," Mason muttered. "Then did his vanishing act."

"Okay," Vickers said, lowering herself into the chair by his desk. "Maybe he's just not into it...?"

"He is," Mason snapped. Then, after taking a breath, continuing in a calmer voice. "I think he is. The way he…ah." He made a frustrated noise and rubbed his face. "Forget it."

"Here's a novel idea. Have you tried just talking to him?"

"I said forget it. We've got two bodies in the morgue, an AWOL chief suspect and a missing person. This is not the time to get distracted."

"If you say so," Vickers said, giving him a long knowing look before returning her attention to her phone. "In which case… Apart from that fingerprint, the Fort was forensically dry. But Chuckles from last night? We're doing an extensive background check. There's a lot to go through, too. We may get lucky."

"Walker. Vickers." Amelia stepped into the doorway, looking smart and groomed, but Mason could see her eyes were heavy. "Progress report?"

"We're working on several things, ma'am," he said with a pointed look at Vickers.

"And what were you working on all night long, exactly?"

Mason lowered his eyes. "Trying to figure out how Heron got word to the Fort to clear out, and how they did such a thorough job of it."

"But that's telling in itself, right?" Amelia said quietly.

"Right," Mason said. "It feels professional. All of it."

"So we're looking at professional, resourced, secretive," Amelia said, coming into the office and closing the door. "What does that remind you of?"

Vickers chewed her lip.

"Government," Mason said.

"Government." Amelia nodded. "What was Ford-Byerson's official title again?"

Mason blinked. "Legal Counsel on Haemophile Affairs. Ma'am, you're not suggesting…"

"I'm not suggesting anything," Amelia said carefully. "But the missing person works for the government. She's in a unique position — the right hand of Ivor Novák, the haemophile parliamentary representative. She vanished without a trace…"

"*After* Heron got busted out of hospital," Mason protested.

"Someone with that kind of reach doesn't do the dirty work themselves."

"But, ma'am," Vickers said. "Her wife's testimony…"

"When have you ever known me to jump to any conclusions, Vickers?"

Vickers looked abashed. "Never, ma'am."

"I'm simply saying it's an angle we should explore," she said. "Victim or perpetrator, we need to know more about Honor. Ask Bracken. He probably knows more than is in the files."

"Yes, ma'am," Mason said, clicking his mouse and pretending to look at something on the screen.

He sensed Amelia's gaze. "Vickers, would you give us a moment?"

Vickers did not need to be asked a second time. She fled the room just short of a run.

"Are you having a problem with SO Bracken, DI Walker?"

"No," Mason said shortly. "There's no problem."

"Good," Amelia said, opening the door. "Then you'll have no problem consulting him about this the second the sun has set."

"That's *if* he appears."

"Why wouldn't he?"

"No reason," Mason hedged. "But I only get to talk to him when he chooses to show up at my office."

"You have his phone number, don't you?"

"He doesn't seem to answer his phone to me much."

"Okay then," she said, lowering her voice. "So go to his lodgings. Then you can talk to him as soon as the sun goes down."

Mason blinked. "You know where he's staying?"

"Think about it, Walker. It'll come to you."

* * * *

Sunset was still an hour away when Mason pulled in at Oswald House, but the day already felt like it had lasted twice as long as any other he had lived through. Fatigue from the sleepless night was like an undertow tugging at his brain. But his heart was skipping about when he pressed the doorbell.

Jesse Truelove opened the door. He blinked when he recognized Mason.

"Any news?" he asked as he stepped back to allow Mason inside.

"Not yet I'm afraid," he said, glancing up the stairs. "I'm here to see SO Bracken."

Truelove raised his eyebrows. "No one's supposed to know he's here...not even you."

"I am a detective, you know. And I have a matter of some urgency to discuss with him."

"Well, you're a little early, mate," Truelove drawled, glancing at his watch.

"I know," Mason said awkwardly. "If there's just somewhere I could maybe wait? I don't want to be in the way."

"Detective Inspector Walker?"

Mason turned. Tom Addams was there. His face was strained. There were shadows under his eyes. "Anything?"

"I'm sorry...no, not yet," Mason said with sincere regret.

"He's here to see Cai," Truelove said.

"There is one thing I wanted to ask you about, actually, Mr. Truelove."

"Mate, please," Truelove said, opening the door to the same sitting room as before. "Call me Jesse. I'm changing my name soon anyway."

"Jesse," Mason said, taking a seat on the sofa as Tom took the armchair and Jesse perched on the sofa arm. "It was that that I wanted to talk to you about. I don't want to sound insensitive, but have you and the Baron considered postponing your wedding?"

Jesse exchanged glances with Tom. "Yes. We considered it. I did more than consider it, if I'm honest."

"I heard their shouting match from the other end of the house," Tom said with a smile.

Jesse made a noisy sigh. "We're not postponing."

"Jesse," Mason started, but Tom interrupted him.

"Darragh fought very long and hard for Emory and Jesse's wedding to be allowed to happen," he said. "He would want it to go ahead. Otherwise, there's no point to any of it."

"Okay," Mason said. "I understand. I just wanted to make sure someone had mentioned the idea."

"They've both mentioned it," Tom said. "And I told them the same thing I told you. The wedding is going ahead."

"You're a stubborn asshole, you know that?" Jesse said to Tom, but he was smiling.

"Darragh would never forgive me if we just gave up."

"It's not giving up," Jesse argued. "It's just looking at the bigger picture."

"And what did Emory say when you said that to him?"

Jesse rolled his eyes. "Let's not have this argument again."

"Okay, we won't," Tom said with a shaky smile and stood. "Now, if you don't need anything else, I have a security sweep to run."

Tom left, and Jesse stared after him with a haunted expression.

"I'm very sorry you're having to go through all this."

"Not your fault," Jesse murmured. "Just catch the bastard. That's all we want." Mason nodded, even though Jesse wasn't looking at him. Jesse stood. "You can wait here if you want. Get you anything? Coffee? Something stronger?"

"I'm fine, thank you," Mason said. "I'll just wait here, if that's okay."

"Knock yourself out," Jesse said and left.

The room was warm. The sofa was comfortable. The light grew dimmer, and Mason's eyes began to droop.

A touch on Mason's hand brought him out of a soft, pleasant dream. He blinked groggily. Bracken was sitting in the armchair.

"You should get some proper sleep."

Mason sat up, rubbing his eyes. "I'm sorry. I shouldn't have nodded off." He blinked at Bracken, all the feelings he'd told himself he'd keep suppressed rushing to the surface. "You didn't call back."

Bracken's expression closed. He stood. "Not here."

Mason followed Bracken along a corridor, down some stairs and through a series of locked doors to a comfortably furnished room. There was a wardrobe, a sofa, a desk covered in papers and an open laptop. There were minimalist paintings on the walls, several shelves of books and a large TV. It was airy and comfortable, but with no windows. No bed.

"This is where you sleep?"

Bracken indicated an inner door locked with a numbered keypad. "I have a secure sleeping cell through there, completely up to grade." Bracken gave him a pained look. "Walker, no one's supposed to know I'm here."

"Why not?"

"It's not exactly neutral ground, is it? But it's not like I can check into the nearest hotel, either."

"I think you're capable of keeping your sleeping arrangements separate from your professional duties."

Bracken lifted an eyebrow. "Well, that's loaded."

Mason sank onto the sofa. "I'm sorry. I...I didn't sleep last night."

Bracken's expression softened. "Mason, let me explain. About last night—"

"Truelove and Magnusson won't postpone the wedding."

Bracken held himself very still. "Nor should they."

"I agree. But we need to be prepared."

"We are. The location is a secret. Even I don't know where they're doing it. Intelligence is monitoring internet chatter. But the best thing we can do for them is catch this murderer."

"Fletcher wanted me to talk to you about Ford-Byerson."

"Has she been found?"

Mason shook his head. "But the DCI's wondering if someone at government level is involved in all this."

"Ford-Byerson is a victim, not a criminal."

Mason studied him. "You seem very sure of that."

"I know her…well."

"You do?"

Cai nodded. "Whatever this job is, I wouldn't even have that without her."

"I thought you liked your job?"

"I love my job, but I can't be seen to be doing it. I no longer have an official rank. My old team either has no idea I'm still alive or don't want to know if they do."

"That's awful," Mason replied.

Bracken's eyes flickered. "I believe in what I do. If the only way I can do it is in secret, then so be it. But having to hide, like I'm something to be ashamed of…"

"You're not," Mason said firmly.

Bracken looked taken aback. "Either way, Honor was the one who got me this position. She's also the one who helps me stay under the radar, so I can work without ruffling too many feathers."

Mason brushed absently at the sofa arm. "It doesn't follow that she'd be trying to make changes for haemophiles on one hand and have them quietly murdered on the other."

Bracken leaned against the bookshelf and crossed his arms. "No. It doesn't."

"But she's involved at the highest level. If not her, maybe it's someone she has worked with…or against." Mason raised his eyes when Bracken didn't answer. "You've thought the same thing."

"I've dealt with criminal gangs before," he said carefully. "Well-resourced and organized ones. None have felt quite like this."

"Like what?" Mason asked.

Bracken frowned, still not looking at him. "I don't know. Almost personal."

Mason weighed his words before speaking. "You said yourself, it is personal. Kelly was working for the rights of haemophiles. Ford-Byerson, too."

Bracken looked like he might say more but took a breath. "Anything flag in her background check?"

Mason shook his head. "She's an exemplary civil servant. Several humanitarian awards. A resume as long as my arm. And she's worked with haemophiles ever since they first came out of hiding. Kelly and Novák are just the start. She's even organized meetings with that Dragomir Soroka character and members of parliament."

Bracken blanched. "Rather her than me."

"I have, unfortunately, had the pleasure of meeting him. There's someone everyone's going to need to keep a close eye on."

"He doesn't know much about compromise," Bracken mused.

"Have you met him, too?"

Bracken shook his head. "No, thank goodness. From what I know of his politics he would hate what I'm doing." His eyes were far away.

"We haven't looked at him in all this," Mason said quietly. "What do we actually know about him?"

"He doesn't make a secret of anything. Originally from Russia, turned at the beginning of the eighteenth century. He was one of the first to come out of hiding...and to campaign for equality."

"You know more than I do."

"One of the conditions of my position is knowing as much as I can about prominent haemophiles and their agendas. But anyone with a phone knows who he is and that he's vocal. Active. He wants haemophiles to have more power, more advantages."

Mason remembered his black eyes. His blank stare. "Is he dangerous?"

Bracken winced. "Maybe. But he wants the same things Kelly did. He just thinks a more direct approach is needed."

Mason studied his face. "You don't like him, do you?"

Bracken met his eyes. "Like I say, I've never met the man. I just get, what do you say these days?" He smiled though it didn't reach his eyes. "Bad vibes."

Mason glanced around the room. "Yeah. Me, too."

"And it's not just my gut," Bracken said, sitting straighter. "Emory told me some things."

"Fletcher told me they know each other."

Bracken nodded. "They had some sort of fight…years ago. Emory didn't tell me much, but he knows it's good for me in my position to know about our history."

"What was the fight about?"

"They were friends, at one point, I think," Bracken said, his eyes far away, "after Lucien left him. You know Lucien and Emory were once…?"

"Lucien 'turned' Magnusson. Yes, I know."

"More than that," Bracken said, looking at Mason's face. "They were a couple. A deeply bonded couple."

Mason's face warmed. "But Lucien left?"

"Guess even those sorts of relationships aren't safe from change."

Mason blinked.

"Then Emory and Soroka found each other," Bracken continued, gazing at the wall. "My kind often pair up. Or find groups. Historically and now…for protection. Emory and Soroka traveled together, I think." Bracken frowned thoughtfully. "I think they all used to travel around a lot, so as not to leave a trail."

"A trail of dead bodies." Mason handled his reaction to that carefully. "Magnusson and Soroka. Were they…involved, too?"

"Not in the way you're thinking." Mason wondered again if Bracken was looking at him differently. "As far as I can gather, it was a practical arrangement…for safety. Emory watched over his family's descendants for generations. Soroka helped with that. In exchange, Emory helped Soroka keep watch on European politics. Apparently Soroka rallied haemophiles to come out of the shadows for centuries before they eventually did it."

"So, what happened?"

"Soroka wanted to turn someone. Emory didn't."

"Turn a human into a haemophile?"

Bracken nodded. "Emory was hazy on the details, but she was some kind of political figure. Or possibly someone royal. Someone with power. Influence. Soroka always had a tactical mind, Emory said. But Emory didn't want to do it. He didn't believe any more haemophiles should be made, even then. he believed that there were too many of them already."

"When was this?"

"I'm not sure. But it was part of their 'coming out' plan, so I'm guessing sometime in the last century. Either way, they fell out about it. Emory left. I think there's been bad feeling ever since."

"Do we know if Soroka went ahead? Turned whoever it was?"

"Emory either doesn't know or wouldn't tell me. He just wanted me to understand the sort of man Soroka is. Ruthless. Determined."

"But, at the end of it all, on the same side as Kelly and Ford-Byerson."

"Unwillingly, perhaps," Bracken picked at one of his long, clawed fingernails. "But yes."

"So we're back to the haters. Even though it's hard to believe a human managed to vanish Honor from her own bed with her wife right there."

Bracken nodded.

Mason tried to make himself focus, to continue running down the thoughts to some sort of conclusion. But his attention kept returning to Bracken, standing so close but not moving any closer.

"You said we should talk," Mason said.

There was a long silence. Finally, Bracken took a seat next to him. "Walker, you have to understand…"

"Please," Mason begged. "Call me Mason, will you?"

Bracken's expression seemed to both lighten and darken simultaneously. "Okay. If you call me Cai."

Mason blinked. He tried the name out in his mind. It made his blood rush. Bracken's…*Cai's* he mentally corrected himself…face shifted, like he sensed Mason's thoughts.

"Mason." Cai's voice was low. Careful. "I know what you think you're feeling. But you have to understand. It's not real."

Mason didn't know what he'd been expecting. But it wasn't that. "What are you talking about?"

Bracken twined his fingers in his lap.

"Humans…" he eventually continued. "They're often attracted to us. We're so different and, well" — he frowned — "intense. And our Blood gives off this" — he waved his hand in the air, like he was trying to find words — "I don't know. Pheromones or something? Some sort of sex chemical. They think it may have been a way to attract you to us, in days gone by." He winced. "Made it easier to lure you in. Whatever the reason, it's powerful. That's why people get addicted to drinking it." Mason shifted uncomfortably. Cai gave him a sympathetic look and continued. "We have no control of it. And some humans are more susceptible than others."

"I still don't know what you're saying."

"I'm saying, humans often think they have feelings for us when they don't."

"You're wrong," Mason breathed.

"Mason —"

"This is hard enough for me as it is. I've never felt this way before about anyone, let alone a man. You don't think it's scaring me?"

Cai gave him a pained look.

"I'm trying to get my head around it. But I'm happy to admit it. And work on it. But the way you kissed me back, Cai…" Mason reached out and took his hand. Just feeling his skin was enough to send jolts through Mason's body, but he made himself focus on Cai's face. "This isn't pheromones. And it isn't in my head. There's something here."

Cai closed his eyes. "It's just because of what I am. That's all it is."

Mason gripped his hand tighter. "That's not true."

"How do you know?"

Mason swallowed. "Because I felt this way when I first met you." Cai opened his eyes and stared at him. "That talk you gave. At my college. We were in a classroom. There were desks. A whiteboard on the wall. I can picture it like it was yesterday. I was sixteen. I dated girls. But the way you talked about your work…the way you made me feel…" Mason's breath caught in his throat.

"I wish I remembered it." Cai's voice was husky. The pain in his eyes was deep. "Remembered you."

Mason couldn't decide if he wanted to pull Cai to him or stand and back away. He was being torn in two, finally saying these things out loud. But he also knew they'd gone unsaid too long.

"I was obsessed with you for weeks. But I had a girlfriend. I told myself I'd get over it. And I did." He looked at their joined hands. "My girlfriend and I were together until we went off to university. Then she met someone else. And so did I. Another girl." Mason's heart was pounding. His skin was tingling. Cai was staring fixedly ahead and wouldn't meet his gaze. "It never happened again, so I ignored it. But then you showed up here."

"You're a great detective," Cai said. "I can't tell you how happy I am that I made you do this for a career. You care. You really care. The force needs people like you. The strength of your feelings? It almost drowned me, that day we met. You see what matters, not just what people tell you matters. And you've given your life to making the world a better place." He withdrew his hand. "I really admire all that."

"Just admire?"

Cai winced. "Maybe more than admire. But I can't do this with you, even though I want to. *Especially* because I want to."

"Why?" Mason breathed, the word as painful as a hook in his throat.

They sat in silence, both breathing hard. Cai opened his mouth to speak but instead Mason kissed him. He made a helpless noise and shivered under Mason's touch. Mason's desire blossomed. When he didn't draw away, Mason urged Cai back into the sofa, kissing him deeply, drinking in his taste, his blood singing to feel Cai's firm, strong body yielding to his own. He broke the kiss and mouthed his neck, unable to quite believe how amazing it tasted. Cai let out a low noise that made Mason's cock jump in his pants. He had no idea what he wanted to do, but he knew he wanted Cai.

"Mason," he breathed in a voice choked with arousal, and at the sound, Mason knew exactly what to do. He slid his hand between them and cupped Cai's hardening cock through his trousers. Cai clutched Mason's wrist hard. Mason gasped, and Cai went rigid.

Mason lifted his head. Cai's face was flushed. His lips were parted. He looked so amazing Mason's whole body would have caught fire, he was sure, apart from the naked fear darkening the blue eyes.

Mason's desire ebbed.

"What is it?"

Cai pushed him away and stood. "I told you. I can't."

"Why?" Mason begged again, standing. "Please tell me why."

"Because—" Cai snapped, running his hands through his hair, taking a deep breath and letting them drop. "Because it's too much."

"I don't understand."

Cai made a noise somewhere between a cry and a moan of frustration. "You don't know what it's like," he said, his voice hoarse. "Being *this*." He gestured at himself. "My senses are off the charts. So are my emotions. Even my damn clothes feel like too much half the time."

"So take them off," Mason said, trying for a smile.

"I'm serious," Cai said. The look on his face sent regret spiking through Mason like a skewer. "People think we don't feel anything. It's completely the opposite. We feel too much. All the time. Sights, smells, touch." Cai closed his eyes and balled his fists at his temples. "It takes every bit of strength I have not to just fall apart with every breath."

Mason sat on the arm of the sofa, legs suddenly weak. "But you seem so in control."

Cai lowered his hands. They were shaking. "I fight...hard. All the time. It's slowly getting easier, but I still can't control it." His face filled with pain. "I move too fast for you to see, but I don't know I'm doing it. I sense everything a human being is feeling just by being in the room with them. And a lot of the time that's fear. Or hatred. But with you..." He took a shaking breath. "It's amazing, Mason. But it also terrifies me."

"I won't hurt you, Cai. I promise."

"No. But *I* will hurt *you*."

"I'm a big boy. I can look out for myself."

"I didn't mean emotionally," Cai said frustratedly. "I mean *literally* hurt you. Injure you. Or worse."

"I don't believe that."

"The last guy I slept with..." Cai closed his mouth. Then his eyes. Mason buried the spark of excitement he felt at the confirmation that Cai slept with men and made himself listen. "I broke one of his arms. I dislocated the other." He opened his eyes again and stared at Mason. Mason couldn't move. "He had to have surgery. He's probably got permanent nerve damage."

"Cai—"

"I didn't mean to do it," Cai cut him off. "But I don't know my own strength. And I can't control it. Especially when I'm…" His cheeks colored. "Especially when I like someone."

Mason stood and drifted closer. "You won't hurt me."

"I will," Cai said. "I won't mean to, but I will."

Mason stepped close, watching Cai breathe, gazing at his mouth with his own blood pooling in his groin. He dipped his head and spoke into the hollow under his jaw that had been driving Mason crazy ever since he first saw it.

"I trust you."

Cai moaned softly, half pleasure, half pain, then pushed Mason back. "Please, Mason. Don't."

Despair and frustration threatened to come spilling out his mouth in distraught protests. But then his phone started ringing.

He swore and pulled it out. It was Fletcher.

"Ma'am," Mason said, watching the color drain back out of Cai's face. "What is it?"

Amelia didn't answer immediately. "They've found Ford-Byerson."

Chapter Six

It took over four hours to drive to London. As if by mutual agreement, Mason and Cai didn't talk about anything that wasn't work-related. They barely even exchanged glances.

"The press are having an absolute field day," Cai murmured as he scrolled on his phone. "So much for letting the poor woman's family grieve in peace. Dragomir Soroka's already released a statement."

Mason took a sip of cooling coffee to give him time to get his voice under control. "That man's like a hurricane blowing in in the wake of a tornado."

Cai pressed play on a video.

"This is premeditated murder. This is weaponized hate. This is designed to obstruct the pursuit of equal rights. It is a disgrace and an injustice, and if the authorities continue to refuse to punish those involved, they can't be surprised when we are forced to take matters into our own hands."

"That's all we bloody need," Mason muttered. "Soroka inciting a riot."

Cai didn't answer. When Mason looked over, his face was troubled.

"What is it?"

"Nothing," Cai said, shaking his head and putting his phone away.

Mason wanted to press the matter, but the uneasiness that lay between them in that moment was as impenetrable as a steel door.

Mason bit the inside of his cheek and focused on the road.

It was getting near one in the morning by the time Mason, caffeine-fueled and edgy, turned in at New Scotland Yard.

He made for the front doors, but Cai stopped him.

"This way."

Cai took them round the back, down an access alley filled with bins, to a heavy-duty door almost hidden in the shadows. Cai entered a mind-bogglingly long code into a keypad in the wall and took Mason along a long, dim corridor to a narrow lift.

"What is this?"

"My own private entrance. Aren't I lucky?"

His eyes were shadowed. For a moment, Mason would have given anything just to be able to take his hand. But seeing the set look in his eyes, he resisted.

He could still taste him…feel him. The memory and the need for more rocked in him like waves on a stormy ocean. But the urgency of the present situation had to be the center of his attention. It had to be.

He kept telling himself that over and over.

Cai's eyes slid to him. His face changed like he was reading everything in Mason's face. Mason opened his mouth to speak, but the lift doors opened.

Cai went ahead of him. Another windowless hall. Mason could hear voices and ringing phones muffled behind the walls.

They came to a door with a peephole. Cai put his eye to it, waited a few heartbeats then opened it.

Mason blinked into the sudden light of a large, brightly lit office. A man in a rumpled shirt and a loose tie sat behind the desk, yammering into a phone. He looked up as they came in and frowned.

"Yeah. Yeah, mate, I know. Just stall him, will you? I'll call you back." He hung up. "Bracken," he said with a wary look at Mason. "Wish I could say it was good to see you."

"Detective Superintendent Okeke, this is DI Mason Walker, North Yorkshire Police. We heard about Honor."

"I know. What a shit show." The big man stood and shook Mason's hand. "Good to meet you, Walker. Shame it's under such shitty circumstances."

"Likewise, sir."

"So" — Okeke put his hands on his hips — "you think this is linked with your case up there, Bracken?"

"Honor worked with Kelly, the first victim," Cai said. "And was doing a lot of her own work in that area."

"Including employment rights, I know. Don't think I haven't considered the implications, Bracken. It's on my mind. Trust me."

"Implications?" Mason asked carefully.

Okeke looked hard at Cai, who gave him a nod. The older man sighed and pulled out his chair. "Honor was trying to get Bracken his job back...officially. Now she's... Well, it's gonna be longer than we thought."

"I don't care about that right now," Cai said. "Boss, what happened to her?"

Okeke's eyes darkened. He handed over a widescreen tablet. Cai activated the screen and Mason peered over his shoulder as he swiped. Crime scene photographs. She lay in a shallow grave. They'd cleared away most of the soil, but it still clung to her silk pajamas and bright hair. Her eyes were hooded and bruised-looking. The bullet hole in her head was neat and dead center.

"Snatched. Restrained. Executed. Found in a woodland outside the city."

"Like Kelly," Cai said.

"And Alonso," Mason said.

The superintendent's face fell. "Yes, I heard about your man. I'm sorry. Look, fellas. I wanna give you everything we have on this. This scumbag needs to be brought in...yesterday. The press is clamoring for statements. Not to mention—"

The office door banged open. In stepped a large haemophile so tall he didn't look real.

What makes them all grow so big?

Mason hurriedly suppressed the thought before it showed on his face.

The newcomer was in a long, navy overcoat and patent-leather oxfords. His black hair was secured in a dark tail down his back, and his walnut-brown skin shone in the low light. He was breathtaking, literally, but the midnight blue of his large, serious eyes was blazing with anger as deep and fierce as a furnace.

"Ivor Novák, sir." The superintendent hurried to his feet. "First, let me say how sorry I am—"

"I don't need you to be sorry, Okeke," the haemophile rumbled, voice like a quake through granite. "I need you to tell me how this has been allowed to happen."

"Sir, let me assure you —"

"Who's this?" The haemophile turned his blazing eyes on Cai and Mason. "Who are you?"

"Sir, I'm Specialist Officer Cai Bracken, of the Met. This is DI Walker, North Yorkshire. We're here for the same reasons you are."

"Bracken, yes. I've heard of you. Honor talked about you a lot."

"I knew her well."

"It's a shame it seems we'll be needing you more than ever."

"It's like Blood Winter all over again," Okeke said, shaking his head.

"It's worse than that, Superintendent," Novák said. "That was one rogue haemophile with delusions of grandeur. This is much bigger. It could be what triggers an all-out war between our kinds. And, believe me, it's not my kind I'm worried about in that scenario."

Mason looked at him hard. "Is that a threat, sir?"

Novák's eyes darkened. Cai stepped between them.

"We should all calm down. If we start fighting among ourselves, there's no chance for anyone."

"Bracken's right," Okeke said after a breathless pause. "We need to think rationally. These aren't random targets."

"Far from it," Novák said. "But the thing is, however disgraceful they are, these murders won't stop anything. The wheels are already in motion. This will delay things. Muddy the waters. Make our lives hell while we make the changes." He tilted his chin. "But they are not stopping anything. I won't allow it. Kelly and Honor wouldn't have allowed it."

"What *would* stop it, sir?" Mason asked after a moment's reflection.

Novák blinked slowly, considering. "The only thing that could stop the equal rights movement now would be a wholesale review of haemophile classification on a global scale."

"Which would happen if haemophiles start openly attacking humans?" Mason said.

Okeke swore. "Could that happen, Novák?"

Novák looked grave. "The mood at the moment? Yes, it could."

"We have to find Damon before a haemophile does," Cai said.

"Sir," Mason stepped forward, "our suspect isn't acting alone. Is there anyone on the inside, in your world, with strong enough feelings to orchestrate something like this?"

"Are you suggesting one of our own kind is working against us?"

Mason didn't allow himself to waver. "Honor was taken from her home, right from under her wife's nose. A human couldn't do that."

"Why would one of our own want to hurt the people trying to make things better for them?"

"Maybe they don't all feel like you do?"

Novák shook his head. "Is Sadie Ford-Byerson even sure about what happened?"

"Sir, please," Mason insisted. "Is there anything you know that might help?"

Novák's eyes flickered.

"Anything, sir?" Okeke said.

"I will cooperate fully with whatever you need. You," he said, pointing at Cai then Mason, "can have full access to my files. No one else, Okeke," he said, shooting a sharp glance at the superintendent. "The situation is fragile enough as it is. And if what you say is right, I really don't know who to trust."

"Does that mean you have someone in mind, sir?" Cai asked quietly.

When Novák spoke again, his voice was low as a storm on the horizon. "This does not leave these walls, understand?"

"Of course," Mason said eagerly.

Novák looked at each of them in turn then took a step closer, lowering his voice further. "Not one of mine, but one with connections to us — and more power than she lets on."

"Who?" Mason pressed.

"The Lord Mayor of York. Emerald Lomax."

Mason started. "The Mayor?"

Novák inclined his large, leonine head. "Let's just say that some curious...roadblocks have come up in our efforts to change things in that area of the country."

"But she publicly welcomed Baron Emory Von Magnusson," Mason argued. "She spoke out for him during his custody case."

"I'm aware of that. But I have to ask myself why there was such violent opposition in the first place. And her own brother threatened the Baron's home during those same protests. Then he was arrested for kidnapping a haemophile, by you I believe, DI Walker."

Cai's eyes were on Mason.

"That's not as straightforward a situation as it first seemed, sir."

"Nothing ever is. And there has certainly been violence and protest and discontent everywhere, but it seems very concentrated around your city, DI Walker.

Perhaps you should be looking at why. Superintendent"—Novák rounded on Okeke—"I will expect to be kept in the loop on this."

"Everything, sir. You'll be the first to know."

"Good." His face softened. "Thank you."

He was gone.

Okeke shook his head in the shocked silence he left behind. "What a mess."

"Okeke?" They looked up. A woman stood in the doorway. Her tanned face was drawn. She wore a designer overcoat, but underneath she was in rumpled sweats. Her highlighted hair was tangled up in a messy bun, and her eyes were red.

"Sadie," Okeke ushered her gently inside. "What are you doing here? You should be at home."

"Is that who I thought it was?" Her voice was raw. Tears trembled in her eyes. "Was that Ivor Novák?"

Okeke grimaced. "Honor was his assistant, Sadie," he said, urging her to sit. "He is just as upset by this as the rest of us."

"He's one of *them*," she cried, gripping the arms of her chair. "You can't trust them. Can't you see? Honor did. Look what's happened to her."

"We don't know what happened to her," the superintendent said soothingly. "But we will. I swear."

The woman opened and closed her mouth then stared at Mason with desperate eyes.

"This is DI Walker, Sadie," Okeke said. "He's helping with the case."

Mason looked around then hurried to school his face when he realized Cai had gone.

"It was one of *them*, Detective." The woman's voice shook. Her knuckles stood out white as she clutched the chair arms. "She was right there. In bed. With me.

We were just going to sleep. Then she just…vanished. And now…" She covered her mouth with her hand.

Mason stepped forward. "We will find who did this, Mrs. Ford-Byerson. You have my word."

"Sadie, come on," Okeke said, putting a hand under her elbow and helping her to stand. "Let me get you a lift. You need to go home and rest."

"No. I need to *do* something."

"Leave all that to us." Okeke sent Mason a look over his shoulder then guided the shaking woman from the room.

"Mason?" Mason jumped and turned. Cai was there again. "That was Honor's wife."

"I gathered." Mason shook his head. "Jesus."

Okeke returned shaking his head. "They've been together twenty years." Okeke sighed noisily and lowered himself into his chair. "So, what are you boys thinking?"

"About Sadie's thoughts?" Cai said. "Or Novák's?"

"Emerald Lomax?" Mason frowned. "Really?"

"Do you know the woman, Walker?" Okeke's gaze was keen.

"We've met," Mason hedged.

"We've both met her," Cai said. "We interviewed her about her brother."

"And?" Okeke demanded.

Mason searched for words. Cai got in first. "We'll look into it, sir."

"Good. I suggest you start now."

They were both silent until they were back in the car.

Mason stared out the windscreen rather than starting the car. "Do we really think Emerald's behind this?"

"I don't see it," Cai said quietly.

"You think Novák is barking up the wrong tree?"

"I think we need to see his files," Cai said, tapping on his phone. "I'll put in a request for anything he has."

"I wouldn't put much past Emerald Lomax," Mason muttered. "But multiple murders? For what? It's her pro-haemophile stuff that's raised her political profile. Don't get me wrong, I'm sure the profile is more her reason than any great desire to change the world for the better. But still... I don't see what she'd get out of this."

"She and Honor will have crossed paths," Cai ventured. "During the Baron's custody case, if nothing else. Honor was in York a lot during that time."

Mason rubbed his eyes. "Well, we've got nothing else. Better get on it."

"Mason, you've been awake for nearly forty-eight hours."

"I'm fine," he said, starting the car and steering toward the gates.

"Even if I believed that," Cai said, "we're not going to make it back to York before dawn."

Mason turned the car to join the slow crawl of traffic. "Damn. You're right."

"My place isn't far," Cai said after a barely perceptible pause. "They should be able to put you up for one night."

"They?"

"My commune. There are ten of us, plus our Magister." He smiled. "Don't worry. They're nice." His smile tilted. "Weird. But nice."

"Weird?"

"The old ones are all weird. And most of them are old. I don't understand them half the time. The rest of the time they scare the hell out of me. But they protect me. And they're all I've got."

Mason swallowed. "I'm sorry."

"Sorry for what?"

"I've been so wrapped up in what I'm feeling. I haven't been listening to what you've been trying to tell me." He looked over at Cai and away again. "I really have no idea what you're going through."

"That makes two of us."

He was smiling. The tightness in Mason's chest loosened.

He followed Cai's directions out of the city center to where the buildings were smaller and less crowded together. Cai instructed him to pull over and opened the window to tap a code into a keypad Mason hadn't even seen. What had looked like a blank wall slowly shunted open, and he drove down a ramp into an underground car park. They got out and Cai took them through a steel door, secured with yet more locks.

"It's like Fort Knox," Mason said.

"It has to be."

Mason was almost asleep on his feet as they rode a lift even deeper underground. But when the doors opened, he was wide awake again. It was like they'd stepped into the lobby of a luxury hotel. There were couches, pictures on the walls, artificial plants and soft mood-lighting. The only thing missing was windows.

Three haemophiles were watching the news on the widescreen television. They all looked up as they entered.

"Cai." A tall woman with jet-black hair cut into a sharp bob rose from her seat and came over. Her features were pointed. Her gray eyes were huge and shone like gunmetal. Her dark skin had the same gleam as Cai's, glowing even in the low light. Her eyes went over Mason then back to Cai. "We weren't expecting you back so soon."

"Magister Khan," Cai said with a strange smile. "This is sort of a flying visit."

"Everything all right?"

"Everything's fine. This is DI Walker. He's a colleague. We're just here to rest for the day. We return to York tomorrow night."

"Of course," Khan said, her angled face still empty of expression. "Anything we can do." She gestured to the television and the news report on Honor Ford-Byerson's murder. "We heard about what happened. It's all so terrible. Everyone's nervous."

"We're doing everything we can."

"I'm sure you are," she said, squeezing his shoulder in what Mason couldn't help but feel was a possessive manner. He wasn't prepared for the strength of the reaction it triggered in him.

Khan looked at him again, her fine brows drawing together, and he clamped down on the feelings.

"DI Walker, we're grateful for everything you're doing. These are troubled times."

The eyes of the other haemophiles in the room were also fixed, unblinking, on him.

"They are," he said. "But we're working hard to make them better."

Khan inclined her head. "Let us know if we can do anything. Anything at all." She smiled at Cai, but the expression didn't reach her eyes. "It's good to see you again, Cai. I've been thinking about you. The season is turning. You've missed some beautiful nights."

Cai's smile was wry. "Still doing that? Even after all this?"

"Of course. It is my right, after all. Now, go. You're tired. Make sure you feed, like we talked about."

"Yes, Magister," Cai said, drawing Mason toward the door.

Mason suppressed a shudder as Cai led them away from the room down a wide, warmly lit hall. "You're right. They are weird."

Cai chuckled softly. "They can hear you, you know."

Mason closed his mouth.

Cai took them to a furnished apartment, complete with a sitting area, bathroom and kitchen area. A door stood open onto what looked like a bedroom, apart from the fact that there was no bed. Instead, there was a large box, like a chest freezer, in the corner.

"My sleeping cell," Cai said. "You can't open it when I'm in it, but best you don't even go near it."

"I won't," Mason said, glancing around, noticing the only equipment in the kitchen was a large fridge. Cai followed his gaze.

"I have to eat. I hope you don't mind."

"Of course," Mason said, not quite sure where to look and took off his coat. "What was that about beautiful nights?" he asked, as casually as he could.

Cai smiled a tired smile as he took a flask from the fridge. "Magister Khan takes a walk in St. James's Park most evenings. She's done it for years, ever since she founded our commune. But recently someone took a video, and it went viral." He opened the flask but just stared at it and didn't drink. "All she's doing in the video is walking, looking at the stars. But it has divided people. Some say it's her right to walk where she pleases. Others say she's a danger and shouldn't be allowed to roam at large on her own." He made a face.

"So now she makes sure to do it every night, just to make a point."

"I remember it now. It made the news."

"It did." Cai drank without making eye contact. "I used to go with her, especially when I first started leaving the commune." He looked around the comfortable but windowless room. "It was a long time before I could trust myself to leave."

"You're not a danger to anyone, Cai," Mason said softly.

Cai met his eyes briefly. "You can have the sofa," he said, taking a drink from the flask. "It's pretty comfy."

"Cai…"

"This is how I have to live, Mason," he said, gesturing around the room. "It's good for you to see it. Now you can see how different we are. How we can't…" He winced and looked away. He drank more deeply. He closed his eyes. His pale skin flushed with obvious warmth. Mason fought the confusing mix of reactions it conjured in his body.

Cai opened his eyes and moved to the bedroom. "I'm going to turn in. We've got a lot to do tomorrow."

"Cai, wait."

But he'd already shut the door.

Mason collapsed on the sofa, fully clothed, and stared at the ceiling. He strained his hearing for the sounds of Cai preparing for bed, desperate for even an illusion of normality, but it was eerily silent behind the door.

Fatigue weighed his whole body, but whenever he closed his eyes, his thoughts crowded against them. Thoughts of Kelly. Of Honor Ford-Byerson. Of her wife's haunted expression. The taste of Cai's mouth mixed with the fear in his eyes.

Mason swore under his breath, pulled out his phone and began scouring the internet for information on haemophiles. He already knew all the stuff from the government briefings and training sessions by heart. That hadn't prepared him for this — for the realities of knowing one. Of…wanting one.

A video link came up in his search list.

Living With An Immortal. The Reality of Sleeping with a Vampire, by Trixy Jazz.

Mason glanced at the door. All was silent. He checked his watch. It was after sunrise.

He pressed play.

Chapter Seven

Mason knew about the Influencer Trixy Jazz and her viral documentary about the sex lives of haemophiles. It had come up during Magnusson's custody case, among other things. But he'd never felt the urge to watch it himself.

Until now.

His skin tightened at the sight of Darragh Kelly sitting beside Tom Addams on a purple sofa. Kelly's face was inexpressive. Tom's face shone with anticipation. Kelly was in a gray suit and a red tie, Tom in a sports shirt and jeans. They couldn't have looked more different, but they sat with their fingers entwined, and the looks they exchanged during the interview left very little to the imagination.

Mason watched, fascinated, as Jazz asked increasingly personal questions about their relationship. Tom laughed and colored but answered easily. The most reaction Kelly showed was a flicker in his green eyes or a twitch of his pale lips. But he never hesitated in his answers, either.

"Our sex life is vibrant and engaged," Kelly said smoothly. "The only difference between us and any other couple is that I am physically very different from Tom...from any human."

"Different, how, exactly?"

"My nervous system is highly tuned," Kelly said, matter-of-factly, but there was an undercurrent in his voice that had the blood pumping in Mason's veins. "It's hard to describe. But my skin is very sensitive. My senses are very strong. Heightened."

He glanced at Tom, who replied with a smile and a fiery look in his brown eyes. Kelly looked back at the camera, something like regret tightening his expression.

"It takes us decades to master our senses...our emotions. It takes us years just to learn to cope." A flash of vulnerability went through his eyes. "Just because we look like we're not feeling anything doesn't mean we aren't. But relationships, sex, physical touch, displays of emotion...?" He looked at Tom again. "They are deeper. Stronger. And take longer to manifest. So we have to be careful. That's all."

"Careful?" the interviewer said, off camera. "Are you saying you're dangerous? That you're not in control?"

"No," Kelly said. "I'm very much in control of both my body and my emotions." He blinked, his green eyes burning. "But a human can't know either of them entirely. Or understand them. So an open mind is required...and trust. Lucky for me, I've found someone who's patient, understanding—and who recognizes both the advantages and pitfalls of having great strength."

The couple looked at each other again, and Mason's chest tightened.

"We're different," Tom said quietly. "And we always will be. But we recognize those differences. We embrace them. *Allow* for them, if that's what's needed. And, somehow, it works."

"But how do you handle it, Darragh?" Jazz asked after a pause. "Knowing, one day, it will end? Even if you never break up, you will live on long after Tom is gone. How do you handle that?"

Kelly's blank solemnity had returned, but there was still that wild unruliness brightening the green of his eyes.

"Everything comes to an end, Miss Jazz. Life is fragile. That's why it's precious."

"There are no guarantees in anything," Tom put in. "In life. In love. We could break up tomorrow. Or we could be together until the day I die." He laughed, an unfettered sound that Mason had only known the ghost of back at Oswald house. "There's no way to know what will happen, so we live for now. We enjoy the moment." His grin widened. "In every way we can."

"And now we get down to it." Jazz's voice changed. "The main reason we're here. Tom, Darragh. For all those haemo-human couples out there, what advice do you have for a satisfying, healthy and safe sex life?"

Tom colored again but his eyes were alive. Kelly's eyes darkened as he looked at his partner.

"Unfortunately, the most valuable bit of advice I can think to give," he started, "isn't very sexy and not all that original." Kelly drew Tom's hand closer. "Listen to each other. Talk. Communicate. Tell each other what works. What doesn't."

"And, if you're different," Tom put in, "appreciate those differences. Accommodate them." He grinned again. "Turn them to your advantage."

"How, exactly, Tom?" Jazz pressed, and Mason could hear the grin in her voice. "Give us some juicy details."

Tom looked at Kelly, who nodded. "Haemophiles are the powerful one...every time. It's just physical fact. But they like to feel cherished and wanted as much as anyone else. You can't outmatch them, but you can help them feel safe. Supported. Wanted." He gazed at Kelly with a love and desire both shining in his eyes. "If they care about you, they won't hurt you. But they are different. If you're unsure about how you're feeling, tell them. And they should do the same." Tom squeezed Kelly's hand. "Oh. And don't be afraid of aids if you need them. And toys. They can keep things fun and exciting. But they can also help keep things safe."

"What sort of aids?"

Mason's throat had already dried out. His trousers were uncomfortably tight and only got worse as discussion got more explicit. Mason kept glancing at the door, even though he knew Cai wouldn't stir for hours.

Still, he turned the volume down and watched, fascinated, ignoring the dull ache that undercut his excitement whenever he remembered that only one of this couple remained alive.

* * * *

When Cai shook him awake hours later, it took Mason several moments to adjust. His dreams had been so vivid and intense that he gasped when he registered Cai standing over him.

He almost reached for him, the need so strong in his body that it was like an ache. Even after reason returned and he told himself, firmly, that he'd been dreaming, his palms itched, and his skin was tight with need.

Cai's smile fell as he studied Mason's face. Mason sat up, keeping his blanket over his lap.

"Sorry I don't have any food," Cai said, a little flatly. "But I can do coffee."

"Sounds good."

The silence between them deepened as Cai made the coffee. The delicious smell filled the room as Mason turned his attention to his phone and the messages and reports waiting in his inbox.

"We should be back in York by midnight," Cai said as he handed Mason his cup, avoiding his gaze as he did so. Mason swallowed the pain and the coffee in one.

"I'd like to make a quick stop first."

"Where?"

"The Ford-Byersons' place."

"Why?"

"I want to talk to Sadie again, get more about what she really saw that night."

"I don't think she's going to say anything different."

"Something's not adding up," Mason said. "She said she was falling asleep. Maybe she was dreaming. Maybe not. But you might be able to tell if we're missing anything. If you stay in the room this time, that is."

Cai gave him a level look. "She's not the biggest fan of my kind at the moment. I'm not sure how she'd feel knowing I was working on her wife's murder case."

"What was it you said? You have to show people when they're wrong?"

Cai weighed him up for a moment. "Okay," he said, draining a flask of blood and throwing away the empty. "Maybe you're right."

"It can't hurt to try."

The Ford-Byerson home was an elegant townhouse on a wealthy street in Marylebone. Under normal circumstances Mason would have taken a moment to gawp at the three-story terrace, set back from the road and clearly worth more money than he could even imagine making. But the awkward car ride with Cai, coupled with a deep, ominous feeling he couldn't shake, came to head as they climbed the stairs to the front door and found it open.

Cai put his hand on his arm to stop him from entering.

"What is it?"

Cai didn't answer. In the streetlight, his face was tense.

"Cai?"

"There's no one there," Cai said, pulling Mason away.

"The door's open. Something's wrong."

"Mason," Cai said as Mason pushed the door wider to reveal the shadowed hallway.

"Mrs. Ford-Byerson?" he called softly.

"We should call a team out here."

"I want to take a look first," Mason insisted. He stepped inside.

Cai followed him in. His movements were stiff. "There's no sign of a struggle. No blood anywhere. I don't think she was taken."

"Then where is she? And why did she leave the door open?" Mason moved into the living room. The dark shapes of couches and armchairs stood around a large open fire which stood cold and empty. He scanned the open-plan kitchen. A barely touched plate of chicken salad sat on the side. There was an open bottle of wine next to the sink. The half-drunk glass was on the kitchen table beside a discarded iPad. Several kitchen knives were scattered next to a half-empty knife block.

"We don't have a warrant," Cai said.

"People are dying, Cai," Mason said, stepping closer and frowning at the knives. "And the usual methods aren't cutting it. We need every advantage we can get. See what you can see, will you?"

Cai made an impatient noise and began leafing through the magazines on the coffee table. "What are we looking for?"

"I don't know. A link to Emerald Lomax? Anything."

Cai's face was masked in shadow, so Mason couldn't read his expression as he continued searching.

Mason tapped the discarded iPad's screen and muttered to find it PIN-protected.

"What is it?" Cai said, coming over.

"It looks like she was on this before she left, but it's locked."

"Here." Cai held out his hand and Mason handed over the tablet. Cai tapped at it for a few seconds, and it opened.

"Okay, how?"

"I can see where the fingerprints are most concentrated," Cai said, scanning the screen then handing the iPad back. "She hasn't checked her messages in days, by the look of it."

"Something she saw made her leave in a hurry," Mason murmured, opening the browser. "Shit."

"What is it?"

Mason turned the screen round.

Cai's face shifted in the shadows. "That's Khan."

"An article about those bloody walks of hers," Mason breathed, glancing back at the knives on the kitchen counter. There were two in the block. Three on the side.

The block had space for six.

Cai followed his gaze. "Oh God."

Mason was already moving for the door.

Cai was on the phone before they'd reached the car.

"The police are on their way to St. James'," Cai said as he hung up and Mason unlocked the doors. "Mason, I need to be there."

"Get in," Mason said. "We can be there in twenty."

"I can be there in less time than that." He gave Mason a regretful look. "Hurry, Mason."

Cai vanished.

Mason swore and climbed into the car. He turned on his lights and siren and floored it. Traffic parted but not fast enough. He swore and steered into back streets, cutting corners, mounting pavements where he could.

His phone was ringing.

"Walker." It was Okeke. "Are you with Bracken?"

"On my way to him now, sir."

"What the hell is going on? He's called half the Met out and isn't answering his phone."

"It's Sadie Ford-Byerson, sir. We think she's gone after Cai's Magister."

"Khan? Why?"

"On my way to find out."

Mason cut the call and turned a corner with a screech of tires.

He left the car on a cycle path, vaulted the park fence and raced into the shadowed interior. All was deadly silent around him. He paused, panting. Still nothing. He tried to ring Cai but he didn't pick up.

Mason swore at the distant sound of sirens.

Then he heard the shouting.

He raced toward the sound, dodging round late-night joggers that had stopped to gawp, narrowly avoiding staggering into ponds or tripping on undergrowth.

He reached a clearing in a small patch of trees. Magister Khan's face was a twisted mask of horror in the starlight. Her teeth were bared. Her eyes burned black fire. She was clutching at her neck where dark Blood leaked from between her fingers.

The smell stopped Mason in his tracks. Bonfires. Hot wine. Death and beauty and sex, blood and metal and pain. He blinked until the dizziness passed and made himself focus.

Cai was desperately holding on to Khan. His muscles bulged as his Magister strained against his grip.

Sadie Ford-Byerson was screaming and ranting and waving a bloody knife. Tears streaked her face. Her eyes were wide and wild.

"You took her," she screamed over and over. "You took her. You took her. She wanted to help you. You took her."

"Magister," Cai panted as Khan roared and reached for Sadie. "Keep control. Please."

"Murderer," Sadie cried, pointing the knife. "*Monster.*"

Mason rushed to Sadie.

"Mrs. Ford-Byerson," he said. "Please. Put the knife down."

"They took her," she sobbed. "Honor's *dead*. She wanted to help them. And they killed her."

"It wasn't Khan."

"I don't care," Sadie cried. "Look at her. Look at them both." She pointed the knife.

Khan continued to strain and growl. An animal fury twisted her face. Cai's clawed fingers clutched her clothing, the tendons standing out with effort. His sharp teeth were bared, and his eyes burned with a fierce light.

"*Look at them,*" Sadie screamed. "Freaks. Monsters. They'll kill us all."

Khan lunged. Cai, somehow, held on. Mason grabbed Sadie and spun her away.

"Sadie, please. Drop the knife. Honor wouldn't want this."

Her large eyes shone, wet and swollen, in the starlight. The pain in them burned like cold fire. She shook, hung her head and dropped the knife.

Khan's breathing slowed. She blinked. The twisted lines of her face softened. She straightened.

Cai eased his grip. His breathing was ragged. "Magister?"

Khan blinked, still clutching the wound in her neck with one hand. "Cai?"

"Can I see?" he said, gesturing to her injury.

Khan blinked again, like she was waking from a deep sleep, then drew her hand away from her throat.

"Is she okay?" Mason asked.

Cai nodded. "It's already healing."

Sadie's sobs became wracking cries.

"Get her away from here, Walker." Khan's voice was low. "The police have entered the park. No one can know of this."

"But Magister," Cai started.

"She's in pain. She lashed out. But the world won't understand. If this comes out, it will only make things worse."

"Magister Khan," Mason said firmly, now half-supporting Sadie, who swayed on her feet, "she attacked you. We can't ignore this."

"I'm not asking you to ignore it," Khan said, turning up her collar to obscure the worst of the blood. "Quite the opposite. But reporting it would not be wise."

"I don't understand," Sadie croaked, her head hanging, her shoulders shuddering. "I don't understand."

"Take her home, Mason," Cai said. "I'll meet you there."

Mason blinked, and he was alone in the clearing with Sadie. Her sobs had faded to exhausted panting. Blue lights flashed between the trees with bobbing torch beams. The crackle of radios got louder.

He took Sadie's hands and looked her in the face. "Sadie, I'm going to take you home. Okay?"

She stared dumbly at the knife on the grass. Mason scooped it up, tucked it into his jacket, took her elbow and hurried her back toward his car.

Somehow he got her there without them being seen. She got in without protest. His phone was ringing. He ignored it.

Sadie didn't speak during the drive back to her house. When they arrived, she walked inside like a zombie, turning on lights as she went. Khan's Blood stained her clothes and hands and face. She went to the kitchen and stopped. She stared at the knife block.

Mason went to the sink, filled a glass with cold water, pressed it into her hand, then filled the sink with warm water.

"Sadie," he said softly, holding out his hand, "let's get you cleaned up."

She raised pain-filled eyes to him. "I'm sorry."

Mason opened his mouth to reply, but words had left him.

"Mason…"

Mason turned. Cai was in the doorway. "Is she okay?"

Sadie stared at the sink, unblinking.

Mason went over to him and lowered his voice. "What about Khan?"

"She's fine," Cai said. He kept glancing round the room. "It was just bad luck Sadie got an artery. Khan's Blood went on the defense."

"Khan's…what?"

"It takes over," Cai whispered, examining Sadie, "when it thinks there's a threat. It fights back, whether we want to fight or not. She's very lucky she's not dead."

"Lucky you were there."

Sadie took off her jacket and began to mechanically wash her hands.

"Mrs. Ford-Byerson," Cai said, moving forward carefully, "you should drink water and eat something. You're in shock."

"Please leave," she said quietly as she scrubbed her hands, over and over.

"Sadie," Mason started, "can you tell us exactly what you remember from that night?"

She stopped washing. She lifted her vacant gaze to Cai. His face was set as stone. Mason frowned.

Sadie began to shake again. "Leave. Please."

Mason moved to approach her, but Cai put his hand on his arm and shook his head.

Sadie started washing her hands again. They left.

They sat in the car while Cai spoke to Okeke on the phone, persuading him it had been a false alarm. After he hung up, they sat in silence. Time was ticking on, but Mason didn't start the car.

"I don't like leaving her like this."

"Me either," Cai said. "But Khan is right. We need to keep this quiet."

"You think haemophiles would retaliate?"

"Anyone under threat is unpredictable. And we're already on a knife's edge."

"None of this is making any sense."

"We need to speak to Emerald Lomax again," Cai said as they pulled out into the traffic.

"You think she'll talk to us?"

"If you ask her outright," Cai said softly, "I'll tell you if she's lying."

* * * *

They didn't talk much on the drive back. Cai spent most of it glued to his phone, reading through the material that had been sent through from Ivor Novák.

"It's all what you'd expect," he said as he scrolled. "The Baron's registration documents. Details of Oswald House. The security measures there. Policy proposals with Honor and Kelly about employment and marriage rights." He shook his head. "I can't see anything linked to Emerald…or Damon."

"We'll keep looking," Mason said as he turned off the motorway.

Cai frowned when Mason took the roundabout for the city center. "We're heading there now?"

"No time like the present."

"It's three a.m."

"There are too many loose ends in this case. Let's tie up at least one."

To Mason's surprise, lights again were shining between the curtains on the ground floor of Emerald Lomax's mansion. This time she was fully clothed when she answered the door, though the jacket of her business suit was thrown over a chair, and her patent heels were tossed aside by the sofa. The vodka bottle was on the coffee table, a glass next to it, clearly visible over her shoulder as she blocked the doorway and glared at them.

"Let me guess," she muttered. "Another time-sensitive matter that needs addressing outside of working hours?"

"We work all hours, ma'am," Mason replied, glancing at the files and papers on the coffee table. "Like yourself, it would seem."

She sighed and stepped aside.

"I heard about Honor," she said as she topped up her glass. "I'm sorry."

"We are, too," Cai said, his eyes taking in the Mayor's every movement.

"And you still haven't found Heron? Damon?"

"Don't you think you'd have heard if we had?" Mason added carefully.

She gave him a sharp look then sat, downed the drink and started spreading the papers out. "Go on, then. What do you want?" Mason sat opposite the Mayor and remained silent until she finally looked up. "Walker? Come on. Out with it."

"We were just wondering if you had any insight as to why a lot of this violence appears concentrated around here. Your brother. Your citizens. Your city."

"Pardon me?"

Mason held her penetrating look. "It's been suggested that York is the hub of all this unrest. And you know this city better than anyone. Is there any reason you can think of why it all seems to be happening here?"

She transferred her angry glare from Walker to Cai. Cai was silent, watching keenly. "What exactly are you implying, Detective Inspector?"

Mason spread his hands. "Damon is working with someone with resources and connections. Someone with a private agenda. Someone who would benefit from haemophile-human relations being strained."

"And you think that's me?"

"We're considering every possibility."

Emerald was frozen for a long moment. Then she leaned back in her chair and crossed her arms. "And how is having the species out for each other's blood good for me, exactly?"

"You wouldn't be the first to benefit from apparently stabilizing a restless political situation," Cai put in carefully.

Her face was cold. "That's quite a statement."

Walker held his ground. "What about Tyler?"

"What about him?"

"We could really do with talking to him. Maybe he's the link. Not you."

"He's gone, Detective Inspector," she snapped. "He's fucked off and left me to clean up after him...as bloody usual. If you *do* find him, I'd like a word with him myself."

"Is there anything else you can think of?" Cai said with an earnest expression. "Anything that could explain why all this is happening in York?"

"Get out. Both of you."

"Mayor Lomax," Mason started but she went to the door and wrenched it open.

"I said get out, Walker," she said. "I honestly thought you two had this. Now that it's clear you haven't, I guess I'll have to do your job for you. Please leave so I can make a start."

"We had to ask, ma'am," Cai said calmly, not moving from his spot behind the sofa. "It's not a question York is in the epicenter of all this."

"And that couldn't possibly be because of the Baron?" Emerald said. "Publicly reclaiming ancestral lands? One of the first haemophiles to successfully campaign to live independently from a commune? Oh, yes, and winning a ground-breaking child custody case while also going viral on the internet with a sex video of him with a human man?"

Mason looked at Cai, but he was still focused on Emerald.

"You're right, ma'am," he said softly and moved toward the door. "That's something we should consider, too."

"Next time you come around here accusing me of a conspiracy," she said, her eyes flashing, "I suggest you have some real evidence."

She slammed the door.

"So?"

Cai turned and walked back to the car. "She's hiding something," he murmured. "But I can't tell what."

"Why does the case keep leading back to her?" Mason asked impatiently as he climbed into the car.

"Or possibly back to *Tyler* Lomax, like you said?"

Mason made an impatient noise and started the car. "That bastard's a pain in my ass, even after he's left the country."

Cai chuckled. "You should go home. It's been a long night. I'll do some more digging before dawn then—"

"Would you come with me?"

Cai looked at him. "Where?"

"Home. With me." Mason glanced at him, fought the heat rising into his face and looked out of the windscreen. "I'm not going to sleep any time soon. And I think we both need a break from the case."

Cai was quiet a moment. "You could be right. But, Mason—"

"I'd like to talk."

Cai sighed. He didn't answer but he didn't protest as Mason turned his car toward home.

Chapter Eight

Mason felt oddly exposed, letting Cai into his house. He looked around the sparsely furnished space in a way he hadn't before. The bookcase held a few crime thrillers mixed in with law journals. The sofa faced the large TV, but the remote was by the set, not handy on the empty coffee table or sofa arm. There were no pictures on the walls, which were the same off-white they had been when he'd first moved in.

Cai looked around in silence then turned a half-smile his way.

"Nice place."

"It does the job."

"How long have you been here?"

Mason had to stop and think. "Almost eight years now."

Cai nodded, examining the shelves.

"I don't really spend much time here," he found himself explaining. "Work and all."

Cai didn't respond. Instead, he lifted one of the books to read the blurb.

"Uh, are you hungry?"

Cai smiled awkwardly as he turned back round. "I am, as it happens," he said softly. "But something tells me you don't have what I need in your fridge?"

Mason tried for a smile. "Coffee, water or wine is about all I can offer."

"Wine would be nice," Cai said. "For now. But I will have to head off soon."

Mason fled to the kitchen. He uncorked the half-drunk bottle of red that had been on the side since Amelia's last visit and poured two glasses. Then he stood staring at them.

"Why the hell are you doing, Mason?" he muttered under his breath.

He shook his head then carried the wine through to the living room. Cai had removed his coat and sat on the sofa. He took the wine and sipped. It stained his top lip red, and Mason had to look away.

He could feel Cai's eyes on him as drank from his own glass.

"Why am I here, Mason?" he asked quietly.

"I want…" Mason choked. He unstuck his throat with more wine and made himself continue. "I want you, Cai."

"Mason…"

Mason sat near him. "I can't stop thinking about it."

Cai set his wine aside. "You're a great guy. I like you. You know I do. But we've been through this."

"You're feeling something, too. I know you are. You hide lots of things. But you can't hide that."

"I don't want to hide anything from you."

"Then why are you resisting this?"

"I…" Cai's face changed. He retreated behind his mask, even the blue of his eyes going dull. "I told you why. I'm afraid of hurting you."

Mason put down his glass. He slid along the sofa, moving cautiously, like someone approaching a skittish animal. "We can find a way."

Cai sat very still. Mason's breathing deepened. He could smell Cai, the fresh, strong scent of his hair and skin. He could see each individual eyelash, long and sweeping, framing the tropical blue of his eyes.

Cai's lips parted.

Mason lifted his hand, hesitated then ran his thumb down Cai's jaw. Cai inhaled. His eyes lowered to Mason's mouth. Mason's pulse slugged in his throat. He ran his thumb over his chin then over his bottom lip.

Cai's eyes fluttered. "Mason," he whispered.

Mason lowered his hand and hovered his lips over Cai's. "If you tell me to stop, I'll stop."

Cai made a low sound in his throat. He ran his hand up Mason's leg. Mason quivered. He slid his fingers around the back of Cai's neck and drew him closer. Cai's pulse was slow but strong under his palm.

They panted in each other's mouth for a torturously long second then Cai melted against him. Mason couldn't stop the sound of desperation that escaped him. Cai's tongue was in his mouth. Cai's fingers were in his hair. Mason groaned again and drank it all in.

Even when his tongue rasped over a razor-sharp canine, his pleasure flickered and flared. He slid another hand inside Cai's shirt, quivering to feel the cool, strong flesh under his fingers. Cai moaned into his mouth, and his grip tightened on Mason's thigh, so tight Mason winced.

Cai went rigid. He broke away, breathing heavily against Mason's mouth, his eyes wide, then moved out of reach.

"Wait, Cai."

"Stop, Mason. I'm telling you to stop."

"But—"

"No," Cai said, grabbing his coat. "Please. I can't resist you when you do this. But I refuse to put you at risk."

Mason grabbed his wrist to stop him leaving. He knew Cai could break the grip and vanish quicker than thought. But he didn't. He held Cai's gaze and didn't blink.

"I have a way through this."

"What do you mean?"

"Let me show you."

Cai hesitated but then nodded. Mason led the way upstairs with his heart thumping against his ribs. Embarrassment and dread weighed his insides, but they were nothing compared to the excitement that coursed through him when Cai stepped with him into his bedroom.

He purposely didn't think about the scattered clothes, the empty walls, the rumpled bed linen. He went straight to the wardrobe and dug around in the back until he found what he was looking for.

Cai eyed the box Mason produced doubtfully. "What is it?"

Mason held it out. Cai hesitated then took it and opened it. He raised his eyebrows.

Mason made himself stand still, even though he wanted more than anything to rush forward and reclaim Cai's mouth.

"I think this will help," Mason said. He drew the silk rope from the box. "You're afraid of hurting me. This will mean you can't. And this" — he took out the blindfold — "will help you just feel, Cai. Help you to stay present. Forget about being afraid. You can just concentrate on feeling. On feeling good."

Cai gnawed his lip. Uncertainty clouded his eyes, but color had filled his cheeks.

"I bought them to use with someone else," Mason said quietly. "But it never really worked. I didn't really know what I wanted. But I think this will work for us. You and me. This is how we can be together."

"What if it's not strong enough?"

"I trust you, Cai," Mason said "You can leave now, and I promise I will finally take the hint. I'll work on forgetting the idea of us being more than colleagues. Or you can let me try to help you. Try to free you. Try to stop you being scared of what you feel."

Cai swallowed. He raised his eyes. "You'd do this for me?" The desperation in his eyes made Mason's cock twitch in his pants.

"I watched the video. Trixy Jazz's video. I think I understand more about you now. About how much everything is. How overwhelming. It must be scary. But all I care about is being with you, Cai. I want you. And I think I can make you feel amazing."

"You already do."

Mason stepped forward. "Let me make it even better."

Mason kissed him again. Cai dropped the box and thrust his hands inside Mason's shirt. Mason gasped as the sharp fingernail drew over his skin. Part of him still couldn't believe it. He was kissing Cai Bracken. Holding him. The young detective he'd had horny fantasies about as a teenager. Fantasies he'd never understood but were now becoming a reality. His hands were in his clothing, and Cai's own hands were on his skin.

His control hung by a thread, but he clutched to it like a lifeline as he loosened Cai's tie.

Cai wrestled with his belt. As soon as Mason's trousers loosened and Cai slid his hands into his boxers, Mason trembled and Cai moaned as he kneaded Mason's ass.

"My God," Cai groaned into his mouth. "Mason, I—"

He cut off with a groan as Mason moved his mouth down to lick his neck. Finally, he got Cai's shirt undone and stripped him out of it. His torso was toned and sleek, his skin as delectable as heavy cream. Mason thought he might come just from touching and kissing it, feeling the sleek quiver of his responsive flesh under his fingers.

But he needed so much more.

"Lie down," Mason whispered.

Cai backed toward the bed. Mason shed his own shirt and the rest of his clothes then assisted Cai with what remained of his before he lay back on the bed, dragging Mason with him.

"I can't believe this," Mason gasped, running his hands down Cai's sides, his thighs, over the flat, hard pectorals. "You're so beautiful. I can't even say."

"Mason"—Cai was breathing heavily but looking at him intently—"are you sure you want this?"

Mason raised himself on his elbows. Cai's mouth was open. His immaculate hair was disheveled. Heat warmed his cheeks, and his eyes were storm-blue with obvious arousal. His chest was hairless but broad and flat. His muscles bulged in his arms and slid at a tantalizing angle to his groin, which was dusted with dark blond hair. His cock lay, semi-hard, against his inner thigh. He was unquestionable male, human or not. And Mason knew what he was asking.

But Mason could no more stop himself now than he could stop himself from falling if he'd jumped off a cliff. It was like something in him had clicked into place, something that had always been slightly askew. And now it lined up and pumped his blood so fast and hard around his body that he wondered if he would stay conscious.

"I want *you*."

"Fuck," Cai said, thrusting his still-soft groin against Mason's belly. "Quick, Mason. I'm not sure how long I can hold on."

"Here," Mason panted, helping Cai move up so his head was on the pillows. His fingers dug into Mason's back so hard that his nails broke the skin.

Cai swore under his breath and forced his hands away, but Mason grabbed his wrist. "It's okay," he said. "It's all okay."

"Tie me up, Mason. Hurry."

Mason retrieved the rope and returned to lavishing his ministrations on Cai's irresistible collarbone. He drew his wrists above his head, wrapped the rope around them and secured them to the bed frame.

"Is that okay?" Mason said, making himself stop to meet Cai's eyes. "You must tell me if it hurts."

Cai shook his head. "It doesn't hurt." Cai tensed his arms and pulled. His biceps swelled and the bed frame groaned. "But I'm not sure it'll hold…"

Mason bent his head and nibbled at Cai's earlobe. "You won't hurt me, Cai," he whispered. "I trust you."

Cai whimpered and closed his eyes. "I…I'm scared."

Mason's heart sank. "We can stop—"

"No," Cai cried out. "No, please, don't stop Mason." He opened his eyes. "I don't want to stop."

Mason's pulse quickened again, and he fetched the blindfold. "You just need to feel," he whispered. "And not be afraid of it. Forget I'm human. Forget I'm here. Just let yourself feel this."

Cai took a breath then nodded.

Mason placed the blindfold over his eyes. He took a moment to sit back on his heels and take in the sight of Cai on his back, bound and blinded, panting, restrained. He was dizzy with the anticipation but made himself concentrate. This was about Cai. Not him.

He kissed him again—a long, slow kiss and no other contact. A kiss that was meant to reassure, comfort, speak without words. Cai's body relaxed one muscle at a time. Mason smiled and trailed kisses down his neck. He grazed his fingers up his belly and over his chest, and Cai shivered.

It was his first time touching a man's body. Mason thought he'd be more hesitant. All women were different, but he was still used to the female form. Cai was not a woman.

But Mason's hands roamed without him having to think. He ran them over Cai's chest, his belly, his nipples.

Cai gasped. Mason followed the path of his fingers with his lips.

"Mason...God."

The sound of his name in Cai's voice, guttural with need, drove arousal through his body. He ran his hands down the powerful thighs and up again, drinking in the sight and feel of the muscles in his hips and groin. But he made himself pause and consider Cai's cock, still only half-hard.

He swallowed. "Am I not doing it right?"

"No," Cai said, shaking his head and pulling the rope taut. "You're doing everything right. It just…it takes a while, Mason. Please don't stop."

Relief flooded Mason. He lowered his mouth to one of Cai's dusky nipples. Cai gasped, and Mason continued to lick as he brushed his fingers over the other. His cock pulsed and ached. He pushed it against Cai's hip, enjoying the friction, but made himself move slow. Cai's noises became more needy.

Mason got onto his knees, straddling Cai's legs and mouthed his way down his chest to his belly. The smell of his skin was dizzying. He traced everything could reach with his fingers and his mouth, still not quite able to believe what he was doing, how much he needed this, how strong the desire was to know every inch of Cai's body.

Cai whimpered and moaned. He strained against the rope. The bed frame creaked but held. Cai opened his mouth wide, and Mason caved and took his own cock in his hand, unable to bear the lack of contact any longer. He choked back a cry and forced back his orgasm. He opened his eyes. Cai was finally hard, his cock standing straight from the nest of hair.

Mason made a noise of satisfaction and grasped the tender flesh with his free hand.

Cai gasped. Mason closed his own eyes, the sight now too much, even for him. He concentrated on matching his strokes to the rhythm he was using on Cai.

He made his shaking knees take his weight and kissed his way up Cai's body, never stopping his pumping of both their cocks together.

He kissed Cai, deep and hard, plundering his mouth as he stroked his cock, swallowing his cries, hearing his own strangled in his ears.

This was something he'd never felt before, something he'd never expected to feel. He'd jerked himself off innumerable times, both alone and with a partner. But this time he was working himself with one hand and working another man with the other. The scent and sound of Cai's arousal was intoxicating. The heat in his body was stifling. The sound of Cai's increasingly desperate noises deafened him. The thought that Cai was bound and blind and had completely surrendered to Mason made his orgasm explode under his abdomen like a slow bomb.

The pleasure rocked him. It rode through his limbs in waves. He grunted into Cai's mouth and hot, sticky liquid spurted over both his hands and filled the air with the smell of sex.

He pressed his forehead to Cai's. His body was trembling. His skin was sheened in sweat. Cai's was smooth and cool. He was breathing deeply but was quiet.

Mason undid the rope with shaking hands. Cai lowered his arms then removed the blindfold. It was a moment before he met Mason's eyes. A dark heat flickered in his own.

"I never thought I'd feel like that again."

Mason let out the breath he hadn't realized he'd been holding. "It was good?"

Cai smiled. "It was good." His smile flickered. "Was it good for you?"

Mason kissed him in answer.

They sighed and sank back into the pillows. Mason wanted to put his arm around Cai and draw him close but was suddenly unsure of himself. Would a man like that? He wanted to do it. He would like it if Cai did it to him. But still, he doubted.

Cai's soft words broke into his thoughts. "I wish I didn't have to go."

Mason's mood dimmed. "I wish you didn't, either."

"Some things," Cai said, fingering the rope thoughtfully, "we don't have any control over."

"What are you thinking?" Mason asked as the silence lingered, half-afraid of the answer.

"We did it. We slept together."

Mason frowned. "Okay..."

"It's out of your system now."

Mason's stomach dipped. "What are you saying?"

"I'm not saying anything. I'm asking... I guess I'm asking if that's it?"

Mason's mind was crowded with unsayable things and feelings he didn't understand.

"I was an unresolved teenage crush," Cai went on quietly. "Or you craved something new, maybe. You saw me, and you wondered. I guess I'm asking if it really was what you thought it would be."

Mason tilted Cai's face to meet his eyes. "It was more."

Cai's eyes flickered again. Mason pressed a kiss to his lips. He wanted to say more but wasn't sure how. Wasn't sure if he was ready. But Cai made a low noise of contentment, returned the kiss then broke away, smiling.

He sat up, the smile vanishing. "I really have to go."

"What would happen? If you stayed?"

Cai didn't make eye contact as he began gathering his clothes. "You don't want to know."

"Obviously I do, or I wouldn't ask."

Cai looked at him and Mason regretted his tone. But then Cai shrugged and began dressing.

"Sunlight hurts my skin…and my eyes. Prolonged exposure would be dangerous. The Blood doesn't like it."

"What does that mean?"

"Like I said, it does its own thing." Cai shrugged his shirt on, his movements now stiff. "It responds to threats. Daylight is a threat." He reached for his belt. "If we didn't put ourselves away somewhere dark and safe, it would do it for us — and destroy anything that got in the way."

The warmth was stolen from Mason's body as quickly as if someone had opened a window.

"And there's nothing anyone can do?" he asked quietly.

"Do?"

"You know. To cure you?"

Cai sat on the edge of the bed to pull on his socks. "I'm not ill, Mason."

Mason swallowed a mix of shame and annoyance, but he couldn't think of anything else to say. He watched Cai dress in silence.

"But I'll see you tomorrow night?"

"You will," Cai said. He was smiling again as he opened the bedroom door. "We still have a case to solve, right?"

"Cai," he said, reaching for his dressing gown. "Before you go…"

"What is it?"

Mason belted the gown and stood awkwardly by the bed. "I can't spend another day wondering. Not after this. After what we shared tonight."

"Wondering what?" Cai looked perplexed.

"What you aren't telling me."

Cai's expression hardened.

"Please. I don't care if it doesn't make sense. Please, just tell me."

"I don't know what you're talking about."

"Something bothered you. About Kelly's body. About Alonso's."

"They were dead people, Mason. Of course they bothered me."

"It happened at Honor Ford-Byerson's house, too. There was no body there. But I saw something in your face. Something…scared you."

Cai's grip tightened on the door. It was several moments before he replied.

"How about that wine?"

Mason sat on the sofa, watching Cai swirl wine around in his glass. He resisted the urge to fidget and fought the sensation that another barrier was solidifying between them.

When Cai finally spoke, it was barely above a whisper. "You were right. I sensed something. Something about both the bodies. Something I can't explain."

"What?"

Cai grimaced and swallowed some wine. "A haemophile."

Mason held himself very still. "What do you mean?"

"A haemophile touched them. Both of them. The same one."

Mason held himself very still. "Why didn't you say something at the time?"

"Because it's not the same as knowing about the human that touched them. That was a physical trace I could smell and taste. This is…something different."

Mason paused. "And it was at the Ford-Byerson place, too?"

"I...I think so. I'm not sure."

"What do you mean you're not sure?"

"I mean exactly that, Mason. I don't really understand how I know this. It's just something I *feel*."

Mason stared at the wall. "So, a haemophile really did take Honor."

Cai nodded. "I think so."

"And helped Damon murder the others?"

"Probably." Silence filled the room. When Mason was finally able to speak his voice was raw. "Why didn't you mention this before?"

"I told you. Because I don't know how I know. It's not sight, smell or anything like that. I just know."

"*So?*"

Cai tightened his hold on the glass. "My entire career is based around providing evidence. Proof. I don't have either. And I can't explain it. How am I supposed to expect you to trust that? I don't even trust it myself."

Mason downed a large mouthful of wine, stood and began pacing. "If Damon's associate really is a haemophile, we've been looking at this completely the wrong way around."

"And we're in more trouble than we realized."

"Who?" Mason said. "Who is it?"

"I don't know."

"The Baron? Lucien?"

Cai shook his head. "I...I don't think so."

Mason reached deep for patience. "Can you explain why?"

Cai grimaced. "No. I know a haemophile was involved. I don't know how I know it. And I can't tell who it was."

Mason drained his wine and sat again.

"This is something," he said quietly. "We have a direction."

Cai didn't look at him. "What direction, Mason? Why do I even know this, huh? Seeing things, smelling things, tasting things... Khan explained all that. We can detect the most minute traces of physical evidence. And telling what human beings are feeling or thinking? That's all physical, too. It's just changes in the chemicals of your blood. We can detect those easily. It's all physiology. But *feeling* someone's touch on a dead body, or their presence in a room, even though there's no physical trace?" Cai shook his head. "She's never mentioned anything like this to me before. No one has."

"At this point I don't care how you know. I just care that we finally know something."

Cai raised his eyes. "I did get something else, too. Something both coroners missed."

"What?"

"It could be explained with Kelly and Alonso, considering where they were found. But I could smell it in Ford-Byerson's house, too. And smell I get." He straightened. "Smell is real. There's no doubt about it."

"What could you smell?"

"Traces of a plant. Eyebright. The traces were so minute forensics didn't differentiate it from the rest of the plant debris found on the bodies. And as they were found in the countryside, I didn't think anything of it either. But then I smelled it at Ford-Byerson's, too." He set his glass aside. "Detecting it there, so out of context, it triggered something. It brought back a memory. One I thought was gone forever."

"Memory of what?"

"A trip to Wales as a child." Cai's face grew solemn. "My family are from there originally. I know we used to go regularly, but there are so few of those memories left. But I remember the smell of Eyebright. Mason. It grows in heaths and grasslands. Not woodlands. And certainly not in London."

Mason's pulse flickered. "Why didn't you say something while we were there?"

Cai winced. "I was…distracted by sensing that haemophile and not knowing how I was doing it. I'm sorry. I was going to tell you. But then Khan happened, then we got back here and, well…" He smiled a small, intimate smile that made Mason's pulse flurry. "I got distracted again."

Mason took a moment to make himself focus. "So, these victims have all been on and around heathland? Like the moors?"

"Or the murderer has. Yes."

Mason stood. "Christ. What are we waiting for? We need to start hunting on the moors."

Cai stood. "Dawn is less than an hour away."

"That wedding is only a few weeks away. We can't afford to waste any more time. I'll take backup."

Cai stepped close, grasping Mason's hands in a grip like iron. "Mason, promise me you'll wait."

"But—"

"You can't tackle a haemophile alone. Backup won't help. Even if you approach during the day. *Especially* if you approach during the day. Please, Mason. You promised you wouldn't allow yourself to be hurt. This is part of that promise."

Mason made an impatient noise. "What if they kill again?"

"I won't have *you* killed," Cai said firmly. "I won't."

Mason stared at him. The raw emotion in his eyes struck him like a blow. He took a deep breath. "Okay, Cai. I promise I'll wait."

Cai visibly relaxed. He moved to the door.

"Get some sleep. We both need to be prepared."

Mason stared at the front door after he'd left. Then he made a noise of frustration and did as he was told and returned to bed, knowing Cai was right.

Even so, he highly doubted he'd be able to sleep. He took his phone to bed, thinking to update Amelia and Vickers, go through the forensics again, maybe find out more about Eyebright. But when he got into the bed he was surrounded by the smells of him and Cai together. His racing mind stilled. His eyes were heavy. He slept.

* * * *

He was woken by his phone buzzing. He had no idea how long he'd been asleep, but he was groggy and aching and daylight was bleeding in under the blinds.

He blinked at the screen.

Unknown Number.

"Hello?"

"Walker?"

Mason was instantly awake. "Lomax?"

There was a pause on the other end of the phone. "I don't have long. But tell me you're not goin' after my sister for all this, you moron."

Mason sat upright. "Tyler, what do you know?"

"I said I've not got long, didn't I? Not got time to explain myself to you, at any rate."

"Where are you? I need to talk to you."

"No, you don't. You need to do your job. Stop whatever's happening before —"

"Before what?"

Tyler was silent for so long Mason thought he'd hung up.

Finally, he continued. "Look... It's all my fault, okay? I know that now. I just wanna try to stop this before it gets any worse."

"How is this your fault, Tyler? What do you know?"

"Damon wouldn't be on the rampage if it weren't for me, would he? I let him off the leash. And all because..."

"Because you didn't know what you wanted."

Tyler muttered under his breath. "Look, cop. I heard that you reckon Damon's working with someone. Someone that gives him his money. His toys. That all makes sense now."

"Who is it?"

"I don't know who, all right? I just know it ain't my sister. She'd do many things, but this doesn't work for her. She don't like mess in her town. She's got nothin' to gain from stirring shit up like this."

"I know that," Mason said.

"If you know it, why are you paying her calls in the middle of the bloody night?"

"How do you —?"

"Never mind how I know. Answer the question."

"I'm not accountable to you, Tyler. In fact, it's the other way around. And if you really want to help, you should come home, come to the station and talk to me."

"I...can't."

Mason was surprised at the frustration in his tone. "Why not?"

"I just can't, okay? Look... I'll tell you what I know about Damon. The stuff I should've told you before I left."

Mason's pulse quickened. "I'm listening."

"He's not normal. He's unhinged. Obsessive. Single-minded."

"I'd figured that much out myself."

"He's *determined*, Walker. The only way he works with someone else is if they want exactly what he wants and are as obsessed about it as he is. He looked down his nose at me and at the other hunters he hung out with. All of them. He thought he was the dogs' bollocks. The chosen one. To be working with someone else...? It'll be someone as mental as him, is all I'm saying."

Mason hesitated. "Would he work with a haemophile?"

Tyler's silence was loaded. "No," he said after a long pause. "He wants them dead. All of them. No way would he work with one."

"And if I told you we had evidence of him teaming up with a haemophile?"

Silence. "Only way he'd work with one would be if he was *using* one. Manipulating one. Maybe to help him kill others. He was never strong. He used his weapons, and sometimes they weren't enough. Now he's injured, yeah, so maybe he thinks he has to have some muscle. But I wouldn't bet on that haemo surviving a partnership with Damon."

"Tyler, I really need you to come in and give an official statement. Please."

"Can't help you," Tyler said. A pause. "I want to. If I thought I could clear up this mess myself, I would. But I can't. Lucien can't come back into the country. And I'm not going anywhere without Lucien." He paused. "You've got the balls, Walker. You can sort this out."

"I'm flattered."

"Just do it." His tone changed. "I've not seen Lucien scared before, but he is. Not for himself. But for what the world is teetering on the edge of. If the haemos rise up, we won't escape it, even out here."

"And where is that?"

"Somewhere far away. But not far enough to be safe if all hell breaks loose, apparently."

Mason raised his blinds and blinked out on the low, cloudy sky. He took a deep breath. "How do you do it, Tyler?"

"Do what?"

"How do you...be with one of them? When you want them, need them...but they're so removed. Locked away every day. Wired in so different they don't even understand it themselves."

A low chuckle. "Someone got a haemo crush?"

"Lomax," he growled.

"Chill, Walker. It's just nice to have some evidence you're actually a red-blooded human being."

"Yeah. And perhaps that's the problem."

"It ain't, mate. Doesn't have to be, anyway."

"So, what's the answer?"

"It's like any relationship, ain't it? They're all different. We're all different. It's never easy, but if it's worth it, you find a way." His voice lowered. "But if you want a bloody chance, you need to stop this thing before they make enemies of us all."

He hung up.

Chapter Nine

"Boss, *there* you are." Vickers hurried over as soon as he entered the station. "I've been trying to get you on the phone."

"Sorry," he said, making for his office. "It's all been a bit full on."

"Oh," Vickers expression changed, and she closed the office door behind her. "Do tell."

"Can we focus, please?" Mason said. "The body count is mounting, and now it appears forensics are missing things. Even Tyler bloody Lomax is ringing me from exile to tell me I'm missing things."

"What? Wait," Vickers said, raising her hands. "Back up. Tyler Lomax contacted you?"

"To tell me to lay off his sister, among other things." Mason sighed loudly and opened his laptop. "At least I know what she's been hiding now."

"What?"

"They're in touch," he grated. "They must be. How else would Tyler know I'd been to speak to her?"

"Bloody politicians," Vickers ground out. "She could have saved us so much time if she'd just been straight with us. At this point, what do we care if she's texting her scumbag brother on the quiet?"

"Exactly…when there are other things we should be looking at."

Vickers frowned. "Like what?"

"Ever heard of Eyebright?"

She blinked. "No. What is it?"

"It's a plant." He pushed the forensics file toward her. "It was found on both Kelly and Alonso. And in Ford-Byerson's house."

"I don't remember that from the report," she said, taking the file.

"The amounts were too small for forensics to identify."

"Then who identified them?"

"SO Bracken."

Vickers raised her eyebrows. "Wow. It's like working with a supercomputer."

Mason winced. "Yeah. Sometimes."

She looked at him with amusement then returned to the file. "So that may be an impressive party trick, but how does it help us? All three bodies were dumped in the countryside."

"They were all dumped in and around woodland. Eyebright only grows on heathland. Moors."

"It's a link, sir," Vickers admitted. Her face had become serious. "But half of this bloody county is moorland. You really think this is gonna help narrow things down?"

"I'll take anything at this point. What did you want to tell me?"

Vickers' face fell. "You've not been on social media today?"

Mason's stomach sank. "What is it?"

She offered her phone.

Dragomir Soroka had clearly filmed himself on a phone. Even in the still image raw, cold fury filled his night-black eyes. Mason shuddered. He pressed play.

"Any other minority meeting such treatment would induce public outcry. Protests in the streets. A demand for reform. But what's being done? Nothing. Darragh Kelly, murdered. Honor Ford-Byerson, also dead. And now another of our own attacked in cold blood. Assaulted with a knife as she walked through St. James's park..." Mason's blood ran cold. "Hatred and criminality are running rampant. We need to take matters into our own hands. We can't trust the authorities. They've had their chance. Hear me, fellow haemophiles. Now is the time for action."

The video cut.

"The attack in St. James's," Mason breathed. "Where did that come from?"

"You got me," Vickers said, shaking her head. "I didn't see a report." She narrowed her eyes at him. "Do you know something, boss?"

Mason handed the phone back. "It's a need-to-know thing."

"Soroka knows," Vickers said.

"He's doing more damage than this killer ever could," Mason muttered. "Can't someone send Novák after him or something?"

"I suspect Soroka has more clout than Novák at this point."

"Then what's the bloody point of him?" Mason rubbed his forehead. "I'm sorry. It just feels like the sands are shifting under our feet by the minute. I mean, does Soroka really think this is going to help?"

Vickers' face was uncharacteristically solemn. "Depends who you ask, boss. And he's not the only one doing it, either. The original supporters of Magister Morak, the one that executed those Blood dealers during Blood Winter? They're speaking out the same way. Magisters from some of the more isolated communes, too, the ones that have resisted registration. Even a few independent haemophiles. They're all coming out of the woodwork. Posting statements online. Warning us if action isn't taken soon, then they'll take it themselves."

Mason shivered, even though his office was warm.

"Can't help but see where they're coming from," Vickers said softly. "You gotta admit, boss. Turn the tables. How would you feel if you were on their side?"

Mason thought of Cai. His heart fluttered. He wrenched his focus back to Vickers. "We need to know everything there is to know about Eyebright. Where exactly do you find it? Let's try to narrow this down."

"I'll give it a go, sir. There may be someone at the university's ecology department I can call."

"Do it," Mason said, standing. "Oh and, Vickers..." She turned in the door. "Keep this between us, all right?"

She hesitated. "Is that because you think this is as thin as I do...or because of something else?"

"Just do me this favor," he said quietly and moved to open the door wider. "I'm going to report to Fletcher."

Amelia was on the phone when he got to her office, but she waved him in.

"Yes. I repeat, yes. Right away. Thank you." She hung up. "Mason, tell me you have some good news for me."

Mason guarded his face and closed the door. "Cai thinks he has a lead. We're running it down now."

"Tell me."

Mason searched for words. "He thinks a haemophile was involved in all the killings."

Amelia stared at him. "What?"

"That's what he says."

"How does he know?"

"He can't explain it." Mason shrugged. "But I believe him."

Amelia looked at him closely. "I'm glad you're finally getting along."

Mason hoped his facial expression was neutral. "There's one more thing, something he caught on all the victims and in the Ford-Byerson home. A plant. Eyebright."

Amelia frowned. "Not a single forensics department picked it up?"

"Apparently not. The traces are too small. But Cai could distinguish it from other plant material found on the bodies. And he knows it grows on heathland."

"So, we find out where this plant comes from, and we find where the murders happened?"

Mason nodded. "Vickers is getting on to the university."

"Good. We need to accelerate on this. Trouble's brewing. I've had Ivor Novák's people on the phone most of the day. I gather you spoke to him in London?"

Mason flinched. "That was fun."

"The pressure is on, Mason. I hope you and Bracken are up to this."

"We are. He…" Mason hesitated. "He's an excellent cop."

Amelia searched his face. She opened her mouth to speak when her phone rang again. She sighed and picked it up.

"DCI Fletcher." Her face fell. "When? Shit. Does anyone know how long he's been gone?" She raised her eyes to Mason's. "And why are we only just hearing about this? I'm sending DI Walker now." She hung up. "Another haemophile's gone missing."

Mason went cold. "Who?"

"Emmanuel Woodburn. A registered independent. Lives out in the sticks. Someone tripped his silent alarm yesterday. When uniforms got there, his sleeping cell was gone. It only just occurred to them to kick this up to us."

"Shit," Mason said, moving to the door. "Taking the sleeping cell? That's Damon's MO."

"My thoughts exactly. Get out there and get eyes on this. We need to find him," Amelia said gravely. "Another body will mean a riot. And I don't want to be around if haemophiles riot."

Mason hurried from the room, ringing Cai's number. "Cai, when you wake up, come straight to the office. Something new has come up."

Mason called Vickers and hurried out to his car.

"Shit, another one?" Vickers shook her head as she buckled in.

"Do we know anything about this Woodburn?"

"Not much," Vickers said as she scrolled through reports on her phone. "The Haemo Affairs file is thin, basically just his registration and a Kill List. No human deaths for over a century. He's law-abiding, it seems.

His place was up to spec. Remote. Never came near human habitation, as far as I can see."

"So, he didn't know Kelly? Wasn't working with him?"

"No links to Kelly," Vickers went on. "No obvious links to anyone."

"Not an activist, then? That doesn't fit the profile…"

"Then maybe our profile is wrong. Or he was just easy pickings?" Vickers made a noise between her teeth. "I hope we find him before — "

"Yes," Mason said, pressing his foot on the accelerator. "Me, too."

Woodburn's house was a converted barn at the end of a long, rocky track. It nestled in a narrow valley down which the wind blasted, scraping the warmth from Mason's face and bringing with it the first sniff of winter.

Every light was on, and every door stood open as crime scene investigators swarmed over it in white overalls.

"Any signs of forced entry?" Mason asked a forensic tech as he hovered on the doorstep.

"Right here," the tech said, pointing at the scrapes in the door frame. "This took some force, too. There were three separate locks. But inside, the door to the cellar where he slept," the tech beckoned Mason and Vickers to follow. They moved through a cluttered living room to a steel door with a chunky keypad set in the wall. It was flashing red. The door stood open and was easily half a foot thick. "This wasn't forced."

"So how did he get in?"

"Techs are working on it," the man said, shaking his head. "But it was above spec, even for a haemo lock-up.

I can't see how you'd get in if you didn't have the code."

"And no one's found anything to say why he was targeted?"

The man shook his head again. "Think he was just a run-of-the-mill vamp. Private income from some old...*very* old...investments, according to some bank statements on his desk. His donated blood supply was delivered once a month by a private courier. As far as anyone can tell, he barely even left the house."

Mason examined the heavy door and the dark stairwell. There were scrapes where something heavy had knocked against the paintwork. A small table was knocked over in the living room. The broken fragments of a vase were scattered on the carpet.

"This was planned, and they had specialist equipment," Mason murmured. "And it happened in the daylight."

"So a human," Vickers said. "Damon?"

Mason glanced out the window. The day was darkening. The clouds were low and angry. "I want prints and DNA as soon as they come in," Mason instructed the tech and left.

Mason tried to concentrate on the reports when they arrived from Woodburn's but found himself pacing — to the window, checking the progress of the sunset, then back to his desk. Then back to the window again.

Finally, darkness fell. He stared at his office door. No Cai.

He swore, fired off emails, made a couple of calls, paced again.

Two hours passed. Still no Cai.

He rang him. It went to voicemail. "Cai? Where the hell are you?"

He hung up.

Another hour went by. Vickers found him at his desk with his hands in his hair, staring at his phone.

"Sir?"

Mason swore and got to his feet. "Keep chasing forensics," he said, rushing past her and grabbing his coat. "And move up the door-to-door. I know there's not much out there, but that sleeping cell didn't grow wings and fly away. Someone must have seen a van, a lorry, *something*."

"Where are you going?"

"We need Bracken."

Mason didn't want to acknowledge the concern that weighed in him like lead as he drove to Oswald House. His phone sat ominously dark on the passenger seat for the whole trip.

Jesse Truelove was waiting at the open door with the Baron at his shoulder.

"DI Walker," Magnusson said, his face grave. "Any news?"

"I need to speak to Cai."

Jesse raised his eyebrows. "He's not here."

"What?"

"We thought he was with you," Magnusson said.

Mason's heart lurched. "He didn't come back at sunrise?"

Magnusson shook his head.

Mason raced past the pair toward Cai's room.

"I don't know what you expect to find, DI Walker," Magnusson was at his back as he entered. Everything was neat and tidy. The inner door was open. Mason rushed to it. The sleeping cell was open. It was empty. "Cai didn't sleep here today."

"People are kidnapping and murdering haemophiles. Don't you think you should have reported this?"

Magnusson frowned. "He's a police officer in the middle of an investigation. He's not required to run his movements past me. I would say the more pertinent question is why didn't you notice he was gone?"

Heat filled Mason's face. "We trusted you to keep him safe."

Jesse stepped between Magnusson and Mason. "Okay, mate. Just calm down. I'm sure Cai is fine. When did you last see him?"

"Last night," Mason said, the memories warming his blood even as the cold pit deepened in his stomach. "Just before sunrise."

"He probably just spent the day somewhere else," Jesse said. "There are other secure places he could be."

"Then where is he now?" Mason said, his voice catching. "The sun's been down for hours."

"I'm here."

Mason whipped around. Cai stood in the hallway, glancing between them all. "I'm here. I'm fine."

"Where have you been?" Mason demanded. "Why didn't you answer your phone?"

"Is everything well, SO Bracken?" Magnusson cut in in a voice that drowned Mason's.

"I'm fine, Baron. Thank you."

"Come on, Em," Jesse said, taking the Baron's hand and stepping back. "Let's leave them to it."

"There was nothing to worry about," Cai said when they were alone.

"Another haemophile is missing," Mason snapped. "And you weren't answering your phone."

Cai's expression tightened. "Who?"

"A man called Emmanuel Woodburn," Mason said, keeping his voice steady with an effort. "He was taken, sleeping cell and all, from his home yesterday. Then when you didn't show up at sunset..."

"I'm sorry," he said quietly. "I didn't mean to frighten you. Who's this Woodburn? How's he connected?"

"He doesn't appear to be connected at all," Mason said a little gloomily. "But he was taken in daylight, just like Lucien was taken by Damon."

"No body?"

"Not yet."

"Then we need to get moving."

"Wait," Mason grabbed his elbow. "Where were you? Why didn't you answer?"

"It's just been a couple of hours, Mason."

"I thought you were avoiding me," Mason said with his voice caught in his chest. "Or worse..."

"I'm not avoiding you. Why would I?"

Mason's face warmed. "I...I don't know. Maybe you were regretting —"

"Hey." Cai put his hand on his face. "No." His smile was warm, but his eyes sparked with uncertainty. "Are you?"

"No," Mason said huskily. He took Cai by the arms and drew him into the room. "But I feel like I don't want to let you out of my sight."

"I'm a grown man — older than you, in fact." His sharp teeth glinted as he smiled. "I can look after myself."

Mason kissed him, feverishly, possessively. Cai went rigid for a moment then sank into it.

"I've spent years waiting to find you again," Mason mumbled between kisses as he backed Cai against the wall. "I don't want to lose you."

"You won't," Cai said, clinging to Mason's arms and tilting his head to let Mason kiss his neck. He gasped when Mason slid a hand into his shirt. Then his grip tightened, and he pushed Mason back. "We can't. Not without the rope."

"We can," Mason said, pulling off his tie.

Cai's eyes burned. "What if it doesn't hold?"

"It will." Mason drew Cai's hands together. He looped the silk tie around his wrists, nibbling Cai's ear as he did so. Cai's breathing deepened. His skin warmed under Mason's touch.

"How do you do this to me, Mason?" Cai breathed as Mason pulled the bonds tighter and lifted Cai's arms over his head. "How do you know this was what I needed? Even I didn't know."

Mason kissed him deeply, swallowing his taste and pinned his bound wrists against the wall over his head. Feeling the lithe body trapped between him and the wall, the quivering strength restrained under his hands, Mason's entire body sang.

"Sometimes you just feel things. Right?" He breathed against his mouth then reached up and looped the tie around a decorative picture rail. He tied the knot tight, kissing and nibbling Cai's mouth, jaw and lips. "Is that okay?"

Cai exhaled and pulled on the tie. His muscles bulged and Mason swallowed, his throat thick. There was an alarming groan of strained masonry, but the rail held.

"My tie, too, Mason," he panted. "My eyes…"

Mason undid Cai's tie then flicked open his top button. He lowered his lips to Cai's collarbone. He ran his hands up Cai's thighs, making him shiver.

"Don't you want to see this time?" Mason whispered. "Watch what I'm going to do?"

"What are you going to do?" Cai's voice was deep and ragged. Color flushed his pale cheeks, and his lips were wet and swollen. Mason tilted his hips against Cai's, shuddering at the pressure against his aching erection.

He put his lips against Cai's ear. He licked his lips. "I want to taste you," he whispered. "I've never tasted a man before. I've never wanted to. But you..." He drew his earlobe into his mouth and thrust against his crotch again, his whole body taut as wire. "I want everything to do with you."

"God, Mason."

Mason pulled back and looked into his face. He had trouble getting his breath into his chest at the sight of the arousal darkening Cai's eyes. "Will you watch me?"

Cai took a breath. His face flushed deeper red. "You want me to?"

"God, yes. The thought..." His throat closed over. "I trust you, Cai. You won't hurt me. Be in this with me. Watch me make you feel good again."

Cai closed his eyes and swallowed but then nodded. "I'll watch," Cai breathed. "But if this starts to break," he pulled at the tie, "you have to stop. Stop and get away."

"I will." Mason managed to get the words out then unbuttoned Cai's shirt with one hand while he wrestled with the belt with the other. He exposed Cai's toned chest just as he got his hand into his own pants and started stroking himself. The taste and feel of Cai under his tongue as he pumped his own cock filled him with liquid fire. He moaned against Cai's chest and delighted in the feel of his breath shuddering in and out.

Mason increased his pace on his cock as he used the flat of his tongue on one of Cai's nipples. Cai was moaning. Mason could feel the slow slug of his heartbeat under his mouth.

He made himself slow down, remembering the night before, the slow build of Cai's desire, the glorious anticipation as it grew. He reluctantly let go of his own cock to undo Cai's trousers and pushed them and his pants down, straightening to kiss him again as he did so. Mason grasped the hardening flesh of his cock, and Cai moaned into his mouth.

This should feel alien, he told himself. *This should feel too different to be good.* But his body moved on instinct, like it was finally doing what it had wanted to do his whole life.

"You're amazing," Mason panted into his neck as he kneaded Cai's cock to hardness. "Just turning you on is making me want to come right here."

"I don't know how you're doing this, Mason," Cai breathed heavily. "But don't stop."

Mason couldn't wait any longer. He dropped to his knees. He registered Cai's gasp somewhere beyond the roaring in his ears. He met Cai's eyes as he stroked him fast, taking his own cock back in hand.

Cai's eyes flashed blue fire. Mason opened his mouth, breathed on the end of Cai's cock. Cai shivered and tensed. He strained against the tie. There was a low cracking sound, but Mason couldn't stop now, even if Oswald House came crashing down on their heads.

He leaned forward and took the end of Cai's cock into his mouth. Cai collapsed against the wall.

Mason's flesh tightened. The taste was strange and familiar, all at once. Salty-sweet. A little bitter. But also with an undercurrent of something more than human. Woodsmoke and rich liqueurs. Red wine and liquid copper.

Mason wanted more. He moved his head forward and took him deeper. Cai opened his mouth in a silent cry. Mason fought the sensation of invasion as Cai's cock pressed against the back of his throat. He tried swallowing. Cai shivered. Mason drew back. He beat his own cock lazily, tantalizingly, lighting fires along his veins.

He started to move his head in time with his strokes, taking Cai deep then sliding back, running his tongue over the tip then back again.

Cai was saying his name now, over and over, low and breathy, almost a growl.

Mason drew back just long enough to say, "Watch me, Cai."

Cai looked down. They locked eyes as Mason continued to suck and lick, stroke himself and run his free hand over Cai's thigh.

"Christ," Cai panted. His legs quivered under Mason's fingers. "God, Mason. I'm close. I'm really close. Do you want me to tell you…?"

Mason pulled back and rubbed Cai's cock, slick with his saliva. "I want to taste you," he breathed. "All of you."

Cai inhaled sharply and nodded. "Christ. Yes. Keep going. And —"

"What?" Mason said, still stroking, a furnace lighting in his belly at the look in Cai's eyes. "Is there something else you want? What? Tell me."

Cai bit his lip and shivered. "How do you feel about…using your fingers?"

Mason paused. It wasn't somewhere his mind had gone. But now the thought was planted, and it flowed through him like lava.

"Do you want me to?"

"Not if you don't want to."

Mason grinned. "Will you like it?"

"Fuck." Cai shook, his arms tugging at the tie. "Yes."

"Then tell me what to do."

Cai inhaled deep. "Get your fingers wet."

The command that had crept into Cai's tone sent Mason's desire through his body like an arrow. He sucked at three of his middle fingers, licking them and coating them with saliva.

"Like this?" he said, moving his hand around Cai's hip.

Cai nodded and stepped wider. The movement made Mason's whole body clamp down on itself. The expectation was almost too much. He closed his eyes and took Cai back into his mouth to help ground himself. Then he reached around Cai's beautifully taut ass and pushed a finger into the hot, tender space there.

Cai bucked. Mason hesitated, but then Cai urged him on. He sucked and licked his cock and pushed farther through the tight ring of muscle.

Cai sagged against the wall, moaning. His cock jerked in Mason's mouth. His mouth opened wide, the sharp canines glinting. Mason pushed deeper, his own insides clenching.

"Fuck," Cai cried. "Mason…Fuck. More. Please." Mason slid another finger in. Cai swore again. "Deeper."

Mason obeyed, the tightness around his fingers unusual but not unpleasant. Far from unpleasant. And when he pushed deeper and swept his fingers around when Cai asked him to, the reaction in Cai's body was incendiary. He quivered and groaned.

Mason beat his own cock fast. He swallowed Cai's cock deep. He slid a third finger deep into Cai and reached for the spot that made him buck into his mouth. Cai jerked and cried and came in Mason's throat. Mason swallowed greedily. Cai's muscles clamped on Mason's fingers. Mason wondered what that tight, intimate place might feel like clenching around his cock.

The thought was all it took. He came, hard and fast, his vision rolling away as the fire ripped through his body.

It was several moments before Mason could see straight again. Cai was slumped against the wall, his eyes closed. Color still suffused his cheeks, and he breathed heavily through his mouth.

He was so damn gorgeous that desire again pumped again in Mason's veins. But then Cai blinked his eyes open and smiled. He spread his bound hands.

"I'm gonna need you to let me down."

Mason smiled a smile he felt through his whole body. He straightened, a little shakily, and reached up to unhook the tie.

The picture rail had come loose from the wall, and there were some cracks in the plaster. But he unwound the silk from around his lover's wrists without giving it a second thought.

Cai kissed him on the corner of the mouth, softer than a feather brushing against his skin. Then he retrieved some tissues from the other room and cleaned them both off. "That was amazing."

Mason kissed him harder but then sighed heavily and closed his eyes.

"I'm going to ask again. You know I am."

When he opened his eyes again Cai's face was solemn. "Shall we shower first?"

The suggestion combined with the low fire in the back of Cai's eyes was sorely tempting. But Mason shook his head and stepped out of reach, tucking himself back into his pants. "Christ, I want to. But we can't."

Cai began to button his shirt. "You're right."

"Cai..."

"I stayed in an unregistered hide today, farther out in the countryside. Then, after sunset, I was out on the moors," he said, tucking his shirt back into his trousers. "Trying to find Eyebright."

Mason's fingertips tingled. "And?"

Cai hesitated. His face was unreadable. "I found something."

"Found what?"

"A place. *The* place."

Mason froze. "What place?"

"Where all this happened," he said softly.

Mason went very still. "Are you sure?"

"It stank of blood. Of fear."

Mason swallowed. "Was he there? Damon?"

"I didn't get close. I came back to tell you. Just in case..."

"In case what?"

"In case anything happens when I go in there, so you know where to look."

"Cai, no," Mason said, shaking his head. "You're not going back. Not alone. We get a team. We do this right."

"We *can't* take a team," Cai said in a hushed voice, his eyes serious. "We can't tell anyone. Remember what happened at the Fort?"

Mason blinked. "What do you mean? Damon warned them."

"Did he leak the story about Kelly, too? When it was clear we weren't even meant to find him that soon?"

Mason went cold. "You think someone on my team…?"

Mason wondered if Cai really hesitated or if he imagined it. "I don't know. But we can't risk this getting out, not before I've got the culprits under control."

"You can't do this alone."

Cai's face changed. His eyes were hard, deep and darkened like a tropical storm. For the first time, Mason felt a frisson of fear. "I can handle this."

"They killed Kelly. They took Woodburn."

"Mason—"

"I can't lose you."

Cai's mouth softened. Mason's breath was trapped in his chest. He wanted to grab onto Cai and hold on, never let him go. But he couldn't move.

Cai smiled and the spell broke. "You won't lose me, Mason. I promise. I know what I'm doing."

"I'll be your backup," Mason said firmly. "We go together, Cai, or not at all."

Emotions flitted through his eyes but then he smiled. "Deal."

Chapter Ten

Mason was careful not to make too much eye contact with the armory guard as he checked out his handgun. But he'd known Steve for years, and the only comment the older man made was about the football results, though his eyes slid warily to Cai more often than Mason was comfortable with.

Mason was glad to head to the exit, but then Steve called him back.

"Boss, I need Fletcher's initials on this," he said, waving the weapon check-out form. "You know if she's still upstairs?"

Mason hesitated. "She said she's gonna come down and get that sorted ASAP," he said with a half-smile. "I wouldn't bug her now, though. She's doing damage control with the Chief Constable. You know what it's like when she's having a ding-dong with Geoff."

Steve blanched. "I hear ya, guv. Cheers for the heads-up."

Mason let himself breathe freely only when they were back in the car. He looked over at Cai's face, which was pale and grim in the glow of the headlights.

"We need a plan."

"I go first," Cai stated. "That's the plan."

"We're partners," Mason insisted. "We go together."

"This isn't a normal situation, Mason. This is not a danger you've ever faced before."

"I've faced violent criminals before," Mason argued. "I know what I'm doing."

"I know you do," Cai continued, his voice softer. "And I can't think of anyone else I'd rather have as backup. But this is different. I'm not saying you're not up to it. But you have to promise you'll follow my lead, or I'm going alone."

Mason continued to wrestle with a number of responses, gripping the wheel tight. But in the end, he made himself nod.

"Good," Cai said. "Left here."

The drive felt like hours. The farther they went, the darker the night seemed to become. The roads grew narrower, rougher and began to slope uphill. Eventually they were bumping along a dirt track between rusted wire fences.

"Lights off," Cai instructed. "Slow down."

Mason obeyed, his heart hammering as he drove in almost total darkness.

"Right a little," Cai murmured. "Straighten. Okay. Stop."

They climbed out into the darkness. There was no breeze. Mason could smell heather, damp soil, the musty tinge of the start of autumn. The sky arched high and star-speckled above but there was no moon.

Somewhere a sheep bleated then all was silent.

Cai's hand on his elbow made him start.

"Sorry," he whispered. "This way."

Cai helped him climb over the fence then they struck out across naked heath. The ground undulated with uneven tussocks, shrubs and ditches. Cai went ahead, finding as even a path as possible. Mason kept close, swearing under his breath at every stumble. He scanned the horizon but could see nothing—no buildings, no lights.

His feet were soon soaked, and he felt like he'd been struggling over the impossible ground forever when Cai touched his arm. They stopped. Mason narrowed his eyes. In the starlight he could just make out something ahead. Something solid, with straight lines.

"Is that a wall?"

"Ten feet high," Cai murmured. "Barbed wire around the top. Motion-detector daylight floods on either side, too."

"What would a daylight flood do?"

"Nothing to you. But it would blind me. Burn me. And, of course, alert whoever's in there that someone's here."

"Great."

"Don't worry. I have a plan."

"I don't like the sound of that."

"This way," Cai said, and drew Mason away. They crept along, parallel to the wall, for an agonizing amount of time. Mason's palms sweated. He sensed more than saw the wall looming on their right. Then Cai stopped.

"There's a gate ahead," he whispered. "It has a key code lock. There's a flood right over it, but if you crawl slowly, you may stay under the motion detectors."

"*May*?"

Cai shrugged. Mason thought he saw a half-smile in the dark.

"Can't you do your superman mega-speed thing?"

"The motion detectors are designed to pick up the superman mega-speed thing. If you go slow and low, I think you've got a chance."

"How exactly were you planning to do this by yourself?"

"I was planning to get blinded and burned."

"What?"

"We're more dangerous when we're hurt," Cai replied softly. "Sometimes that's an advantage. But given the chance, I'd prefer to stay in control. You seem to be able to help me with that."

Despite Cai's pleasing tone, Mason's mind reeled in a number of unpleasant directions. "This lock, then. Do you know the code?"

"No. But if you send me a photo, I'll be able to tell which keys get pressed the most…like Sadie's iPad."

"That's how Damon got into Woodburn's basement," he mused. "A haemophile had looked at the keypad and gave him the code."

Cai winced. "A real partnership."

"Like ours, do you mean?"

Mason couldn't see Cai's face, but he sensed his smile. "I think ours is a little different. So, are you ready to do this?"

Mason blinked into the shadows of Cai's face. "Sorry, sweetie, but this doesn't sound like much of a plan."

Cai paused. "Sweetie?" There was an equal mix of tenderness and amusement in his tone.

Mason shifted. "That just came out."

Cai squeezed his arm. "I liked it." He let his hand drop. "But we need to focus. Think you can do this?"

"I haven't crawled since my survival training," Mason muttered. "But sure. Here it goes."

"Mason," Cai stopped him. "If the floods go off, just run, okay? Don't think. Just run."

"I will if you will."

Cai hesitated before agreeing. The hesitation made Mason's heart drop. But the silent night swelled around them, and whatever it was that lurked beyond that wall pressed in on him like a physical weight. The faces of all the dead people rose before his eyes. He took a breath, got down onto his belly and began to crawl.

"Slow, Mason," Cai breathed. "Slow as you can go."

Mason bit back a reply and used his elbows and knees to shimmy over the uneven ground. The cold wetness of well-trodden mud soaked into his clothes. He reached the gate and froze, expecting lights, alarms or both. Nothing happened.

His entire body burned with the effort of getting to his feet as slow as humanly possible. But finally, he was up. He drew out his phone, clenched his teeth as he turned on the flash and took a picture of the keypad.

A low glow appeared in the night as Cai checked the picture from his own phone out of range of the sensors. Then there was a long silence.

"Cai?" Mason whispered, his frame threatening to shake with the effort of keeping still.

Several more silent heartbeats passed. Cai's face remained stony in the glow of his phone screen.

"Seven, eight, two, four, one."

"…you sure?"

"I'm sure."

"How do you know the order?"

"Just trust me."

Mason drew a breath, raised his hand, slowly, and keyed in the numbers.

There was a beep and a clank. The gate slid open. Mason let out a shaking breath but then there was an iron-hard grip on his arm, and he was being dragged forward.

"We're in," Cai whispered in his ear. "Hurry."

"The floods?" Mason managed as they hurried along.

"They must deactivate when the code is put in."

"Why?"

"So the haemophile can get in after the human partner's entered the code. Just like us. Only I bet Damon doesn't crawl through the mud. He just lets the floods light up and the haemophile waits at a safe distance until Damon puts the code in."

Mason didn't let himself think about the similarities between him and Cai and Damon and his murdering haemophile partner.

They hurried over hard ground. A dark shape loomed against the starlight ahead. A low, flat-roofed building.

They stopped at a wide, metal door. Another keypad was set in the wall next to it.

Cai was stiff and silent.

"What is it?"

"There are people in there," he murmured.

"Human? Or haemo?"

"Both."

Mason's blood thrummed. "We've got them," Mason whispered. "We've finally got them."

When Cai answered, his voice was tight. "I'll take the haemophile," Cai said. "You have to leave them to me."

Mason nodded reluctantly. "I know."

"And if they get free…shoot for the head. Promise me. The head."

Mason swallowed but nodded. "I promise."

"Okay, then." Cai drew an audible breath and reached toward the keypad. "Here we go."

He tapped in a code. The door opened. Light spilled out, making Mason blink.

He drew his gun and moved cautiously into a brightly lit hall. There were doors on either side, but Cai made for the one at the end. His expression was troubled, but Mason didn't let himself think about it, instead keeping close behind, scanning, gun ready.

The door at the end opened onto a set of concrete stairs, leading to a basement level. They descended. The temperature dropped.

Lights flickered on as they stepped into a wide, empty space. In the same moment, a roaring accompanied by clanging started up behind one of the steel doors set in the far wall. The sound sent ice along Mason's veins. Cai was already at the door, rattling the handle.

"Cai, wait."

"Stay back," Cai ordered and wrenched the handle off. The metal buckled and the door swung open. The blood curdling roar doubled in volume. Cai was gone, and Mason's stomach dropped into his feet. Slowly, the noise quieted.

Mason hesitated, desperate to move forward but somehow unable to make his feet obey him.

"Mason, quick."

Cai's call broke the spell. He rushed forward.

The tiny cell was empty but for a concrete plinth the size of a church altar. Secured to it with chains that looked strong enough to hold a ship's anchor was a prone haemophile. His eyes were wide open, bloodshot and staring. His black hair stood up in all directions, and his hands balled into fists so tight that his sharp fingernails were digging into his flesh. Red-black Blood stained the concrete and filled the air with its strong smell.

The prisoner strained against the chains.

"Shit. Is that Woodburn?"

"He's drugged," Cai called over the renewed cries. "The Blood's trying to take over. We need to get him out of here."

"Can you break the chains?"

Cai shook his head as Woodburn's mouth opened and a low howl started deep in his chest. "They're too strong. We need the key. Mason, look for a key."

"He'll come," the haemophile rasped. "He's upstairs, right now. He'll come. He'll kill you all."

"Who? Who will come?"

"Mason, *key*. Woodburn, calm down. Take control."

"He's coming," screamed the haemophile and began thrashing.

Mason holstered his gun and hurried from the room. He frantically scanned the basement, finally spotting a cabinet at the far end. He ran to it. It was locked. He raised his gun and shot the lock.

The buckled door swung open. Mason grabbed the large key from inside and hurried back to the cell.

Cai snatched the key then pushed Mason back against the wall. He climbed on top of the chained haemophile, pushing an arm against his chest to hold him against the concrete.

Mason wasn't able to analyze the feelings that arose at the sight of his lover straddling this thrashing, bound stranger. The set of his face and terror in the air stole all rational thought away. Cai kept talking to Woodburn, holding him fast to the concrete, repeating over and over his order to calm down, to take control.

Eventually, Woodburn's thrashing eased, and his breathing slowed. He blinked. The wild look left his eyes. He stared up at Cai, then at Mason, then at Mason's drawn gun. He tensed.

"Who are you? What's happening?"

"Woodburn?" Cai said. "Are you in control?"

Woodburn blinked. "The Blood's cooled," he coughed, shaking his head. "It's me. But it's too late."

Cai slid off the large man with and began unlocking the chains. "We're getting you out of here."

"You don't understand," Woodburn said, looking pleadingly at Cai then Mason. "He's coming. He's on the stairs."

"Who?" Mason insisted, covering the doorway with his gun.

"It's a human," Cai muttered, helping Woodburn to sit up. "Just a human."

"He's *not*." Woodburn was shaking so much Cai was visibly struggling to get him on his feet. "You don't understand."

"First, we get you out of here. Mason?" Cai drew Woodburn's arm over his shoulders. Mason holstered his gun and grabbed the other arm. The bodyweight was crushing, but he got his shoulder under Woodburn's armpit and together, they helped him out of the cell.

A gunshot tore the air apart. The wall over their heads exploded. Shrapnel sliced into Mason's back and shoulders. He cried out and staggered. He lost his hold on Woodburn.

He blinked dust from his eyes and pulled his gun.

A man stood at the foot of the stairs. He held a semi-automatic nine-millimeter leveled at Mason's head. He was painfully thin. His cheekbones were sharp angles in an already-angular face. He was pale, almost pallid. Dark circles enhanced the uncanny silver of his eyes. He looked ill, but he stood perfectly rigid. The gun did not waver, and the cut-glass grin revealed startling sharp teeth. There were wounds on his neck and arms. Bite marks. Scabbed but still oozing.

Mason's blood ran cold.

"Damon," he made himself say, "put the gun down."

"You've seen what a good shot I am," he said. His voice was raw, like he'd been screaming. "It would be very unwise of you to move."

Woodburn was slumped against the wall, his head hanging, apparently unconscious. Cai stood rigid in front of his prone form, appearing to not even be breathing, his face set harder than marble. Mason stepped forward, his brain unable to process what he was seeing, but his body certain he wanted to get himself between Damon and Cai.

"Michael Heron," he stated, "I'm arresting you for the murder of Darragh Kelly, Constable Horatio Alonso, Honor Ford-Byerson and the kidnapping and torture of Emmanuel Woodburn."

The gray eyes landed on him like anvils. The pointed grin widened, showing more teeth than seemed possible. "Detective Inspector Walker." His voice continued to rasp, like metal on stone. His lips were cracked. There were dark stains around his mouth, like he'd been drinking wine. "I've heard a lot about you. Tyler Lomax was very vocal about you. About a lot of things, actually. Shame he was all hot air in the end. No balls. No brains."

"Damon," Cai's voice was level, deliberate but with an undercurrent of threat. "You are not well. Let us help you."

"Not well, am I?" The tip of his tongue appeared between his teeth, very red, then vanished again. His eyes flashed, appearing for a second to glow with silver fire. "If I'm unwell, what are you, demon? I'll tell you what you are. Diseased. Cursed." He tilted his chin. "Doomed."

"You've lost," Cai stated. "It's over."

He laughed, a pained, screeching laugh like nails down a chalkboard. "Your kind. You're all so *arrogant*. Your *infection* makes you so strong you think you own the world. *He*'s no different. He thinks *he's* using *me*. But he's wrong. He'll get me where I need to be. Then I'll kill him, too. I'll put his bullet-riddled head on a spike and every human on the planet will thank me."

"This is your last chance," Mason said quietly. "Put down the gun. It's not too late."

"Too late for you." Damon's finger tightened on the trigger.

Mason fired. Something hot bloomed in his body. Damon jerked like someone had shoved him. Cai thrust Mason to the ground. He tried to move but the world had suddenly taken on a dreamy quality. Then the reassuring weight of Cai's body was gone, and the air was filled with noise and movement.

Mason blinked until his vision cleared. Cai had Damon against the wall. He held the wrist of the hand that held the gun against the concrete, even as Damon continued to fire wildly. Dark Blood spread across Cai's clothing. There were bullet holes in his shirt. His other hand was around Damon's throat. The man's feet kicked frantically a foot from ground. His razor-like nails ripped at Cai's hands, drawing more Blood as he struggled. But Cai stood rigid, his mouth open, sharp canines impossible and white against the redness of his mouth as he leaned into Damon's neck.

"Cai," Mason cried. His voice cracked. He pulled a deep, painful breath. "*Cai.*"

Cai's eyes slid to Mason and locked with his. Madness fought pain in their depths.

Mason shook his head. "Don't."

Cai didn't move. Damon continued to thrash. Mason began to register his own pain. The hot wetness spreading over his skin. "Zero Kills," he croaked. "You have Zero Kills. Don't give that up. Not for him."

Damon began to weaken. He dropped the gun. His eyelids fluttered. Woodburn began to stir, blinking and burbling in the corner. Cai's eyes lightened.

Mason stayed conscious long enough to watch Cai drop Damon to the ground, then he let the darkness swallow him.

Chapter Eleven

Mason came around to a cool breeze and the smell of moorlands. The first thing he processed was an overwhelming sense of relief. The second was blue lights flashing through his eyelids and a burning pain in his neck.

He groaned, gasped and tried to sit up.

"DI Walker." Gloved hands pressed against his bare chest and arms. "You're hurt. Just lie still."

He blinked until the interior of the ambulance came into focus. He pawed at the mask over his mouth.

"DI Walker, please."

"Where's Cai? Where's Damon?"

"Detective Inspector," the paramedic's stern face came into focus above him. "I must insist you lie still."

"Cai—"

"I'm here, Mason."

Cai stepped into his line of sight. His face was pale. His clothes were bloody. "It's all okay. I'm here."

"Sir, you have to move away." The paramedic held out a hand to block Cai's path. "He has an open wound. We can't risk infection—"

"He's not a leper," Mason growled, struggling onto his elbows. "Cai, are you hurt?"

"He shot me, but I'm healing. I'm fine, I promise. But you need to go to the hospital."

"So do you," Mason pleaded, looking at the Blood that soaked Cai's shirt.

"I'm okay, I promise." His voice was steady, but his face was strained.

"Cai, what is it?"

"I can assure you he is quite all right," the paramedic said, urging Cai back. "But that's haemophile Blood on his clothing, and we have very strict infection prevention measures."

"I said he's *not*—"

"Mason." Cai raised his hand. "It's okay. We rescued Woodburn. And we got the bad guy."

"Damon's alive?"

Cai winced. "Mostly."

Mason tried to respond, but Cai glanced at the paramedic who now stood between them with her arms crossed. "Go to the hospital, Mason. I'll see you later."

Between pain medication, sedatives and a pounding headache that the morphine couldn't touch, his treatment at the hospital passed in a blur. The doctor told him it was a million-dollar shot. Damon's bullet had passed a centimeter from his aorta. The stitches pulled and hurt like hell, but he wasn't in danger.

Once they told him that, he refused any more medication, and as soon as his head was clear enough, he discharged himself.

He was signing the discharge forms under the disapproving gaze of a junior doctor, uncomfortably aware of his bloody shirt sticking to his skin, when a noise made him look up. It was a roar, building from a quiet whine to an unholy scream. It sounded like a tortured animal or a person screaming with a torn throat.

"Sir, you can't go in there."

He ignored the doctor and stepped to the doorway of the room at the center of a lot of activity. The young constable guarding the doorway had turned a sickly shade of green.

Mason showed his badge and attempted to see inside, but the constable barred the way. "I'm sorry, sir. You really shouldn't go in."

Another scream, full-bellied and agonized, drowned out all other sound as more doctors, swathed in plastic aprons, face shields and masks, rushed into the room.

"What's going on?"

"It's the perp, sir." The young constable's voice shook. "He's having some sort of attack. The hospital staff have ordered everyone to stay clear."

Mason resisted the urge to cover his ears as the sound came again, but it was like glass shards scraping over the inside of his skull. The constable was examining him with concern.

"Are you all right, sir?"

"I'm fine."

"You should leave."

"We need to talk to this man."

"I'll report in as soon as he's stable."

The constable didn't need to say that wouldn't be any time soon, if at all. It was written on his face and in the eyes of all the medical staff in sight.

Mason made for the exit, desperate to get out of the ward before Damon screamed again.

He blinked stupidly in the bright sunlight outside and cursed. Damon's screams were still echoing in his head. He was sick, tired and sore. He needed Cai. But it was hours until he would see him again.

He remembered the Blood soaking Cai's clothing. Nausea returned with a vengeance. But he breathed through it and pulled out his phone to order an Uber. He started putting in his home address then changed his mind and put in Fulford Road.

He ignored the driver's open stare at his bloodstained clothing and asked him to put his foot down.

"Boss? What the hell?" Vickers chased him along the station corridor. Curious eyes followed their movements, but Mason ignored them. "You should be in the hospital."

"Where's Amelia?"

"She's in a meeting. Seriously, boss. You don't look right."

Mason turned toward the meeting rooms, concentrating on walking in a straight line.

He opened the meeting room door. Amelia looked up from her laptop with a startled expression. It changed to anger then to shock as she took in his appearance.

"Mason," she said. "What on God's green earth—?"

"This isn't over," he said. "Damon wasn't acting alone. We need to get that place turned over—"

A gruff voice came from the laptop. "Is that Walker?"

"It is, Detective Superintendent," Amelia said, folding her arms and glaring at him. "Defying doctor's orders. What a surprise."

"Amelia, you have to listen to me."

"Vickers, get him out of here."

"Come on, sir," Vickers laid a hand on his arm, but Mason shrugged it off.

"Damon thinks he was the one in control, but he's half-mad. Delusional. There's someone else out there."

"We know there's an associate, Mason. That's what we're trying to do now, to identify them."

"It's a man—or someone male. Damon called him 'him'."

"Fletcher," Okeke grumbled from the laptop. "That doesn't fit."

"I know it doesn't," Amelia said pointedly, turning the laptop so the camera took in Mason. Okeke glowered like a thundercloud. "But just take a look at my Detective Inspector, sir. I think we need to wait until he's at least stopped bleeding before he gives an official statement."

"First, it's definitely Mayor Lomax. Now it's an unknown male? We really need to get this straight, Fletcher. I've got Novák and Soroka and the whole bloody lot of them breathing down my neck. And this may not be politically correct, but I *really* don't want any of these people near my neck."

"What are you both talking about?" Mason said, frowning through the returning headache.

"Mason," Amelia snapped, "go with Vickers. She'll fill you in on what we have. Within reason, Vickers," Amelia added with a stern look at the sergeant. "Then you need to go home, understand? We'll take up the little matter of you checking out a firearm and running an op without authorization later." She gestured at Mason's bandaged neck. "As soon as you're well enough, anyway. Now...*go*."

Mason released his hold on the nearest chair, not realizing he'd been sagging.

"Come on, boss," Vickers said gently, taking his elbow. "Let's get you some coffee."

Mason's head was swimming again by the time he was sinking into the chair at Vickers' desk.

"Here," Vickers said, holding out a half-empty pack of chocolate chip cookies. "For blood sugar."

Mason realized he hadn't eaten since early the day before and took one gladly, chomped it down, swallowed some coffee and took another.

"Damon," he said around his mouthful. "Tell me."

Vickers pushed the packet closer. "You're gonna want another cookie before hearing this."

"Why?" said Mason, obediently taking a third biscuit but this time not eating.

"Did you notice anything…weird about him?"

"Be quicker to list the things that weren't weird."

"Doctors are still doing tests. But he had a lot of Blood in him. Capital 'B' Blood."

Mason lowered his coffee. "Haemophile blood?"

Vickers nodded. "Seems someone was — whatever you call it — *turning* him. Into a haemophile. He was only halfway done." She grimaced. "Apparently."

"How?" Mason breathed.

"We're not sure. And he isn't talking. They're hoping the Baron will go to the hospital at sunset to try to answer some questions. But at this point they're not even sure if Heron will survive the day."

Mason remembered the screams with a shiver. "What's happening to him?"

"They gave him enough sedatives to take down a rhino, but he's still able to tear through the hospital restraints. He's crying out for blood. Nothing they've tried has worked. Then they gave him a blood transfusion." She'd gone pale. "That just made him stronger...and more desperate. He's trying to bite people." She shuddered. "I went to see if I could interview him while you were still under. The doctors wouldn't let me in. I got a glimpse through the door, and I'm glad they didn't."

Mason swallowed. "What did you see?"

Vickers hesitated. A look Mason didn't recognize darkened her eyes. "His skin's too tight on his bones. His teeth are too big for his mouth. He was apparently unconscious, but his eyes were open and staring, blood-red and bulging. He's got these slashes all over his body that won't stop bleeding." She raised her coffee mug to her lips. Her hand was shaking. "It's scary stuff, boss. Real scary. I wouldn't wish that on anyone."

Mason's mind conjured images of the same thing happening to Cai, and he reeled. He gripped the arms of the chair until the sick feeling passed.

"They're supposed to be checking in with me again later. But I don't see us being able to talk to him, boss...maybe ever."

"Has he said anything at all? To anyone?"

"Like what?"

"Like who the haemophile was that did this to him?"

"We don't know that it was a haemo, boss."

"How can it not be?" Mason said exasperatedly. "A human couldn't do that to another human."

"We don't know that, either," she said patiently. "They won't talk about how they make new haemos. It involves the Blood, we know that. But any human with know-how can get whole bags of that on the black market."

"But he was covered in bite marks," Mason breathed. "I saw them."

"Puncture marks, for sure," Vickers said, face twisted with distaste. "The doctors are still trying to make sense of it all."

"He said," Mason insisted. "He told us he was working with a haemophile."

"He's saying lots of things, boss," she said carefully. "Christ knows if he even knows what's real and what isn't."

Mason ran a hand through his hair. "It feels like we're learning less at every turn. Did they find anything at that bloody place, at least?"

"You mean besides the torture basement?" Vickers shook her head. "Forensics are there now. It's probably where Kelly died. Poor Alonso, too. The place is a purpose-built haemophile death camp." Her face was unusually grim. "There were no computers, though. No paperwork. No CCTV. No clues about who Damon was working with. Apart from..." She glanced over her shoulder toward the meeting room. The door was still shut.

"What?"

"I'm not sure Fletcher would want you to know this yet."

"Know *what*?"

Vickers pulled over a file that had been buried under a pile of others, drew out a photograph and handed it over. "They found this is one of the rooms upstairs."

It was a picture of a gold statement earring with a heavy emerald set in the center.

"They think it's the Mayor's."

"It is the Mayor's," Mason breathed. He shook his head. "But that can't be right."

"They're testing it for DNA now."

Mason shook his head. "Damon said 'him'. His accomplice is male. He said so."

"Did he say anything else?"

Mason frowned, trying to figure out what was different about her face. But the headache clouded his mind. He shook his head. "Nothing that made much sense."

Vickers looked uncertain then lowered her eyes. "Forensics will go over that whole place — and over his clothing and person, too. If there's a way to identify who did this to him, they'll find it."

"There's no time," Mason muttered. "This was all part of something big, Vickers. Something that's about to break. I can feel it."

"At least we have Damon now, right? And they'll bring in Mayor Lomax. Between them, we gotta learn something."

"Ifs and maybes again." Mason sighed and finished his coffee.

"Sorry, boss," Vickers said. "That's all I got."

"You've got nothing to be sorry for, Vickers. This is me. I'm not used to being so at sea."

She patted his hand. "It'll all come right, sir. You'll see."

"You seem very confident."

"I am." She smiled her bright smile. "Just wait. Now" — she stood and took his mug from him — "I have my orders, sir. Let me drive you home."

He shook his head, but it was pounding, and his body didn't want to protest. "I've got work to do."

"Fletcher said you should rest. And she's right. Let me take you home. You can be back kicking bad-guy ass by this time tomorrow."

"Maybe you're right."

"I'm always right. You should know that by now."

* * * *

205

Mason had to admit as he stripped off his filthy clothes that he was too exhausted to even think straight. Everything ached. The wound in his neck throbbed. The sun was bright out of the window. He drew the blinds.

Just an hour, he promised himself. One hour's sleep. Then he'd head back to the station. He wanted to be there when they brought Emerald Lomax in, whether Amelia approved or not. He wanted to look her into her eyes and make her tell him just what the hell was going on.

He wasn't sure what it was that woke him. The house was silent. It was also dark. He swore and groggily groped for his phone. It was dead. He swore again and scrabbled for his watch. He peered at it in the dimness. He'd been out for hours. The sun had been down for a lot of that, too.

How long had his phone been dead? What had he missed? And what was that sound downstairs that had woken him?

He heard it again. It was the sound of the fridge. He frowned, baffled, grabbed his underwear and searched for the gun among his clothes on the floor, remembering too late that it was locked in the safe in the hall.

He crept to the bedroom door and eased it open. There was a light on downstairs. He could hear liquid pouring.

"It's okay, Mason. It's me."

Relief and joy surged through him. He tied his dressing gown and hurried downstairs.

"Cai, thank God," he said, hurrying into the kitchen. Cai sat at the table with two glasses of wine in front of him. His hands were in his lap, and he was staring at his glass with a blank, empty look in his eyes.

Mason stopped. "What is it?"

Cai raised his eyes. He was quiet for a moment. Then he blinked, breathing in through his nose. "You need some more sugar, Mason. And some more protein. And your cortisol is very high."

"I'm fine," he said, taking the other seat. Cai went back to staring at his untouched drink. "What is it? Has something happened?"

Cai took a sip from his glass and lowered it again. "They've brought in Emerald Lomax."

Mason's neck still throbbed but his mind was clear. And clamoring. "I know."

"This is wrong," Cai said. "Someone's framing the Mayor."

"You know that for sure?" Cai nodded. "How?"

Cai's jaw clenched. Then he downed his wine and poured more. His face was tight. His eyes haunted.

"Cai, tell me what's wrong."

"The Blood that was in Damon... The haemophile Blood... The Blood that was turning him..."

"Yes?" Mason made himself wait.

Cai ran his long fingers around the rim of the glass, making it sing. He didn't look up as he spoke. "It belongs to the same person I could sense on Kelly's body. And Alonso's. And in Honor's house."

Mason unstuck his mouth with his own wine. "So, Damon definitely has a haemophile accomplice. And whoever he is...he was turning Damon into a haemophile?"

"Yes."

"Cai, you have to tell someone. Tell Fletcher. She thinks it's all Emerald."

"There's more."

The unfamiliar severity of Cai's tone made his flesh chill. "What?"

Cai's face crumpled. Pain filled his eyes. He bared his teeth. Whether it was conscious or not it froze Mason's blood. "I figured out how I know…" he whispered.

"Know what?"

"Everything. How I could sense his touch on the victims. How I recognized his Blood corroding Damon's humanity."

Mason was breathless. He wanted to reach out. To touch him. But the look on his face pinned him to the spot. "How, Cai?"

Cai raised his tortured eyes. "Because he did it to me, too."

Mason's blood was ice water in his veins. The pain in Cai's face clenched his heart in his chest. The mental picture of Cai being tortured as Damon was, as Woodburn was, rose in his mind and closed his throat.

"God, Cai…this is the same haemophile that attacked you?"

"I knew the second I touched Damon," Cai said. "His smell. The feel of him." The lines of Cai's face hardened. "I wanted to kill him so badly, Mason. I would have done it, too. Crushed him. Bitten him. Drank him dry. Anything to destroy him. To have that horrid light go from his eyes."

Mason made himself draw his breath in and out. He made himself meet Cai's desperate gaze. Then he dragged his chair closer.

"You didn't," he whispered. "You wanted to. But you didn't."

"Only because of you. I'm not sure anything else would have stopped me. And that terrifies me."

Mason hunted for words. "You're a good man, Cai. This doesn't change that."

"I'm not good — and I'm not a man."

Mason kissed him, desperate to swallow those words and breathe new ones into him. He tasted like wine and sunrise and hope. "You are," he said, over and over. "You are, you are."

Cai whimpered and opened his mouth. He swallowed Mason's kisses, thrust his hands into his hair and tilted his head to slide his tongue deeper.

Mason's whole body caught on fire. He began to grow hard, terrified and horny all at once, but then Cai broke the kiss. "Not like this. Not how I'm feeling now. Even ropes wouldn't hold me."

Mason's pulse was thundering in his throat. Cai's eyes were tinged with sadness, fear and the tiniest spark of rage that made Mason's skin ripple.

"Who is it?" Mason whispered.

Cai swallowed. Mason watched the muscles moving in his throat and the tangled mix of arousal and fear writhed in him like snakes.

"Cai. Who is it? Who did this to them? To you?"

Cai opened his mouth. Closed it again. He took a breath. "I don't know. I told you. I don't remember. It's the same person. But I don't know who."

Mason took Cai's hands and threaded their fingers together. "Think, Cai. Please."

Cai closed his eyes. His lashes were flecked with moisture. Pain twisted Mason's stomach. But he kept his mouth firmly shut. He held Cai's hands...waited.

"It's like he's always there, Mason," he whispered. "Like he's always been there. Ever since it happened. Like someone's been watching me. Right at my shoulder. All these years. But I turn and there's never anyone there." He drew a shaking breath. "I'm so tired of being scared all the time."

Mason tightened his hold on Cai's hands, even as uncertainty gripped his chest. "This is part of it," he said quietly. "You said so yourself. So did the Baron. You have this link with your maker. You didn't choose it. It's not your fault."

"I've been too scared to admit it, to acknowledge that's what I was feeling. If I had, maybe I could have stopped all this."

"You're going to be the one who stops it, Cai. You are the one that brings him down. *You.*"

Cai shook his head. "I know he was at that place. I know he fed Damon his Blood. I know he did *all* this. But I don't know *who* he is."

"You do," Mason said, resting his hand on Cai's chest. "In here. In here you know. He did this to you. You know who he is. You must."

"All I remember is coming back to myself, starving, staggering into A & E before I bit someone. I don't remember what happened or who did it. I just know it was the worst night of my life."

"I'll get him, Cai," Mason promised. "One way or another, I'm going to get the person who's done this to you. I swear."

Cai's eyes flickered. "No one's ever promised me that before."

"No one's ever felt like I do before." He drew Cai closer and drifted his lips over his jawline. "No one in history. No one in the future." He shifted forward, nudging his knee between Cai's and kissed the hollow of his neck. Cai's slow pulse beat against his lips. Mason drew the scent of his skin deep into himself, letting it set his nerves tingling.

"Come upstairs with me."

Cai trembled. "Not now," he breathed, even though his voice had grown hoarse and his grip on Mason's hands tightened. "I don't know what I'll do."

"You won't hurt me," Mason said, tonguing his earlobe and releasing one of his hands to run it up Cai's thigh. "You won't."

"You don't know that."

Mason stood, pulling Cai with him. He tilted his chin, brought their lips together. The kiss was heated, desperate. Mason slid his tongue against Cai's, drawing him toward the stairs.

Cai seemed oblivious as Mason guided him up to the bedroom. Their mouths were locked, their hands ran all over each other. Mason undid Cai's shirt and pushed it off his shoulders. He took a breathless moment to run his fingers over the smooth, unbroken skin.

"You really weren't hurt?"

"I healed," Cai replied and wrestled Mason out of his dressing gown. He kissed him again, possessively, like he was drinking him in.

Mason edged Cai back until the back of his legs hit the bed then eased him down onto it. Cai let out a low groan and dug his fingernails into Mason's back.

Mason gasped. He was desperate for everything all at once. He slid his hands between them to grope at the front of Cai's trousers.

Cai moaned and pushed against his hand. Mason shifted his weight enough to allow both his hands between them to undo Cai's fly. Cai turned his face to the side to inhale. Mason smothered his neck with kisses as Cai's fingernails again pricked delicious points of pain against his back.

"Mason, we have to stop. I don't know what I'll do… Ah."

Mason had got his hand into his pants and had taken his stiffening cock in a firm grip.

"Embrace what you're feeling, Cai. Feel it with me, now. Don't think about what it used to be, or how different it is. Just think about me."

Cai looked at him. He breathed heavily through his mouth. His eyes were hooded and bright with desire. He raked his fingernails up Mason's back, making him shiver with pleasure then took his face in his hands.

"All I want to think about is you."

"Then let me help you do that," he said, stroking Cai slowly but firmly. Cai began to breathe in time with the rhythm, never breaking eye contact. He released Mason's face and brushed his hands down his chest and into his boxer shorts.

Mason groaned and closed his eyes as Cai took his cock in both his hands and began to work him. The world crumbled away and all that was left was the heat of Cai's touch, the pleasure burning under Mason's skin and the sneaking fear that he would never, ever, be able to get enough of this.

"It's all about you," Cai breathed against Mason's mouth. "You and me. I won't hurt you Mason. I won't."

"I know you won't. You're in control. Feel it." He lowered his head to run his tongue over Cai's collarbone. "Feel me."

"Undress me. Let me feel you."

Mason reluctantly released Cai's swelling cock to do as he was told. He yanked his trousers and underwear down then stripped off his remaining clothing with a sort of fevered desperation. Cai pulled Mason's boxers and got to his knees to wrap his arms around him.

Mason ran his hands down Cai's muscled back, over his toned ass, down the back of his hard, slim thighs. Cai shuddered and panted into his mouth and stroked his own hands down Mason's arms and back up, his fingertips gentle, even though the touch blazed trails of fire over his skin.

Mason's cock ached with need. His body cried out for release. The sounds of Cai's desire only made it all hotter, stronger, harder to control.

"Cai," he breathed into his ear, shivering as Cai's hand tightened on his ass, pulling him close. "I want to be in you."

"Christ," Cai gasped.

A jolt of fear made Mason pull back to meet Cai's eyes. "Is that... Would you want that?"

"I need it," he said, face tight with emotion and flushed with desire. "I've needed it from the moment I saw you. I didn't think you'd ever want—"

"I want it," he replied. "I want *you*."

Cai nodded with a dazed look on his face. He thrust himself against Mason, rubbing their cocks together. "Do you need me to show you what to do?"

Mason smiled and brushed his fingers over Cai's nipple, making him gasp. "I think I know what to do."

Amusement flickered through the heat in Cai's expression. Then he turned serious. "It won't be the same as what you're used to."

"How do you know what I'm used to?" Mason teased, speaking against the tender skin of his neck while teasing a nipple with one hand. He slid his other around and down, using a finger to tease Cai's entrance.

Cai's grip tightened. "You're used to women," Cai forced out, his words audibly strained. "Whatever you did with them, they were still women...and human."

Mason took hold of Cai's throbbing cock as he continued to rub his finger over that tight, hot entrance, closing his eyes tight and breathing deep the scent of Cai's skin as his body trembled against him.

"Let's discover this together," he breathed. "Discover how good this can be. You and me."

"You'll still need protection," Cai said, even though his labored breathing made every word sound like he was begging to begin. "They say there's no risk with us, but I want to be sure. And we need lubricant."

"Everything's in the drawer," Mason said with a smile, thrusting lazily against Cai's hip.

Cai showered kisses along his neck and shoulder. "Yes," he panted. "Yes, okay. Come on then, Mason. Fuck me. Fuck me *now*."

"God." Mason had to swallow the feeling that boiled inside him before it threatened to spill everywhere. Cold rushed between them as he reluctantly leaned to scrabble in the bedside drawer for the supplies.

Cai kissed him and took the condom from his hand. Mason moaned when he rolled the cool tightness onto his dick with skilled hands. He squeezed a generous amount of lube into his own hands while kissing as much of Cai's neck, face and shoulders as he could reach. Cai wove their hands together and rubbed them and the lubricant up and down the length of Mason's twitching cock.

Mason swore, his voice husky, then Cai lay back, pulling Mason with him.

Mason brought his mouth back to Cai's and kissed him deeply, desperate to move forward but just as desperate to savor the anticipation forever. But then Cai gripped Mason's hips with his knees and lifted himself, and Mason's control frayed and snapped like a kite string in a strong wind.

He shifted forward between Cai's legs, running his lubed fingers up his thigh, then brushed them against the hot, tight entrance.

Cai whimpered into his mouth and bucked against his fingers. Mason growled and pushed one digit in. Cai flung his head back, his spine curving, clutching Mason's arms with bruising force.

The pain produced no fear. It only made Mason's desire burn hotter. He eased his finger deeper and swept it around, remembering Cai's reaction from last time.

He wasn't disappointed. Cai groaned his name and wrapped a leg around Mason's waist, giving him a better angle. His neglected cock pulsed, but he resisted touching himself, instead running his free hand up Cai's thigh and licking and teasing his nipples as he pushed another finger inside.

Cai's whole body moved with him. He was no longer forming words, just making low, sharp sounds of desperation that threatened to undo Mason at the seams. He hurriedly slid in a third finger and swirled and stretched, concentrating on making sure he was being thorough. He knew if he didn't, he could be the one hurting Cai. And he would die before he ever hurt Cai.

"Mason," Cai growled. "*Now*. Fuck me *now*."

Mason allowed himself a long, low moan, withdrew his fingers, propped his weight on one elbow and guided his cock between Cai's legs.

He made himself slide in slowly. It was like his entire being was torn from his body and balled in his groin, melting in a pleasure so hot it threatened to hurt. But it bubbled on the edge of pain, burning on the right side of ecstasy. He buried himself deep, slowly, so the sensation built and built, distantly hearing Cai's answering pleasure as he lifted himself from the bed to take Mason all the way in.

"Mason," Cai cried and grabbed the back of neck with one hand and his wrist with the other. "Stop. Mason, stop."

Mason froze, trembling, fighting the sensation of teetering on the edge of a cliff. His body cried out for him to move, but he inhaled deep and held himself still. He forced his eyes open.

Cai was pressing his forehead against Mason's. He was shaking.

"Am I hurting you?"

Cai shook his head. His eyes were clenched shut. His lips were drawn back. His over-long canines glinted against the red wetness of his mouth, and Mason's excitement tightened to breaking point.

He made himself speak. "Are you okay? Shall we stop?"

"I…" Cai blinked his eyes open. "This is so amazing. You feel so fucking good, Mason." He shifted against him and gasped. "I'm scared. I'm scared I won't be able to hold on…to hold back."

Mason nipped at his jaw. "Don't hold back. Let it go. Feel it all." Mason pulled back and thrust in again. His body bloomed with pleasure, and Cai groaned, his muscles bunching under and around Mason. Mason repeated the motion, slower still. Cai gasped and relaxed, his head falling back, his death grip loosening. He grasped Mason's ass and brought him close, pulling him deeper.

"Fuck. Yes. Like that."

"Like this?" Mason forced out, tilting forward and up.

Cai jerked and made a noise that was somewhere between Mason's name and God's. Mason grinned and repeated the motion, this time pulling farther out first.

Cai's panted affirmations told him he was reaching everywhere he was supposed to reach with every thrust, which was good because he couldn't follow instructions now, even if they were bellowed in his ear. He was moving on instinct, pushing deep, pushing hard, pushing faster. The tight, hot grip on him was overwhelming. He needed it. Needed Cai. Needed every inch of him, inside and out.

Cai clutched his ass. His fingernails scratched his skin. His grip was threatening to dent his bones. It was like Cai would eat him alive, crush him into nothing and absorb him right into his body. Mason didn't care. He wanted it. Begged for it.

He moved faster.

"Mason," Cai breathed. "Mason, I'm gonna... Mason, please, please, *please.*"

Mason grasped Cai's cock and pumped it fast as his own orgasm built and trembled like a dam about to break. He groaned loudly and pushed forward so hard he lifted Cai's hips from the bed. He was so deep he couldn't tell where he ended and his lover began. He held him tight, buried his face in his neck and came, crying and shaking, jerking inside him, once, twice then once more. That third thrust was answered by Cai crying out. His body clamped tight around Mason's spent cock, sending aftershocks of pleasure through his over-sensitized body. Cai's cock jumped in his hand and fluid spurted against his belly.

Chapter Twelve

Mason collapsed, panting. Cai's arms were around him. Their chests heaved and sweat stuck their skin together.

Eventually, Mason found the strength to raise his head. Cai wasn't smiling but his eyes were swimming with emotion. He pulled Mason's face to his and kissed him slowly with languid strokes of his tongue until their breathing returned to normal.

"That was incredible," Mason said.

"You liked it?"

"*Like*?"

"Your first time all the way with a man," Cai said carefully. "You must have notes."

"I think I could do it forever."

A ghost of something cold filtered through Cai's eyes at the word 'forever', but then they warmed again.

"I didn't think I could feel that way anymore," he murmured. "Not safely. Not so I could cope with it. Thank you."

Mason kissed Cai, deep and long, drawing a deep sigh from him. Then he rolled onto his back and winced, rubbing his neck, feeling the wound again for the first time.

Cai propped his head on his hand and concern creased his brow. "Does it hurt?"

Mason shook his head. "Just a few stitches. It's fine."

Cai ran his fingers over the scratches down Mason's ribs, the redness of early bruises on his biceps. The color drained from his face. "I did this."

"There's nothing you can't throw at me I wouldn't willingly take."

Emotions fought in Cai's eyes. Then they softened, and he kissed Mason's eyebrow. He sighed again, the soft breath ruffling Mason's hair.

"I can't even say how good this is. It sounds stupid but I felt…normal again. I thought I'd forgotten what that means."

"You won't forget," Mason stated. "It's who you are."

"Who I was." Cai lay back, his head next to Mason's and stared up at the ceiling. "But maybe that's okay. Maybe it's okay to let that go."

Mason tried not to doze, but he was so content, so peaceful. It was like all the trouble had been leached away, leaving them in a vacuum of peace and comfort.

But when he opened his eyes again, Cai's face was troubled.

"What is it?" Cai got out of bed and began dressing. "Cai?"

"Has anyone been able to speak to Damon?" he asked as he buttoned his shirt.

Mason winced and pushed the covers back. "He's not really capable of talking."

Cai tucked his half-buttoned shirt into his trousers and sat against the headboard, staring at nothing. Mason pulled on some tracksuit bottoms and a T-shirt then sat beside him, looking into his face.

"He's played dice with the devil," Mason said quietly. "And lost."

"You can't say that," Cai said quietly. "You don't know what he's going through."

Shame flushed through him. "Do you know what's happening to him, exactly?"

Cai didn't answer immediately. "I don't think anyone really knows how it works. All I remember is pain. And sickness. And thirst. Thirst like you've never known. Like fishhooks in your veins. Broken glass in your mouth."

Mason picked at the cover. "I heard him. In the hospital. Screaming. I never knew a human could make sounds like that."

Cai didn't answer. When Mason looked up, his eyes were lit from within with a fearful light.

"What is it?"

"There was screaming." His voice was low. "That night. There was screaming. And crying. A little girl crying."

"What night?"

"*That* night." Cai blinked like he was seeing things that weren't there. "I remember. I was looking for the little girl. Cara. Cara Sullivan."

Mason's pulse quickened. "The missing child."

"I'd had a call...a tip." He frowned. "I went alone...against regulations. But the man on the phone had said come alone, so I went."

Cai's hands were clenched. His neck muscles stood out like cords. Mason held his own breath, longing to take Cai's hand but not daring to touch him.

"I drove for hours. I can't remember where it was. It was dim and shadowy. There was an alley. I heard her crying." He appeared to suddenly see Mason again. "She was alive, Mason. She was there. She was right there."

"You saw her?"

Cai nodded. "She was curled on the ground. Her arms were over her face. She wore a blue cardigan."

"What happened?"

"Then...darkness. Utter darkness." He gazed at his hands. "And...pain. Deep, drawing pain." He frowned. "Something...someone was biting me. On my neck. On my arms. My legs. I fought, but I was tied down."

Mason felt ill. "Where were you?"

"I...I don't know. It all happened in blackness. I never knew he was coming, not until he bit me."

"Jesus, Cai."

Cai didn't appear to hear him. "He drank from me. Over and over. I have no idea how long I was there, chained in the dark. I screamed myself raw. Then he started...feeding me something." He clenched his mouth shut and closed his eyes. "Oh God."

"It's okay." Mason took his hand. "You don't have to go on."

"I do," Cai insisted. "I have to remember. While I can, I have to remember."

Mason braced himself. "He fed you something?"

Cai gripped his hand. "It was metallic. But sweet. Thick. It tasted amazing. It stopped the pain...for a short while. But then he bit me again. Bled me. And fed me. Over. And over. And over."

Cai rubbed his forehead hard. His breath caught in his throat. Mason held his hand and put his other hand on his back. He wanted to take him into his arms, to tell him to stop, that he didn't need to relive this. But he made himself stay silent. He made himself listen.

"You're not supposed to know this," Cai whispered. "We're not supposed to tell."

"You can trust me," Mason insisted.

"Magister Khan said, if I ever remembered, I should go to her. I should never tell anyone human how it happened."

Mason swallowed. "I swear, Cai. I won't tell anyone."

Cai didn't look at him. When he continued, his voice was a hoarse whisper.

"I have no idea how long this took. But then one day...night? One *time,* God knows how long later...I opened my eyes. And I could see." He swallowed. "There was still no light. But I could see. The concrete room. The chair I was chained to. I could see all the blood on the floor..." He shook his head. "My blood? Someone else's? I had no idea. But I could see it, clear as day. And I could smell it. It smelled so strong. Old. Nasty. Like corroded copper and rotten meat. I knew it was old, but, Christ, Mason, I was so desperate for it." He started to shake. "Even if it broke my bones, I wanted out of that chair, just to lick it off the floor. That's how bad it was."

"Shit. I..." Mason couldn't find words to continue.

Cai squeezed his hand but didn't look at him.

"Cara was there, too," he breathed. "She'd been there all along. Curled in the corner, staring wide-eyed at nothing. She couldn't see me, but I could see her. She was crying."

Cai turned tortured eyes on Mason. "I didn't care that she was crying. I didn't care that she was lost and scared. I just cared that she was human, and she was full of blood." Cai bit his lip so hard he split the skin. Dark redness oozed down his chin. The smell filled the air and made Mason dizzy. He felt sick and sore and grotesquely excited, all at once. He lifted a shaking hand, but Cai grabbed his wrist.

"Don't touch it," he whispered. Mason blinked. Cai had gone.

"Cai?" The room was empty. Mason called again then heard the water running in the bathroom.

He padded down the hall. His neck pulsed with every step. He reached the bathroom. His headache was coming back.

Cai was running the hot tap and rinsing his mouth over and over. Mason caught a glimpse of the dark red Blood swilling down the plughole. Cai held a towel to his face.

Mason hovered in the doorway, desperate to move forward but unsure whether he should.

Cai lowered the towel. There was no sign of a cut on his lip. He met Mason's eyes in the steamy glass. "It's healed already."

Mason hovered a long moment more.

"I didn't kill Cara," Cai whispered. "I wanted to. *Needed* to. And I came so, so close." He clenched his eyes shut. "But somehow, I didn't. But then..." His face fell. "*He* was there."

"Who?" Mason breathed.

"The one who'd done it all. Done this to me." He gestured at himself. "He was huge. And strong. He told me to drink from Cara. That her blood would make it all better. That it would make *me* better. Stronger.

Invincible. I refused." He was trembling. Mason tried to draw him close, but he was as unmovable as stone. "He lifted Cara. She was too scared to scream. He dumped her into my lap. The smell was maddening. Somehow, though, I...I got out of the chair. I don't know how. It's a blur. But I got out. I ran. I got out of that place, and I just kept running."

Mason stared into his vacant gaze, willing Cai to see him. "Who was it, Cai? Who did this to you?"

"I left her there."

"None of this... Cai?" Mason waited until Cai met his eyes. "None of this was your fault. Understand me?"

"It is," he breathed. "It's all because of me."

"This doesn't change anything," Mason insists. "You are still you. You are still Cai Bracken."

Cai shook his head. "I left him behind that night, when I abandoned that little girl."

"Listen to me," Mason said and took hold of Cai's chin, forcing him to meet his eyes. "You are still the man you think you are. Nothing has changed. You are still the man I've fallen in love with."

Cai's eyes widened. "Mason..."

"You were assaulted, understand? Kidnapped. Tortured. You are a victim of a crime. This doesn't change who you are — or how I feel about you."

"How can you say that? After I left her there," he breathed again. "I left her with *him*."

Mason gripped Cai's shoulders tight. "Who? Left her with *who*?"

Cai blinked, like he was waking up. He frowned hard at Mason, like he was trying to remember who he was, then drifted past him. Mason followed him down the stairs.

Cai took the TV remote, turned the set on and began flicking through channels. He looked half-dazed. But then he stopped on a news channel and his expression hardened.

"Him."

Mason stared. It was several long heartbeats before he was able to get enough breath to speak. "That can't be right."

"It's him, Mason. It was him all along."

Dragomir Soroka was being asked about the increase of human-on-haemophile violence. He sat, huge and stately, in the studio chair that looked far too small for him. His eyes were black and dead, like a snake's. His clawed fingers were neatly folded in his lap. The sound was off, but Mason could still tell from the way his jaw moved, the way his eyes pinned the interviewer to the spot, that he exuded power, passion and authority.

But there was something else there, something Mason hadn't seen before.

Hatred. Deep, black hatred radiated from his eyes. So complete and encompassing it was almost unseeable. But now Mason could see it.

Mason tried to speak but his throat was closed. He coughed to clear it and began patting his pockets. "We have to call this in."

"No."

"We have to tell Amelia," he said, frantically scrolling his contacts.

Cai turned wide, empty eyes on him. "Mason...run."

"What?" he said, finally finding Amelia's personal number.

"He's here."

Chapter Thirteen

Mason didn't have time to process Cai's words. His body was slammed against the wall. All the wind left his lungs in a rush. He struck out, blind, dazed, gasping. But it was like punching a rockfall. His head was spinning. Pressure on his neck tightened.

"Soroka," Cai's voice came as if from far away, "let him go. *Now.*"

The pressure eased enough for Mason to get breath into his lungs, and his vision finally focused.

Dragomir Soroka was like a creature from a nightmare. He held Mason's six-foot-four, one-ninety-pound frame off the floor effortlessly. His shoulders were sloping folds of muscle under a well-fitted suit. His face was close to Mason's own. The bone-white skin, ice-white hair and black shark eyes looked like something out of a fever dream.

His lips were smiling, baring his predator teeth. The unnaturally long canines were sharper than a cats, longer than a tiger's.

Mason told himself to smack that grinning demon face, to knee him in the guts, to kick him in the balls. Do anything he was trained to do. But his body wouldn't move.

Cai launched himself at the bigger haemophile, but Soroka swatted him away as easily as a fly. Cai crashed into the television set. Red-hot rage surged through Mason's body. He thrashed and punched, but Soroka slammed him so hard against the wall that he saw stars.

"Well, well, well." His voice wasn't like it sounded before. The gravitas was still there. But now it was heavier. Slicker. Like an oil spill. "Here we all are. Finally."

"Dragomir Soroka..." Cai was getting to his feet, shattered glass falling from his clothing like glitter. "You are under arrest for the murders of Darragh Kelly, Horatio Alonso, Honor Ford-Byerson—"

"Let's not do this." Soroka's voice wasn't loud, but it smothered Cai's like an ash cloud. "We all know why we're here, Cai. Why *you're* here."

"Let him go. *Now.*"

"Ah yes." Soroka examined Mason with a distant curiosity tinged with disgust. "Your human plaything. It wasn't exactly the plan I had in mind, but we can make it work."

"I won't tell you again."

Soroka's smile vanished. The cold void it left made Mason feel like he was dangling over airless space. He strained again, clawing at the hand on his throat with all his strength. With an impatient noise, Soroka dumped him to the floor. He drew breath deep into his burning lungs and attempted to get to his feet, but the haemophile grabbed his collar and dragged him close.

"Cai," Mason barked. "Go. Get back up."

"I'm not leaving you," Cai said, his eyes fixed on Soroka.

"Nor should you," Soroka said. "This room, this moment... This is where you choose your side, Cai Bracken. Once and for all."

"There are no sides, Soroka. You are under arrest—"

"Come, now," Soroka said, a little impatiently. "We've covered this, haven't we?"

"You're a murderer. And a torturer. You tortured me."

"I made you what you are." Soroka tilted his chin. "I gave you a gift."

"You delivered me into a living hell."

Soroka shook his head sadly. "You shouldn't have run, Cai. If you'd just stayed that night, all this would have all been so, so different."

"Cai"—Mason strained against the hold—"the safe."

Cai's eyes flicked to him, and Soroka followed the look. Soroka dragged him back, away from Cai.

"You understand," Soroka continued, "what all this was for. What *you* are here for."

"I've never had answers," he said, his voice strained. "Up until tonight, I didn't even have memories."

"That could have been different. If you'd stayed, I would have instructed you. Nurtured you. Taught you everything."

"What happened to Cara?" Cai's voice shook.

"Everyone in this has had a part to play. She was a piece in the game, just like you are."

"A *game*?"

"Pretending you don't know is not helping anything."

"Cai," Mason said, stopping his struggles and staring at the blankness on his lover's face, "what's he talking about?"

"I don't know."

"Of course you know," Soroka said. His eyes narrowed. "Think about it. Why you? Of all the people I could have chosen, why would I choose you?"

Cold fear chilled Cai's eyes. "I don't know. I've never known."

"You're a detective. A good one. With a record for determination. For moral integrity. For fighting for the underdog. And look…" He gestured around the room. "You've done everything you were made to do, even without my guidance."

"I've done *nothing* apart from try to do the right thing."

Soroka subdued Mason's renewed attempts to struggle as easily as if he were controlling an unruly child, never taking his eyes off Cai. "You helped reveal the poison of those extremist groups. You exposed and took control of the Fort. You tracked down and neutralized Damon, their most accomplished weapon. You found the links to Emerald Lomax, an opportunistic leech, jumping on any bandwagon to extend the reach of her own power, no matter the consequences. *You* showed the entire world the fetid underbelly of the cesspool that is humankind."

"*You* did all that." Cai jabbed a finger at him. "You helped Damon capture and torture haemophiles. You helped him kill Darragh Kelly."

"I didn't do anything he wouldn't have done on his own. I just" —Soroka shrugged— "sped the timeline along a little."

"*Why?*"

"Oh, Officer Bracken." Soroka shook his head. "You know. You've always known."

"He wants the war, Cai," Mason said. "He wants haemophiles to rise up. Strike back. Take revenge."

"Not revenge," Soroka said between clenched teeth, giving Mason a shake. "Justice. We are the power in this world. We are the superior beings. These meat-sacks," he shook Mason again, like a doll, "they're *food*, Cai. Fuel. The very *idea* that we should hide from them behind locked doors is as repugnant as they are."

"You're crazy," Cai said, a dangerous light in his eyes. He took a step toward the hall. "And you need to let Mason go this second. This is your last warning, Soroka."

"All you've ever wanted is peace." Soroka spread his free hand. "That is possible. But it's a rocky road." He took a step closer to Cai, tightening his grip on Mason's T-shirt so Mason had to dig his fingers between the fabric and his neck to be able to breathe. "Help me, Cai. Help finish what I've started. You're in a position to make it as smooth as possible. You know the right humans to subdue first. You can access the facilities to hold them. You'll see. Soon humans will be in their rightful place, and there will be no more need for subterfuge."

"This has been tried before, Soroka," Cai said, taking another step to the side. Closer to the safe. "Magister Evgeniya Morak tried this…twice. Blood Winter is still remembered by both sides with nothing but abhorrence. Your plan won't work."

"Evgeniya aimed too low. I strike at the heart, the rotten core of it all."

"That's what you call Kelly, is it?" Mason growled. "And Ford-Byerson? You call them rotten? The ones fighting for your place in this world?"

Soroka shook him again. "Don't you see?" He glowered at Cai. "The more we try to do things *their* way, the worse everything gets. Do you think scum like Damon would exist, spreading their filth, if *we* were in charge? Do you think parasites like Lomax would be able to capitalize on the misfortunes of others?"

"Emerald Lomax is not a parasite," Mason gritted. "She was working with us. Her and her brother. They want a world safe for your kind."

"She's a blood sucker," Soroka insisted, with a feral grin. "In the grotesque, figurative way rather than the open, honest way. She allowed Emory Von Magnusson to buy back his lands. She allowed him to build Oswald House, to encourage integration."

"And that's a *bad* thing?" Mason blurted.

"We are our own people." Soroka's voice deepened. His face hardened. His eyes burned. "We should be moving away from humans, not toward them. Magnusson has always been a coward, too afraid to do the strong thing."

"He's done more for the public perception of haemophiles worldwide than you ever have," Cai snapped.

"By pandering." Soroka sneered. "Crawling. Simpering. Being weak. Refusing to let go of his human life. Adopting a child." He snorted. "I would have *eaten* that child. That's all she is...food. Maybe, when this is done, I'll make Emory feed on her—and on that pathetic human trash he keeps in his bed."

Cai's face contorted. He stepped forward but Soroka yanked Mason between them and gripped his neck from behind. Mason clawed at the hand again, but it was like being chained to concrete.

"You knew it wasn't the Mayor," Soroka's voice lowered, became suggestive. "I knew you'd see through the trail I planted. I knew it would make you face what you'd been denying."

"I've not been denying anything." Cai's voice was hoarse. His face was still wretched with anger.

"Haven't you?" Soroka narrowed his eyes. "You sensed me. This whole time, you knew I was part of this. And you belong to me, Cai. I am in you…forever. There's no undoing that."

Cai flew at Soroka. Mason only caught a glimpse of his face, transformed by hate, but it sent ice through his veins. He tried to get out of the way, but both haemophiles were too fast and too strong. There was less than a second of confused sounds and crashes. Mason was jerked about like a puppet on a string. Then he found himself sprawled on his back, blinking around at his ruined living room.

He tried to roll over when he was grabbed and hauled bodily from the floor. He was on his feet, and Soroka had an arm like a tree trunk around his neck. He gripped Mason's wrist with his other hand in a grip that had Mason's bones on the verge of cracking.

Cai was getting shakily to his feet at the far end of the room. Mason had no idea how he'd got over there, but there was a crack in the plaster near the ceiling, like a heavy weight had been thrown into the wall. The sofa was overturned. Cai was blinking and dazed, but the tendons in his neck stood out like chords.

"You can't fight me, Cai," Soroka said.

"I'm not stopping until you let him go."

"Walker's not going anywhere," Soroka breathed, low and sibilant as a snake.

"What do you want with him?"

Soroka thrust Mason out to arm's length. Mason staggered on shaking knees, but Soroka held him upright.

"He's the final piece of the game."

"I don't play anyone else's games," Mason ground out.

"Kill him, Cai," Soroka said, gripping Mason tighter.

"You're crazy," Mason muttered, though he watched Cai very carefully the whole time. The fact that he was struggling to read the look in his lover's eyes scared him far more than the murderous monster at his back. "And you're only making things worse for yourself, Soroka."

"Think about it," Soroka went on, ignoring Mason. "The DI on the case being killed by one of our kind will send a message. The war has begun. It will tip the avalanche in the right way."

"He's fighting to *stop* all this."

"Humans can't end this. Only *we* can end this. And this is how."

"I don't want any part of any of this," Cai barked. "I never would. I never will. You've fucked up, Soroka, big time. I will stop all this. And I will stop you. Mason's right. The longer you drag this out, the worse it gets for you."

Soroka laughed. It sounded like a volcano rumbling, about to erupt. "I've already won, Cai. It's started. Our kind is wounded...cornered. If we don't spark the keg, something else will. It's only a matter of time. All you can control now is how quickly it will all be over."

Mason eyed the safe in the hall, wondering if he could

reach it if he somehow managed to break Soroka's hold. But then Soroka's fingernails sank into his skin like needles, splitting his skin and pinning him in place. Blood ran down his neck and seeped into his collar. Cai's face altered. Mason's pulse thundered in his ears. He tried to make Cai meet his eyes, but Cai was staring at the blood, breathing hard.

"Bite him," Soroka breathed. "Drain him. You can do it in a way that won't hurt him. He might even enjoy it. And it will take all the pain inside you away forever. Trust me."

"*Trust* you?" Cai's voice cracked.

"If you truly value peace…if Walker does…do this. For him. For all of us."

A deathly silence flooded Mason's senses. All the possibilities of all the possible futures Soroka had hinted at spun out, unstoppable, in his mind. He smelled the blood in the air. He sensed the darkness, impenetrable, lurking just around the corner.

"Maybe he's right, Cai." Mason's croak didn't sound like his own voice. His flesh was numb. His bones ached. He was suddenly so, so tired. "Damon wasn't the first. He won't be the last. We both know what humans are capable of. How evil they can be. How they strike out at what they don't understand."

"Mason, don't talk like that."

"But it's true," Mason murmured. "You know it's true."

"See?" The satisfaction in Soroka's voice was like molten lead. "Even your pet Detective Inspector agrees."

Cai was quiet a long time. A hundred emotions chased themselves through his eyes. Mason's stomach was gnawed by fear and despair.

"If I have to die," Mason whispered, "I'd rather you did it, Cai."

Cai's expression had closed. His gaze shifted over Mason's shoulder to the creature that held him. "I've never killed a human, Soroka. You think I'd start with the man I love?"

It was several moments before Mason could think straight. He was bruised and bleeding, scared and maybe only had seconds left to live, but he was smiling.

"Such a disappointment." Soroka's low rumble shattered the moment. He began to draw Mason toward him.

"I'll fight," Cai snapped, curling his hands into fists. "I'll fight to the end. I'll smash the walls, the windows. The police will come. Even if you kill us both, they'll still know it was a haemophile that did it, did all of it. And they will find out it was you."

"You really shouldn't keep underestimating me," Soroka said, his mouth so close to Mason's ear that his voice filled his head like venom in his blood. "I've had a lot, lot longer to perfect the art of killing."

"You shouldn't underestimate the police," Cai said, taking a step forward. "They already know more than you think they do."

"As it happens, you're right there."

Mason blinked and craned his neck. Vickers stood in the doorway, a gun in her hands.

"Vickers, thank Christ," Mason cried. "Quick. Shoot him. In the head. Shoot him."

But Vickers had her gun aimed at Cai. Cai stared. Her aim was unwavering. Her face was hard.

"Vickers?"

"Shall I do it, Master?" she said. "I could take them both out. Two more bodies dropped ought to do it, don't you think?"

"Vickers," Mason cried, disbelief raising his voice, "what are you doing?"

"I'm sorry, sir," she said, though her voice was without inflection and her gun and eyes remained on Cai. "The greater good and all that."

"I don't understand," Mason said. "You were working with Soroka? This whole time?"

"Fighting with him, sir," she said, her own voice rising a notch. "Fighting to stop the fighting. Don't you see?"

"Phoebe," Mason breathed, his throat tight.

"That's not her name."

Mason stared at Cai. His jaw was clenched. His eyes were swimming. "What?"

"It bloody is," Vickers swore. "And don't you dare say otherwise."

"Cai?"

"Cara," Cai breathed. "Cara Sullivan. I can't believe I didn't recognize you."

"That's not who I am now," Vickers spoke through clenched teeth.

"Phoebe is who Cara became," Soroka said smoothly. "Still just a human. But more than she ever could have been without me."

"Cara, this man tortured and abused you," Cai said carefully. "He's not who you think he is."

"Don't tell me what to think or not think," Vickers said, taking a step closer to Cai. "I've seen evil. I've seen how people work. How sick and depraved and cruel we are."

"What's the alternative?" Mason begged. "Being kept as food? Farmed like animals?"

"Oh, boss," Vickers said, her eyebrows drawing together, "you never got it."

"Too bloody right."

"We need *leadership*, don't you see?" Her eyes begged him to understand. "Sure, they'll control our numbers, feed on some of us. But, really, don't you think it's what we deserve? Look what we do to each other. To the planet. The animals." She shook her head. "We've had our day. We fucked everything up." She nodded toward Cai. "Soroka is right. It's time for a management change."

"And to do that you're going to kill Cai?"

"I'm sorry," she said. "This wasn't part of the plan. I encouraged you, didn't I? When I saw you liked him. I hoped you'd see what I see. I'm the one who first got you thinking a haemophile could be behind all this. I told you a human couldn't kill Kelly alone. I wanted you to start thinking about that. Their power. Their potential. Then, when this moment came, we'd all be together in this. But if you won't join us —"

"He was never gonna spare us, Phoebe," Mason cried. "He wanted Cai to kill me."

Vickers hesitated then took another step toward Cai. "What is it they say? No plan survives contact with the enemy."

"Don't hurt him," Mason begged. "Please. I love him."

Vickers' eyes flickered, but she didn't lower the gun. "I'm sorry, boss. I am." She clicked back the safety. "It's his own fault. If he'd joined us, right from the beginning, none of this would have had to happen this way."

"If I had," Cai said, "you'd be dead."

Vickers' face fell. "Not true. The master needed an ally in the police force. That's what I was for."

"That's what *I* was for," Cai said, his eyes sliding to Soroka. "This whole time. That was what I was supposed to be."

"And you still could be," Vickers said, glancing at Soroka and Mason. "Right, Master? Maybe it's not too late."

"Cara," Cai said, "Soroka chose you for the same reason he chose Damon." Vickers clenched her jaw. Mason held his breath. "You're family. Both of you. *His* family. His descendants."

Soroka's grip tightened.

"You're lying," Vickers spat after a long, shocked silence. She looked over her shoulder at Soroka. Her eyes were wide. "We're not family, are we? *Heron's* not my family. You told me he was a tool, a piece in the game."

"He was," Soroka said smoothly. "He still is. If he survives, he will be part of this. As you will."

"But—"

"I told you from the beginning, Phoebe," Soroka said quietly, "we're a team. We're in this together."

"You're both descendants," Cai said, stepping closer. "You and Michael Heron. Your family immigrated to Ireland from Russia in the eighteenth century."

"You're talking shit, Bracken."

He didn't waver. "They took a new surname. Before they married into the Sullivans...who then married into the Herons. Do you know what they were called?"

"You think this will change something," Soroka rumbled. "It won't. Phoebe can handle the truth. She sees there are bigger things at stake here."

"What was the name?" Vickers muttered, still holding the gun on Cai.

"Kelly," Mason breathed.

Cai looked up at him. Then back at Vickers. "Mason's right."

Vickers was very still.

"Darragh Kelly. Michael Heron. Cara Sullivan," Cai glared at Soroka. "You're family. All of you."

Vickers looked between them all. She returned her tortured look to Soroka. "Kelly was family?"

Mason craned his neck to look over his shoulder. Soroka's face had taken on the look of a cliff face in a storm. "You can't imagine what it was like. To discover my own flesh and blood was doing what he did, after he received the gift of Blood." He scowled. "And living with a human lover, on top of it all." He bared his teeth. "I knew I had to start with him."

"It *was* personal," Mason realized out loud. "He says all of this is about a bigger mission, about a plan. But it's personal, Vickers. It's all about basic, human feelings he can't handle."

Soroka crushed him. "It doesn't change anything."

"He," Cai jabbed a finger at Soroka, "is your ancestor, Cara. Yours and Damon's and Kelly's. He knew this. He didn't say anything. Why?"

Vickers swallowed.

"Could it be because he was ashamed?" Cai spoke softly, but the hatred in his eye was like fire. "Damon. A hate criminal and haemophile hunter. Kelly, a haemophile working to live closer with humans. Your parents were social workers. They did all sorts of projects around community safety, including helping humans work with local haemophile communes.

Helping communication and understanding. I remember it all from their files."

"I don't get it," Vickers muttered. "Why?"

"Soroka saw Magnusson bring his descendent Dimity Hawthorn legally into his family," Cai said, his eyes hard. "Then he looked into his own and didn't like what he saw. *That's* what prompted him to start all this. Shame. Anger. Not pride. Not a grand plan to make the world better."

"You're going to stop talking now," Vickers jabbed her gun at Cai. "Even if you're right, what does it matter? The plan still makes sense. And if I am his family, that just means I'm even more important than he said I was."

"Baron Von Magnusson adopted Dimity," Mason shouted. "He fought for her, tooth and nail. Gave her a home. A future. Safety. Soroka *stole* you from your parents. He's gaslit you and used you as a tool —" He was cut off by Soroka tightening his stranglehold.

"I've taken back control of my family," Soroka said in a low, dangerous voice. "I've punished those who needed to be punished, enlightened those that needed guidance. Phoebe knows this. She understands everything."

Vickers stared at all of them, one by one. Mason pleaded with her with his eyes. She seemed to waver for a moment. Then she squared her shoulders.

"You were right before, boss. The tide is turning. Time to sink or swim." She leveled the gun at Cai again. "So, what are you doing, Bracken? Boss? Swimming? Or sinking?"

Cai had started moving before Vickers had finished speaking. He wasn't fast enough for Soroka, but Vickers was human. She squawked as she was knocked off her feet. The gun went off. The hold on Mason loosened. Mason hit the floor and rolled. Chaos unfolded in his wake. There were crashes, the sound of glass breaking and furniture being smashed as the two haemophiles fought, too fast to watch, more vicious than starved dogs.

Vickers lay dazed against the wall. Mason crawled toward her and reached for the gun. She swore and tried to pull it away. He wrestled her for it. An even louder crash made them turn.

Cai was on the ground, sprawled in the ruins of Mason's coffee table. Soroka straddled him, his hands around his throat. His huge frame dwarfed and crushed Cai, who kicked and choked and ripped at Soroka's hands to no avail.

The white-haired haemophile was grinning. His black eyes were voids of hate.

"Such a disappointment, my boy. Such a disappointment."

Before Mason could gather enough sense to even move, Soroka dragged Cai up off the floor and flung him through the window.

Glass rained down like diamonds. Both Mason and Vickers covered their heads with their arms. Before she recovered, he grabbed the weapon.

"First"—Soroka advanced on them—"I'll deal with you, Walker." He grabbed him by the front of his clothes and hauled him to his feet. "Then, the world."

Soroka's opened his red mouth and bent toward Mason's neck. Mason raised the gun as high as he could. He fired.

Soroka bucked and froze. Darkness stained the front of his shirt. There was a breathless second of stillness. Then the haemophile roared.

He lifted Mason from the floor but then the death-grip on him was gone.

Mason staggered and blinked. Cai had Soroka on the floor. He pounded at him with fists and feet and clawed with his nails. His face was a rictus mask of murderous rage. His lips were drawn back from his teeth. Blood smeared his face and neck, and he looked even more fearsome than the barely controlled frenzy in the eyes of Soroka.

He sensed Vickers frozen at his side, but he couldn't move, either. Soroka reached out to grab Cai's head, Cai flipped them, jerked Soroka around and yanked his head back with a fistful of his white hair.

"Shoot him," Cai cried over the blood-curdling roars. His voice was rocky, raw, deepened by something that wasn't him. "Now. Between the eyes. *Kill him.*"

Mason raised the gun. Soroka's eyes rolled like a mad dog's. His massive frame thrashed but, somehow, Cai held on. A noise like steel rods snapping filled the air, and Soroka screamed even louder. Cai's face was like that of a beautiful but terrifying demon from an ancient religious painting.

Mason's hand shook. He squeezed his eyes shut. He heard Cai call to him in that horrid, Blood-fueled voice.

He opened his eyes. "I can't," Mason called.

"*Mason.*"

"Killing him won't fix anything," he cried over Soroka's unhinged howls. "This only ends if he tells the world the truth."

"He won't," Cai cried. "And I can't hold him. Please, Mason. He'll kill you."

Mason dropped the gun and staggered back. "I can't, Cai. It'll save us for today. But what about tomorrow? What about this ever being over?"

"He'll kill us *all*."

Mason looked deep into his lover's eyes and tears filled his own. "At least then the world will know."

Soroka roared and strained again. Cai fought him just long enough to meet Mason's eyes.

"I love you, Mason."

"I love you, too."

Soroka broke loose.

Mason was never able to describe or even remember clearly what happened next. He was knocked off his feet. His head struck the floor, and the room began to spin. There were sharp, stabbing pains all over his body.

All sounds were muddied. All he could see was the few square inches of carpet in front of his face. He tasted human blood in his mouth and smelled its metallic tang in the air. It was soon mixed with a deeper, headier scent, like copper and wine or fresh fruit burning.

A dark stain appeared on the carpet. It oozed closer. A red liquid, so dark it was almost black. The smell of it filled his body and made his own blood cry out.

Blood. Haemophile Blood. A lot of it.

He tried to sit up, but nothing worked. Then he heard sirens.

There were boots. Lots of boots. The noise increased.

Hands were on him. They were gentle. Someone was saying his name in his ear.

"Mason? Mason, you bastard. You better be alive."

Someone helped him sit up. He cried out. Something, somewhere was broken. The person propped him against the wall. Finally, he could draw a decent breath, though pain shot through his ribs. The face near his finally made sense.

"Amelia?" Relief mixed with terror ripped through him, snapping him out of his daze. He blinked until the room came into focus.

Soroka was kneeling on the floor, his head bent, his arms behind his back. His fine clothing was ripped and stained. Blood was oozing from a deep wound in his thigh. It soaked the carpet and spattered the wall. More Blood seeped from smaller wounds all over his body. Scratches. Bites. Stood around him, holding onto him tight enough to break his skin, were Emory Von Magnusson, Terje Kristiansen and…Mason blinked, not sure if he'd hit his head harder than he thought. But no. The long, black, hair. The set, inexpressive face. The ruby-red eyes.

Lucien.

Armed police swarmed around the room. Some had weapons trained on Soroka. Some held back, holding oversized torches he guessed were daylight floods, their fingers hovering over the power buttons. But Magnusson was talking, low and commanding, saying everything was under control.

"Mason, just hold on, okay?" Amelia said, pressing her balled-up scarf to his shoulder. "Paramedics are on the way."

"What are you doing here?" he mumbled stupidly.

"You *called* me." Mason spotted his phone on the other side of the room, still connected. "My Christ, could you not have rung me *before* the maniac haemophile started running rampant in your house?"

Mason almost threw up. "Where's Cai?" He scanned the room desperately. "Where is he, Amelia?"

Amelia hesitated. Dread flooded Mason's body. "He's in the kitchen," Amelia eventually said. "But, Mason, the Baron says we should stay back. He's in a Blood fury. They both were. They would have killed each other and anyone that got in their way if these three hadn't got here in time."

"He's hurt?"

"They're dangerous when they're hurt, Mason. We need to be careful—"

"He won't hurt me," Mason said with conviction. He tried to stand, but he couldn't get his legs to obey. Amelia tried to get him to stay where he was, but he shook her off and started to crawl.

The three other haemophiles were easing Soroka to his feet. Their faces were all blank and dangerous. Soroka's seethed with fury. His lips were drawn back from blood-stained teeth. His eyes were deep, dark wells in his bloodied face. He was muttering something over and over through his clenched teeth, but Mason couldn't make out the words and didn't care about anything except making it to the kitchen.

His stomach lurched to see the dark red trail that stained the carpet under his hands. It went all the way to the kitchen door. He followed it and pushed open the door.

The Blood trail continued over the tiled floor. Cai was slumped against the stove. His knees were drawn up, and he hung his head. His matted hair hid his face. He was breathing slowly and hard. His hands were clenched into fists. Blood dropped from his split palms onto the floor.

"Cai?"

Cai shivered.

Mason dared to get a little closer. He said his name again. Cai took a deep, rattling breath. Then he raised his head.

There was a deep scratch over one eye. His lips were split. There were bite marks on his neck and face, but he was smiling.

"Mason."

Mason crawled over to him and took his face in his hands. "Thank God."

Cai unclenched his fists and threaded his hands into Mason's hair. "It's over."

Chapter Fourteen

Mason was aware of pain held behind a fuzzy barrier. He could hear beeping, distant voices and the air smelled clinical.

Opening his eyes almost took more strength than he had, but he managed it. The ceiling tiles slowly came into focus. He was on stiff, unfamiliar sheets and the roughness of bandages was around his chest, arms, legs.

His head pounded, but when he tried to lift an arm to rub it, he couldn't.

"Try not to move."

Mason rolled his head on the hard pillow. Cai sat next to his bed. He was in a T-shirt and jeans. His hair was perfect. His skin was unblemished. He was smiling.

The sight filled Mason with warmth. He tried to sit and winced, groaning.

"Here," Cai said and pressed a control on Mason's bed. The head of the bed tilted until Mason was upright. The room was dim, but he could see it was filled with flowers and cards. He blinked groggily around them all.

Cai followed his gaze. "You're a popular guy."

Mason tried to move again and winced. "What happened?" His voice was like sandpaper in his throat.

"You have a concussion, a dislocated knee, broken ribs and a smashed clavicle," Cai said, offering him a plastic cup with a straw. "They had to operate to set your collarbone, but it all went well. They're gonna keep you in here for a few days, but then you should be able to go home."

Mason sipped at the water until his throat unstuck. "That's not what I meant."

Cai lowered the cup. His face grew serious. "Soroka has confessed to everything. He hoped it would trigger the revolution. But instead, it unified everyone." His smile returned, though it was thinner than before. "He's going to be sentenced to a hundred years' incarceration in a specialist holding facility. Magnusson and Novák are working with the International Assembly for Haemophile Affairs to make sure it happens." He took Mason's hand. "We did it, Mason. We got him."

Mason's heart pounded, but his joy was threaded through with despair. "What about Vickers?"

Cai's face fell. "She's been arrested. But Fletcher doubts she'll be charged."

Mason closed his eyes, fighting tears.

"She needs support," Cai said. "Not punishment."

Mason blinked at the ceiling until his vision cleared. "A lifetime of manipulation. How does anyone get over that?"

Cai was quiet for a while. "I think they're hoping she'll agree to see her parents again. They think that might help."

Mason looked at him. Old pain dulled his eyes.

"None of this was your fault. You know that, don't you?"

Cai looked at their joined hands. "He wanted me, Mason. That's why he took Cara. It was all a trap. For me. He wanted someone on the inside of the police force. If I'd just done what he asked—"

"Then Vickers...Cara would be dead. And you too, probably. He'd've got rid of you as soon as he realized you would never be part of something like this."

"But I *was* a part of it, Mason," he whispered. "I did everything he wanted. I helped the police hunt haemophiles that had attacked people...and vice versa. All those crimes were reported. They fed the rumor machine. Then we released the information about the hate groups to the public. That was my idea. And, through Cara, we kept him informed of the investigation every step of the way."

"First, none of that was just you," Mason said firmly. "And second...all that? That's just being a good cop. It's not your fault some megalomaniacal psychopath with some weird psychic link to you was able to take advantage of that situation."

Cai's face brightened a little. "The police commissioner said the same thing. But it means a lot more coming from you."

Mason smiled, not caring that it made his head pound more. He looked at their joined hands and smiled wider. "How did you know? About the link? Between Kelly, Damon and Cara." Mason lifted his eyes. "In all our checks, none of that ever came up."

"Because they're hundreds of years removed. You had to go back generations to even guess at it."

"So how did you know?"

"I...I didn't." He looked awkward. "I sorta just...guessed."

Mason stared at him. "You *guessed*? Vickers aiming a gun at you, and you *guessed*?"

"I was buying time." Cai shrugged. "Or I thought I was." He looked uncomfortable. "I think I know a lot more about Soroka than I realize. A lot more than I want to know just on instinct." He looked thoughtful. "You helped me trust those instincts."

"I think it probably saved our lives."

"You'd guessed it, too. Days ago."

Mason frowned. "I did?"

"You're the one that pointed out the Irish connection. Kelly. Damon. Cara. You have instincts, too. Good ones."

Mason frowned at the ceiling. "Imagine doing that to your own family."

Cai was quiet for a long time. "He told himself he was serving some higher purpose. But in the end, we're all just at the mercy of our emotions."

"That doesn't have to be a bad thing," Mason said. He lifted Cai's hand to his lips and kissed the knuckles. "I do love you, you know."

Cai beamed. He leaned in and kissed his mouth. "I do know." He stayed there, his face pressed to Mason's, then sighed against his cheek.

"What is it?"

Cai drew something from his pocket. Mason took it and opened it. "A warrant card?"

"I'm officially employed by the Met again. They're making an announcement next week."

"And a promotion, too?"

Cai smiled. "Detective Inspector."

Mason looked at the warrant card with conflicting emotions competing in his chest. "You deserve it, Cai." Mason raised his eyes. Cai's face was tight. His smile was gone. "This means you're going back, doesn't it?"

"I have to."

"You don't," Mason ventured, keeping his voice level with an effort. "You really don't."

"I have to go back to my commune, Mason. I've still got a long road ahead of me."

"You're not dangerous," Mason said desperately. "You would never hurt anyone without reason. Doesn't all this just show you that?"

"I lost control last night. When Soroka threw me out of that window something…something just snapped in me. I had no control. I knew he was going to kill you. This…fire just exploded in me, like a match to gunpowder. I *am* dangerous, Mason."

"You *took* control," Mason argued. "You fought. You didn't hurt anyone."

"But I could have…so easily."

Mason's throat threatened to close. "I thought we'd figured this out."

Cai smiled again. It was a sad smile, and his gaze was heavy with mingled joy and sadness. "You helped me to let it go," he whispered, "for a while. You helped me with that struggle, Mason. But I'm still figuring out who I am. *What* I am."

"So stay with me. We'll figure it out together."

Cai kissed him, long, slow and tender. Mason held his head close, not wanting the kiss to end, dreading what would happen when it did.

Cai pulled away. He put his hand on Mason's face. "You helped me not be scared to feel things the way I feel them now. You helped me feel passion without fear. And love." His expression clouded. "But I don't know how any of that works when you're facing an existence of hundreds of years. You don't, either."

"So we do what Tom and Darragh said. We focus on now."

"I want to, Mason. God, I want to." His face twisted. "But I think it would be cruel to you. And I've said, the one thing I could never do is hurt you."

"Why are you so fucking scared of that?" Mason snapped, trying to stop his voice from shaking and failing. "I'm not gonna fall to pieces when things get difficult. And I'm not gonna snap if you get a little rough."

Cai's face didn't change. He stroked Mason's hair back from his face. "There's no negotiation here," he whispered. "Forever is too long a time to live with the guilt of causing you pain."

"*This* is hurting me. Right now. You leaving. *This* is hurting me."

Cai's eyes clouded. "For a short time. Just for a short time, Mason. You'll be better off in the long run. Believe me."

"I've never wanted another man before," Mason's voice rasped. "I've definitely never loved one. But man or woman, human or haemophile, I've never felt about anyone the way I feel about you. I can't ever be better off without it."

"I'm sorry."

Mason wanted to grab him, even if it pulled his stitches, even if it re-cracked his collarbone. He wanted to take hold of Cai and never let go. But Cai stood, and

Mason didn't move. He didn't even breathe. He watched him leave the room without so much as lifting a finger.

Then he was alone. Alone with the beeping machines and the disinfectant stink. Alone with the cold, dark depths of the night all around him and unable to feel anything but the stiff hospital sheets and the drug-dulled pain in his limbs.

* * * *

Days crawled by. Mason was sent home. He didn't recognize the place. It wasn't just the new windows and carpet. He didn't recognize himself in it. He couldn't remember what it had been like to live there before, alone, and that be normal.

He went to bed. He pulled the covers over his head. He willed oblivion to take him.

He got up to pee and eat then he returned to the darkness under the covers. He lost track of days and nights. He didn't care. Sunset didn't mean anything anymore.

When someone rang the doorbell an unknowable amount of time later, he fully intended to ignore it. But then they rang again…then a third time.

It took an ungodly amount of time to get down the stairs. He cursed every step of the way, his entire body protesting at the movement.

Amelia stood on the doorstep. She looked far too good in a navy pants suit and mahogany silk blouse that matched her eyes. The sight clashed with his mood so much he scowled. The bright sunshine brought out the natural highlights in her hair, but her expression was anything but sunny.

"Wow, Mason. You look like shit."

"Thanks, boss."

"Can I come in?"

He shrugged, then limped back into the living room. He lowered himself gingerly onto the new sofa. It took him a second to try to get comfy in its unfamiliar angles. Amelia shut the door behind her.

"Unusual weather for October," she said, taking a seat in the chair opposite. "Never known it to be so bright this time of year."

"Is there something you need?"

Amelia sighed. "Mason, I'm sorry about Cai."

"I don't want to talk about it."

She paused, looking him over then nodded. "Understood. So, how are you feeling?"

"Like Superman beat me up, and they won't give me any more pain meds."

Amelia grimaced. "Fun."

"Yeah."

"HR says you can come back to desk duties next week, though, if you want. That's good news, right?"

Mason didn't answer.

Amelia looked around at the new furniture and TV. "Glad insurance got you sorted, anyway. How's the couch? I had to choose it for you. I wasn't sure what sort of thing you'd like."

"Is that why you're here? To ask about my sofa?"

"No. I'm sorry. You know I've never been very good at the touchy-feely thing."

Mason gave a grudging smile. "I think that's why we get on so well."

That won a small smile back. "I genuinely did come to see how you are," she said. "And to see if you've been following the news?"

"A little," he said.

"New legislation allowing haemophiles to be legally employed? Open forums established to discuss the improvement of inter-species relationships? Discussions on abolishing compulsory haemophile registration?" She spread her hands. "This is all good stuff, Mason. Conflict is down. Protests are down. Things are moving forward. Everything's better."

Mason picked at a loose thread on the new, horrible sofa rather than answering.

"I've also had a word with the Chief Constable," Amelia continued. "And he agrees with me." Mason raised his head. "How does Detective Chief Inspector Walker sound to you?"

Mason blinked. "Seriously?"

"You've earned this, Mason. You handled a delicate situation with finesse, and you got to the truth before anyone else was killed."

"That was Cai," he whispered. "It was all Cai."

"Bullshit," Amelia said. "Don't get me wrong, Bracken's a great cop. But he could barely function in our world when he first arrived, barely understood how to translate what he knew into anything we could use. You did all that. And you guided him on the best way to handle things. You were an incredible team. And you both deserve these promotions."

Mason rubbed his aching head. "Thanks, boss. I appreciate it, I really do. Can I think about it?"

A pause. "Of course," Amelia said and stood. "But really think about it, Mason. We'll be working closer with haemophiles in the future. We're arranging more training on behavior analysis, forensics, the works. We could really do with someone like you to help bridge the gap."

"Just because I slept with one haemophile doesn't mean I'm an expert," he muttered.

Amelia sighed and sat next to him. She put her hand on his knee. The contact was surprisingly comforting. "You *saw* him. Understood him. Even when he couldn't do that himself." She patted his knee and moved to the door. "I'd say that makes you more than an expert."

"I'll think about it, Amelia. I promise."

She didn't reply. She was looking at a silver envelope on the coffee table. She raised her eyes. "You know you should go."

Mason stared at the new carpet, trying not to remember the old one, soaked with blood and peppered with glass shards.

"Mason, you're a huge part of why that wedding is able to happen at all."

"They invited Cai."

"So?"

Mason hesitated. "I'm not sure I'm ready."

"If it helps, last I heard, he hadn't RSVPed."

The cool hollow in his chest solidified into something harder.

Amelia frowned at him. "So that's not good news either?"

"I don't know."

Amelia sighed. "No one's ever ready for this sort of thing, Mason. But you do it anyway."

"I've had my fill of giving everything I am for other people."

"I hate to break it to you, Mason, but that's who you are." Amelia squeezed his shoulder. "But fine. Don't do this for them. Do it for yourself. Come and see what you helped become a reality."

"Darragh Kelly and Honor Ford-Byerson. They're the ones that made this possible. And they're dead." He raised his head. "Was it worth that?"

"How do you know if you don't come and see for yourself?"

He closed his eyes and nodded. "I'll think about it."

"You're still in shock, Mason," she said gently. "I promise things will get better. And I'm here for you until they do."

Mason dredged a smile from somewhere. "Thanks, Amelia."

"Hey, that's what boss-friend-exes are for, right?"

He blinked at her in surprise. "I'm still all those things, aren't I?"

He smiled. "You are."

Her face changed. There was a flash of something vulnerable and very beautiful in her eyes. Then she blinked and it was gone. "Good," she said, patting his arm. She moved again for the door. "Remember... You don't have to come back to work if you don't want to. Technically, you're signed off for at least another fortnight."

"I know," he muttered.

She considered him a moment longer. "Look after yourself, Mason. I'm sending some food over tonight. Make sure you answer the door this time, okay?"

She left. He sat in silence. He picked up the envelope and turned it over in his hands. He made himself open it.

You are cordially invited to celebrate the marriage of
Baron Emory Von Magnusson and Jesse Alexander Truelove
31st October
Fountains Abbey, Ripon, North Yorkshire.
Sunset-till-Sunrise.

He stared at the bold, looping script for a long time before folding the card, putting it back in the envelope and throwing it into the corner with his unopened junk mail.

* * * *

Mason thought he'd prepared himself for the sight of Vickers' empty desk. But seeing everything cleared away deepened the pit in his stomach.

He was aware of everyone watching him as he limped to his office. He'd refused to bring his cane and was regretting it. He lowered himself into his chair with a grimace. His mood slumped further when he saw the pile of files in his tray and the unread emails in his inbox. He spent a fruitless hour trying to decide where to start then got up and left again.

He'd visited Foss Park Residential Hospital before to interview suspects and victims alike. He'd never been to see someone he knew. The bright corridors seemed to echo more than usual. The strip lighting and hospital smell made his healing body wretch.

By the time he was shown into Vickers' room, he was feeling like he'd aged a decade.

Vickers' bright hair was disheveled and spiky. There were shadows under her eyes. Her white hospital scrubs made her look even smaller than her five-nothing frame. She sat at the plastic table with her shoulders hunched in a way he'd never seen her do before. But her jaw was set, and she met his gaze unflinchingly.

"Here to tear me a new one, boss?"

Mason drew out his plastic chair with a horrible scraping sound. "You think that little of me?"

"I wish you would. I'd know how to handle that. All this bloody sympathy and understanding... I'm not a bloody victim, and I don't need people to suddenly stop taking me seriously."

"I'll always take you seriously..." He stopped himself from saying her name. "What do you want me to call you?"

Her expression tightened. "Cheers for asking, sir, but I'm Phoebe. Vickers. Cara Sullivan has been dead for years."

Mason shifted in the hard chair, taking a moment to choose his words carefully. "They said you don't want to see your parents?"

"What did I just say?"

"Okay. I'm sorry. Just the Phoebe Vickers I know never shies away from a challenge, especially if it's the right thing to do."

"It's not the right thing for me."

"Maybe not. But whoever you are now, Vickers...they lost their little girl. Even if you don't feel you *are* that girl anymore, you could help them understand that. It might ease their pain."

"Their pain isn't my problem."

Mason ran his finger over the tabletop. "You've mentioned your grandma in the past. And your mum. Her phrase about good food and bad problems?" He looked at her. "I don't think you were faking caring about those memories."

"You're going to that wedding, then?" she demanded after a heavy silence. Mason held himself very still. Vickers snorted. "See? Just because you believe in something doesn't make it easy to show up for it."

"No," he said quietly. "No, it doesn't. But you do it anyway. Right?"

She scowled at the wall for a long time. Then she leaned over. "You know I don't believe everything he believed, right?" Her face was intense. "I know Soroka was too far out there. Way, way too far." Her face creased. "But it was the only way, Mason. This was something that couldn't be solved with a burrito and some headspace. A big problem needed a big fucking solution. And he was gonna *fix* it. He was gonna stop people from getting hurt. He *said* so."

Mason flinched inwardly but made sure nothing showed on his face. "I know you believed it, believed it so much you were going to kill me and Cai to make it happen."

Her eyes shone with unshed tears. But when she spoke, her voice was calm and level. "It was the only way."

"It wasn't," he said softly. "Things are better — and are going to keep getting better. And no one had to die for that."

"But they did, didn't they? Kelly…and Honor. Those deaths made people pay attention. It made people *make* things better. Nothing else would have done."

Mason didn't know how to answer that. The sneaking suspicion she was right closed his throat.

"I wish he hadn't killed Alonso, though," she said, almost too quietly to hear. "Wasn't his fault he was assigned to Damon. I would have stopped that. But he didn't tell me."

"Dragomir Soroka is an evil, manipulative abuser," Mason said firmly. "You are not to blame for what he made you do."

"He didn't *make* me do anything. No one ever *makes* me do anything."

Mason wanted to help her understand that that was exactly what Soroka had done. That the appearance of her choice in all these things was an illusion, one he'd created in order to control her. But he glanced at the orderly in the corner of the room. He gave Mason a tiny shake of his head. Mason swallowed his words and took Vickers' small hand in his own.

"You know you can call me, right? If you need anything. Anything at all."

A single tear ran down her cheek. "What happened to Heron?"

Mason took a breath. "It took a long time, but they stabilized him."

Her eyes widened. "He's alive?" Mason nodded. "Is he…human or…what is he?"

"He's a haemophile," he said softly. "Magnusson said the only way to save him was to…finish the process. So they did."

Vickers frowned. "Who did? The Baron?"

"I'm not sure. That was all over my head. Between the Baron and Ivor Novák and the like."

Vickers stared at him. "So Damon is a haemophile now. He became what he despised."

"I don't think he fully understood what was happening to him," Mason said softly. "Soroka needed a human to help operate the daylight flood defenses around his bunker. He needed a human to shoot and kill Kelly and Honor." Mason winced. "And Alonso. He wanted to point the finger at a human being. Damon was vulnerable to manipulation. He told us he was using Soroka. He was too far gone to realize it was the other way around."

"Are we really related? To Kelly, too?"

Mason nodded. "I went and looked it up. It's all very distant, but yes. You're all descended from Soroka's family, if you look far enough back."

She shook her head. "I would never have guessed, not in a million years."

"You are what you allow yourself to be," Mason said softly. "That's who you are. Not what other people say you are."

She gave him a grateful look.

"I meant it, you know. If you need anything..."

"I don't need anything, sir, except..."

"Tell me."

She took a deep breath and wiped her eyes. "Go to that wedding."

"That's what you want?"

She nodded. "Go. See all those people. And those haemophiles. Including Bracken. All of them together, celebrating goodness and love. I need to know if that wedding goes well. Then I'll know it wasn't for nothing."

Mason handled his conflicting responses carefully, not sure which one was the best — or the most honest.

"Will you think about meeting the Sullivans? When you're ready, I mean," he added, seeing her face change. "Not a moment before. But when you feel ready, think about it. For me."

"Do you still love Bracken?"

The opening in Mason's insides yawned wide again. "Yes."

"Think about that," she said. "And I'll think about this. Deal?"

He studied her pale face for a long time. "Even now you've got my back."

"Always, sir," she said, with a weak smile. "Always."

Chapter Fifteen

Mason stared at himself in the mirror. The suit was new, a deep twilight gray that complemented his skin. Amelia had picked out the amber tie to bring out his eyes. He'd gone to the expensive barber in the city center at her insistence, too. His cheeks were still hollow, and his eyes still retained the heaviness they'd acquired ever since Cai had walked out of his life, but he was regaining muscle mass and his sleeping pattern had even started to settle over the last few nights. As he studied himself, he had to admit he looked and felt better than he had in weeks.

So why couldn't he walk out through the door?

The doorbell jerked him out of his reverie. He frowned and went downstairs, trying not to limp. He opened the door and blinked.

A limousine was pulled up at the curb. The driver stood by the passenger door.

"DI Walker?"

"I didn't order a car."

"It was ordered for you, sir," the driver replied and opened the door. Mason hovered in his doorway, unable to suppress the surge of hope when he caught a glimpse of someone inside—someone male, tall, in a smart suit.

The passenger opened the other door and got out. The man's chestnut curls were combed back from his face. His gaze was shadowed, but he was smiling a quiet smile.

"Evening, DI Walker."

"Mr. Addams." Mason hoped his disappointment didn't show on his face.

"Again...Tom."

Mason tried for a smile. "Tom. It's nice to see you. And, remember... Call me Mason."

"Mason," Tom replied, then gestured to the car. "Would you do me the honor of coming with me to the wedding? It would mean so much."

Mason hesitated a broken second longer, just long enough for Tom's pleasant expression to fall. But then he nodded and hobbled down the steps.

The inside of the limo smelled like new leather and Tom's woody cologne. The young man smiled at him as they fastened their seat belts and the car pulled away.

"I wasn't sure you'd come if I didn't come to get you."

Mason twisted his fingers together. "Neither was I."

Tom gave him a sympathetic look. "How are you doing?"

Mason shifted on the seat to straighten his bad leg. "Better. Thank you. But I should be asking you that."

"Also better. I think."

Mason bit the inside of his cheek. "If there's anything I can do—"

"You caught Darragh's killer. You and SO Bracken." He surprised Mason by covering his hand with his own. "Thank you."

Mason nodded, swallowing to clear his throat. "You're welcome."

"I wanted to see you tonight, to say thank you." His voice was raspy with emotion. "So I thought I better actually come get you, to make sure I had the chance to do it."

Mason managed a shaky smile.

Tom withdrew his hand. "I went to see him in the end, you know. Darragh."

Mason nodded. "I heard. How did it go?"

"It was amazing," he said softly. "When I went to see my gran, after she'd died of cancer, she didn't look...right. It was a dreadful experience. But Darragh..." He looked up at the ceiling. "I don't know if it's a haemophile thing or what. But he just looked like he was sleeping. He was so peaceful." He frowned. "The gunshot was horrid. But he still looked like himself." Tom's smile warmed. "I'm glad I saw him like that."

"I'm glad it helped," Mason said, knowing words were inadequate, but knowing they were still important.

"He donated his body, you know," Tom said, his tired-looking face taking on a glimmer of brightness. "So we can learn more." Tom sighed. "Always giving. Right until the end."

"He was a very fine man."

"He was. And so are you." Tom pulled a sympathetic face. "Jesse told me about you and Bracken, which is why I know coming tonight might have been hard for you. But thank you for going through with it. It's important to me, to everyone."

Mason looked out of the window as they began passing trees and dark fields.

"Do you know if he's coming? SO Bracken?"

He watched Tom's face in the reflection but didn't let himself look around in case his face betrayed his own churning emotions.

"He never RSVPed to the invite," Tom replied. "I know his career is taking off in a big way. But I hope he does come, for all the same reasons I wanted you to be there. But, honestly, I don't know."

Mason nodded, closing his eyes for a moment until he was sure he could control his expression then turned to give Tom a reassuring smile. He was rewarded with one in return.

Mason couldn't quite believe it when the limo pulled into the Fountains Abbey car park. Fairy lights had been woven through the trees and fences. Burning torches lit the path up to the ruins. The abbey shell was floodlit from below, making it glow like gold. The place was crowded and raucous with talking and laughter. The torchlight glinted on jewelry, gowns and fine suits worn by a mix of humans and haemophiles alike. Mason stared around as he climbed out of the car, shivering in the crisp, autumn air. He'd never seen so many haemophiles in one place before. They were all sizes and shapes, but all had long limbs, glowing eyes, skin so smooth it appeared painted. Photographers lined the verges, and the flashes flooded the night with light, each flash glinting off sharp-toothed smiles and eyes that shone like jewels.

"Quite something, huh?" Tom whispered.

"How did Magnusson swing all this?"

"Emory has some powerful connections," Tom said, his smile turning slightly shy. "And Jesse's fond of the abbey, which I like to think I had a hand in." His smile twitched. "I brought him on a date here, actually. But we soon realized we weren't meant for each other, not the way him and Emory are. Either way, they both agreed, eventually, tonight should be a real occasion."

"No protestors," Mason said, scanning on all sides, a tension he hadn't even realized he'd had dissolving.

"So far so good. Shall we?"

Mason nodded and followed Tom to the gate. The sound of music reached him on the soft night breeze. The clouds parted and a cool, white moon shone, burnishing the surrounding grass and naked trees to silver.

A canopy had been erected over the ruined abbey's interior, and a wooden dance floor had been laid over the grass. The walls were draped in twinkling lights, and there were candles on every table. Instead of flowers, there were wreathes of autumn leaves and pumpkins carved with vines and pinecones and animals. The color scheme was gold and walnut and burnished orange. Fall woodland colors.

Serving staff drifted among the guests with trays of champagne. All the guests, human and otherwise, were sipping from glasses, smiling, talking. Faces were lit in the soft lighting but also seemed to glow from within with happiness and relaxation. There were even some children chasing each other, blowing bubbles from the little bubble wands scattered on all the tables.

Mason recognized Dimity Hawthorn, though she was bigger now, in a powder blue gown, clapping and chasing the bubbles being blown by a young, dark-haired boy that looked so much like Jesse Truelove that Mason knew he must be a relative.

The children chittered and pranced with joy. Watchful adults smiled and looked on. The music provided a comforting backdrop, like the velvet curtains that draped the stonework all around. It was like walking into a dream.

But Mason couldn't help scanning the faces of everyone in sight or stop the slump of disappointment when Cai was not among them.

Tom put his hand on his elbow. "I'm sorry."

Mason forced a smile. "It's fine," he said and nodded to the bar. "Shall we?"

Tom turned to lead the way but paused.

Baron Emory Von Magnusson was making his way over. He looked stunning in his charcoal suit and navy tie. The blue rose in his buttonhole was the same deep, ocean shade as his eyes. He smiled as he approached, and Tom's expression brightened, though Mason, remembering how terrifying the haemophile had looked when he was subduing Soroka, felt a stab of wariness.

"Tom," Magnusson said, his voice deep and gentle, "could you give us a moment?"

"Of course," Tom said, giving Mason a nod. "I'll be at the bar."

Mason was left with the Baron, feeling an intensity coming off him like heat from a furnace.

"Congratulations," he made himself say. "The place looks amazing."

"Thank you," Magnusson said. "We really wanted this to be special. It's not just the most important day of my life. It's important for a lot of people."

"You're right," Mason said awkwardly. "There is a lot riding on today."

"There is. And I'm so glad you were able to come, Detective Inspector. The fact that this is happening at all is down to you."

"Not just me."

"Everyone who helped make this happen is forever in my favor. If you ever need anything from me, you need only ask."

"I think all I need from you, Baron, is an assurance that Soroka, or anyone like him, will never be able to do anything like this again."

"You have my word on that."

"It was you, wasn't it?" Mason asked quietly. "The reason he did all this around here, around York. Framing Emerald. Enlisting Damon and the others to concentrate their activity in this area."

Mason couldn't tell if the look in the Baron's eyes had changed or if it was just the low light.

"Yes," he said, eventually. "It was my fault."

"That's not what I said."

"Nevertheless." He gazed at the ruins around them. "I was born here many lifetimes ago. This is where my human life was taken from me and where everything I once loved was destroyed." He straightened his cuffs without making eye contact. "Soroka knew me, then. He knew Lucien, too. He's made it his business, his entire haemophile existence, to keep tabs on us all. On what we did. Where we hunted. Who we loved." His smile didn't reach his eyes. "He knew I was connected to this land. He probably knew I'd return even before I did, that I'd want to raise my family here."

He stepped closer and lowered his voice. "I was appealing for closer links with humankind and better ways to integrate. He wanted something bigger. More final. And he wanted our kind in charge."

"I think he was jealous," Mason said in a low voice. "I think he looked at what you were doing, how close you were to your people, and he looked at how far removed he was from his own." Mason tore his eyes off the Baron to scan the room. "I've read that haemophiles need connection to something, or someone, to stay present, so the years don't become too much." He shook his head. "Feels to me like Soroka would have benefited from following your example instead of condemning it."

He sensed Magnusson's eyes on him. He lifted his own.

"You're an extraordinary man, DI Walker. To demonstrate so much understanding, even of someone so far removed from yourself."

"It's sort of my job."

"It's more than that." Magnusson looked away and heaved a deep sigh. "It's a terrible thing, knowing Soroka used my attempts to make the world better as a chance to destroy it." His eyes clearly landed on Dimity as she chased another child toward the buffet. "It's even more terrible knowing that even if I had the chance over again, I would do everything the same." He raised his head, smiling a smile that, this time, reached his eyes. "Though I hope in that reality, I would have made sure Darragh Kelly lived to see the triumph of his work."

Mason searched out Tom at the bar. He was staring at a glass of champagne with a distant expression.

"He's going to be missed."

"He is," Magnusson said, following Masons' gaze. "By all of us." Mason jumped when Magnusson put a hand on his shoulder. "We will take care of Tom. Don't take on his pain along with your own."

Mason blinked at him.

"If you take anything away from this, Detective Inspector, make sure it's the strength to fight for what you want. Trust me. It's worth it."

Magnusson was gazing over Mason's shoulder. Mason turned. Jesse Truelove stood in the curtained entranceway. He was in a white suit, fitted snugly to his slime frame, and wearing a white tie. His unruly black hair had been tamed, and he was smiling over at Magnusson with open joy in his eyes. Mason's heart clenched.

"Good luck, Baron." But Mason wasn't sure Magnusson even remembered he was there. Mason stepped aside. Magnusson went straight to his fiancé. Mason limped over to the bar, suddenly needing alcohol more than oxygen.

Tom smiled as he joined him and handed him a brimming champagne flute. He swallowed half the crisp, bubbly liquid in one go. When he looked around, Magnusson and Jesse had disappeared again. Mason finished his glass and reached for another, watching the people that continued to arrive.

"Quite the A-list," Mason remarked, as an actor from TV entered with a beautiful blonde on his arm, followed by an older man with thinning hair and a very expensive suit, talking animatedly to a thinner woman in an even more expensive gown. "He's a judge. And she's an MP."

"Like I said," Tom said, sipping his drink. "Connections. And everyone who comes is showing support. It's a good thing."

Mason went still as a tall haemophile stepped in through the curtains. He had long, pale hair, so light it caught the candlelight and made it look like it was on fire. He had high cheekbones and eyes of ice-blue so intense that Mason had a hard time meeting them, even from across the room. He had a man, a human man, on his arm—a man with dark hair and eyes and a dark suit. His expression was solemn, but whenever he looked at the haemophile, the love and contentment that softened his face was evident, even at this distance.

"Terje Kristensen and Lord Aviemore," Tom murmured. "They're getting married next week."

Mason unstuck his mouth with champagne, feeling it start to buzz in his veins. "I didn't realize..." He coughed. "He's... They're both..."

"I know," Tom said. "Hopelessly gorgeous. And hopelessly in love. Sickening, isn't it?" But there was no malice in Tom's tone or his wry smile.

Kristiansen inclined his head, and Tom raised his glass in reply. Then the pair were swallowed in the crowd.

Emerald Lomax was the next to step through the curtains. She was in an evergreen gown, and her glossy hair was piled high on her head. Diamonds winked in her ears. Her makeup was minimal and tasteful, but her expression was wary. She spotted Mason and froze. Mason was unsure what to make of her expression. Then she glanced behind her and strode directly over.

"I'll leave you to it," Tom said, touching his elbow. "Find me later if you need to."

Mason opened his mouth to stop Tom but then Emerald had reached him. Her eyes were hard.

"Detective Inspector."

"Lord Mayor," Mason replied, equally stiffly.

Her eyes flicked over him. "I heard you were hurt."

"Getting better. Thanks, ma'am."

She narrowed her eyes. "Don't you think we're past the formality, Mason?"

He raised his eyebrows. "Are we?"

"After you seeing me in my pajamas?" She folded her arms. "Oh, and having me arrested and questioned? Yes. I'd say we're past most things."

"That wasn't my idea," Mason said quietly.

"No," Emerald said after a hard pause. "No, I know it wasn't." She grabbed a glass of champagne off a passing waiter's tray and downed it in one go. "Still, we got there in the end. And it worked out for the best." She slid him a sideways look. "While you were going after me, exactly the way the Soroka wanted you to, he let his guard down. My people were looking into the earring that got planted, how someone might have got it. And into the reasons someone might have for framing me." She scanned the crowd. "Soroka's not as fucking clever as he thinks he is. My people found the trail, found the enquiries and freedom of information requests he made of my office." She gave him a triumphant look. "We put that together with what he fed to Ivor Novák and what the Met dug up, once it knew where to look." She grinned. "The case is tight. I think the Assembly might even lengthen his sentence."

"More than a century?" Mason asked in surprise.

"Forever…if I have anything to do with it." She grabbed a second glass but sipped this one more steadily. "I want you to remember this, Mason. Want you to remember how much I helped. And how I'm going to be so generous and forget the wrongful arrest thing."

Mason studied her. "Why?"

"No reason," she said, her gaze lingering on the entrance again. "Just remember. Promise?"

She walked away before he could reply.

Mason watched, puzzled, as more guests, human and haemophile, drifted in.

When Tyler Lomax stepped into the candlelight on the arm of a slender, dark-haired haemophile with eyes red as blood, all Mason could do was stare.

Tyler and Lucien had their heads bent together and were talking softly. Then they spotted Mason.

Being in the haemophile's line of sight was like being in the path of a solar flare. Then he turned to whisper into Tyler's ear. Tyler's eyes never left Mason's face. The haemophile kissed Tyler's cheek and moved away, not sparing Mason another glance.

Tyler hovered for an uncertain moment then turned his back and made for the buffet. Mason strolled over and intercepted him.

"Mr. Lomax. So good of you to join us. And Lucien, too."

"Gonna arrest us, Walker? Not sure the Baron and Truelove would appreciate you ruining their wedding."

"I thought you hated Jesse."

Tyler's expressive face shifted. "I don't hate him. But even if I did, Lucien loves Emory. I'm here for Lucien."

Mason scanned the milling crowds and spotted the red-eyed haemophile lurking in the shadows behind a branch of candles.

"Not a sociable one, Lucien?"

"Would you be?"

Mason didn't answer that.

"He knew this place before it was a ruin," Tyler said, staring round with a grudging wonder in his eyes. "Knows all sorts of stories about the monks that ran it. The power play. The politics. The love stories. I guess nothing ever changes, right?"

Mason wasn't sure how to respond. "Your sister's here."

"I know. She said she'd talk to you."

"She has," Mason considered his words then looked at Tyler. "You get a free pass, Tyler. Tonight. You and Lucien. For the sake of the occasion. No one wants any bad press tonight."

"It would kinda undo the whole thing," Tyler agreed. He hesitated and a flash of vulnerability showed in his eyes. "I didn't think we should come. But Lucien…" He swallowed. "He said we had to be here."

"I think he's right, though he's still a fugitive – and so are you. But I'm not exactly at the top of my game at the moment," he said, putting his hands in his pockets. "And, lucky for you, I seem to have forgotten my phone. So you get tonight. Just tonight. Deal?"

"We'll be gone before morning," Tyler replied, and raised his hand to catch a waiter's attention. "We have to be."

Mason studied his face. "How is it, Tyler?"

"How's what?"

"You know." Mason lowered his voice and looked over to Lucien again, silent in the shadows, watching them. "Being with him."

Tyler drank from his glass. "What exactly are you asking, Walker?"

Mason clenched his hands in his pockets, and his heart thudded against his chest. "You and Lucien. Jesse and Magnusson. Alex MacCarthy and Terje Kristiansen." He shook his head. "All of you…humans and haemophiles…men, too. In relationships." He frowned, fighting back emotions. "How do you make it work?"

Tyler was examining him with interest. "I told you. You just…do." He sipped his drink and smiled. "He's the best thing that ever happened to me, Walker. He makes me understand myself. He makes me challenge things. He helps me see the world differently and to not be afraid of being part of it or afraid of what I want."

Tyler's gaze slid over Mason's shoulder. Mason turned.

Cai stood in the archway. Mason's breath left his body. Cai wore a suit of midnight blue. His shirt was black. He wore no tie, and his collar was unbuttoned to expose his collarbone. The dark fabric against his pale skin was a contrast as striking as it was beautiful.

He'd cut his white-blonde hair short at the back and allowed the top to grow out. A couple of artful strands fell over his eyes. Their blueness shimmered in the candlelight like the ocean under the sun.

Mason wanted to move, to run to him — or to turn and run in the opposite direction. He wasn't sure. Either way, his body wouldn't obey. Then he realized Tyler was gone, and Cai was walking over to him.

Mason put his empty champagne glass down with a shaking hand, not trusting himself not to drop it.

"Mason." Cai's smile was tentative. "It's good to see you. You look great."

"Not as good as you do."

Cai's smile fell. He lifted a hand as if to touch the scar on Mason's neck but then dropped it. "How are you doing?"

Mason reached inside himself for strength. "What exactly are you asking me?"

Cai paused. "I've missed you."

Mason's blood swelled into his chest, making it hard to breathe. "You could have called. Sent a text if you missed me."

Cai looked around the room rather than meeting his eyes. "I couldn't let myself. I knew if I did…"

Mason waited but he didn't continue. He struggled between wanting to reach out and touch him and know he should really turn and walk away before anything else happened. Anything else to deepen the pain when Cai inevitably left again. But the indecision again paralyzed him.

"Can we talk?" Cai's voice was so low Mason barely made out the words.

"What's there to talk about?"

"Please?"

Mason rubbed his eyes but nodded. Cai smiled and gestured toward the back of the canopied room. Mason followed him, feeling more than ever like he was in a dream. The candle flames bobbed as they passed. The people parted to let them through without looking up. Cai held back the soft drapery to reveal an archway into darkness.

Mason stepped through.

There was grass under his feet. Stone walls rose on every side, open to the sky above. The only light came from the moon and stars shining in the deep, dark night overhead. There were stacks of tables to one side, just visible. Chairs on the other side. The air was cool and smelled of autumn leaves. The music and chatter of the wedding drifted through the curtain, but between them, silence hung.

"I meant it, Mason," Cai said. The moonlight played on his cheekbones, in his hair, on his straight, unsmiling mouth.

Mason's chest was so tight he could barely draw the breath to speak. "Meant what?"

"When I said I missed you." He took a step closer. Mason fought the urge to step back. "I don't let myself contact you because I know I'd cave. Nothing's changed, Mason. I'm still figuring things out. My job. Myself." He inhaled. "I can't bear the thought of hurting you. But being away from you just makes me less certain, not more."

Mason wanted to grab him, kiss him and never let go. But with a monumental effort, he held himself still. "What are you saying to me, Cai?"

"I'm saying I love you. And I need you."

The thread that restrained Mason's self-control snapped. He grabbed Cai by the arms and turned him, backing him against the stacked tables. He kissed him, running his tongue over his lips with a low and needy moan.

Cai whimpered and tilted his head, meeting Mason's searching tongue. He hopped onto the table, wrapped his arms and legs around Mason and drew him close.

Mason sighed against his mouth and ran his hands over Cai's fine suit jacket. He was hard already but just focused on the kiss, the moment, allowing himself to believe he was touching Cai again. That he was here. Really here. Wanting him.

He transferred his mouth from Cai's lips to his neck, kissing and nipping in the way he knew he liked until Cai was shivering and tightening his hold.

"Mason," he breathed, "careful."

"Don't hold back," Mason said, thrusting against him. "Give it to me. I can take it."

Cai gasped as Mason slid a hand into his shirt. "You're still healing."

Mason took Cai's chin in his fingers and tilted his face to look into his eyes.

"I want you, Cai. All of you. Who and what you are now. What you can do. What you want to do. I want all of it."

Cai breathed heavily into the silence. "I want to fuck you."

Mason shuddered, his blood heating and throbbing in his crotch. "Then do it."

Cai shook his head. "I'm too strong."

Mason dug his fingers into Cai's arms. "Let me feel it," he whispered, "that strength. I want to feel it. I want you to overpower me." Cai's lips parted. Mason grinned. "I love that you're stronger than me. It's exciting. I want you to do things to me. I want you to do *everything* to me."

"You've never done that," Cai protested, even though he was now rigid with need, and Mason could feel his swelling hardness against his thigh. "You don't even know if you'll like it."

Mason kissed him then whispered into his ear. "If it's you, I'll like it."

Cai grabbed him by the front of his suit and pulled him close. He groaned and kissed Mason so hard, like he might devour him. He crushed their crotches together and Mason shivered with pleasure at the friction but chafed at the clothing separating them. He shrugged his jacket off and Cai removed his own. He swiftly whipped off Mason's tie. They went at each other's buttons as they panted, kissed and thrust at each other.

Cai stood, yanked Mason's belt off and undid his trousers. Heat burned through him at the strength in Cai's movements, and he fumbled at Cai's clothing, undoing his trousers and sliding both his hands into his underwear.

Mason took hold of his hardening cock, and Cai growled and pushed Mason's trousers down. Mason stepped out of them, his erection springing free, without breaking their fevered kiss.

"Here." Cai fumbled a condom into Mason's hand. "Put this on me."

"Are you sure we need — ?"

"Safety first," Cai said, then took Mason's cock and started stroking him, slow but hard.

Mason muttered curses under his breath as he fumbled the packet open then rolled the smooth rubber onto Cai's stiff cock. Cai moaned into the kiss as Mason completed the movement then increased the firmness of his strokes.

Mason cried into Cai's mouth and fought back his climax. But Cai was pumping him faster.

"Come for me, Mason," he ordered, trailing his lips along his jaw to nip his earlobe.

"Cai," Mason whispered, tilting his head back and shivering when Cai ran his sharp teeth over the skin of his neck. "Jesus. Cai."

Cai followed the trail his teeth had burned in Mason's skin with his tongue and pumped Mason hard. Fire flared in Mason's balls. The world splintered into sparking light. The stars whirled overhead. He heard his own cry of ecstasy as if from a great distance and came, helplessly and plentifully, into Cai's hands.

"Fuck," he swore, his knees threatening to buckle.

"We're not done yet," Cai breathed in his ear.

Before Mason had really registered what was happening, Cai spun him around and pushed him against the table. Cai stepped close behind him, sliding an arm around his waist and bending him over.

"Are you sure you want this, Mason?" Cai said in his ear. His voice shook. Mason could feel his long, hard dick against the back of his thigh. He could feel the controlled power in Cai's body, the strength with which he held him still. He wouldn't have been able to break that hold, even if he'd wanted to. The thought sent an electric thrill through his flesh that had his sated cock twitching.

"I want it, Cai," he said, his voice husky.

Cai's breathing was heavy in his ear. Mason heard him slicking his hard cock with Mason's own cum.

"You have to promise me you'll say something if you want me to stop. You have to tell me."

"I don't want you to stop...ever."

"Promise me, Mason." The command in Cai's voice had Mason's blood pumping hard in his neck and pounding in his oversensitive cock.

"I promise," Mason said and pushed his ass back against his lover. "Fuck me, Cai. I want to know what it feels like to have you in me."

Cai made a low, needy sound that Mason would have gladly heard forever. "Wet your fingers," he said as he continued to stroke himself.

Mason obeyed, sucking and licking at the index and middle finger of his right hand.

"You know how you prepped me?" Cai said as his grip slid from Masons' arm to his hip. All Mason could do was nod. "You need to do that to yourself."

Mason shivered, part anticipation, part nervousness. "Could you do it?"

Cai pricked the skin of his hip teasingly with his long, sharp fingernail. "I would love to, Christ, I would." He kissed the back of Mason's neck. "But that's something I can never do."

Mason nodded stiffly and reached behind himself.

"Slowly," Cai ordered, and Mason felt him turn his head so he could watch, making Mason's arousal spike all over again. "Take your time. Find out if you like it."

Mason closed his eyes. He breathed the cold, October air deep into his burning lungs. Cai clutched on to his hip. Mason could feel him stroking himself as he watched Mason's hand.

He found his entrance and hesitated. His whole body was burning. The thought of Cai doing this to him, of being in him, was almost too intense to bear. But he hesitated before touching himself in this way. He'd never done it before. But Cai ghosted soft kisses over the back of his neck and shoulders, and he found he couldn't hold back.

He pushed a finger in. He tensed and clenched his eyes shut. Cai took a gentle hold of his wrist and guided him deeper. He shivered and made himself breathe. He reached. Lightning flashed behind his eyelids. He collapsed against the table, gasping. He swirled his finger again.

He swore, guttural and between clenched teeth.

"That's it, my love," Cai said in his ear. "Another. Move them around."

Mason didn't have the breath to answer. He just did as he was told. Again there was that initial resistance, but as he moved and stretched and rubbed, he relaxed. Then, when he reached, fireworks shot up his body. Stars danced in front of his eyes, and his hardening cock jumped.

"God," Cai breathed. His grip on Mason's hip had tightened, but Mason didn't care. There was too much pleasure for any pain to matter. He repeated the motion that made his whole body spasm a third time and was unable to stifle the strangled cry that left his throat.

Cai gripped his wrist. "Are you ready?"

"God, yes," Mason said, withdrew his hand and propped his weight on his elbows. He panted, staring ahead into the dark, feeling all at once excited and exposed.

Cai loosened his hold on Mason's hip, stroked up and down his thigh before stepping into position. He leaned over Mason so his toned belly brushed the small of Mason's back. Mason quivered.

"I would love to watch your face as we do this," Cai said as the blunt roundness of Cai's sheathed cock press against Mason's tight ring of muscle. "But this will be better for your first time."

"Cai," he started, but then the solid hardness was pushing slowly into him. The power of speech left him and all he could do was moan, sigh and pant as the sensation of being filled by Cai swelled and overwhelmed him.

"God, Mason," Cai panted in his ear when he was fully in. "Fuck. I don't think I can do this."

"You better fucking do it," Mason said, holding Cai's arm around his waist. "Finish what you started, Cai." He pushed back against the penetrating force, and Cai whimpered. "Fuck me…*now*. Show me how it's done."

Cai muttered something inaudible then he shifted his stance. He took hold of Mason's hips with both hands and drew his cock slowly out, sighing as he did so. Then he slid it back in, faster.

The fireworks again. Explosions in Mason's pelvis, behind his eyes, in his chest. He was probably making noises, possibly ones loud enough to be heard beyond the flimsy partition, but he couldn't hear them himself over the rushing in his ears.

Cai was in him. Cai was fucking him. Cai was making love to him. His Cai. They were so together that he didn't think they could ever be separated—and he never wanted them to be.

Cai increased his pace and leaned closer, reaching deeper. The stretch was burning but amazing. Cai's hold on his hips was excruciating but in an impossibly wonderful way. Every thrust had him slamming into the tabletop, but the strength, the power of Cai's body, of every penetration and how he unerringly hit that spot deep inside Mason that made the world flash and break apart was so incredible Mason wasn't sure he'd ever get enough of it.

Cai was saying something, over and over, but Mason could no longer understand words. His nails sliced into Mason's hips. He pushed in so far Mason was lifted onto his toes. Mason groaned from deep in his chest, and Cai grasped his pulsing cock.

He came a second time, so hard it was like time itself had stopped being a thing. All that existed was the wordless, formless wave of ecstasy that overtook every cell in his body and became everything.

He was panting like he'd run a marathon. He was propped on his elbows and his whole body was shaking. His cum was spattered over the table and his belly, glinting in the moonlight.

Cai was against his back, still buried in him, breathing hard. Every swell twitched Cai inside him and sent waves scorching through his insides.

It may have been two minutes or two hours later when Cai finally slid out of him.

"God in heaven, Mason." His voice was hoarse. "You have no idea…"

Mason turned, gingerly, his hips and muscles and shoulders all aching and strained. He grabbed Cai's open shirt and clung on, drawing him close.

"Is that how I made you feel?" he whispered, the words so heavy they hurt, his grip on Cai's shirt so tight his hands also hurt. "When I made love to you, was that how you felt?"

Cai's eyes burned with a low light, visible even in the shadows. "That…and more."

Mason kissed him. His muscles ached. His skin was bruised. His healing bones had been wrenched. But it was the best he'd ever felt.

Their sweat cooled, and the kiss slowed. Cai produced a handkerchief and cleaned them both off. They dressed, quietly, in the dark. Cai helped him fix his tie. He helped Cai fix his hair.

All was quiet beyond the curtain. The chatter had died down.

"We better get back. It must be starting," Cai said, but Mason took hold of his wrist.

"Cai."

Cai turned.

"You have to tell me what this means." Cai was silent. Mason held tighter. "I can't go back out there until I know whether this was you saying goodbye."

The length of time it took Cai to answer was so long Mason went cold. But Cai brushed his face so tenderly that all the fear melted away.

"I already said, Mason. I love you. And I need you."

Mason's heart lifted. "But what exactly does that mean?"

Cai was quiet again. When he spoke, his voice was low. "I thought I had to learn to live on my own. To figure out who I was. Then I realized you'd already shown me that. And I want to share the rest of the journey with you. Here. In your home."

Mason swallowed. "But what about your job? Your commune?"

Mason could see him smiling in the darkness. "They've offered me a job with the West Yorkshire Police. An even better one. I'd be based in Leeds."

Joy swelled in Mason but gave a twisted smile. "You didn't want to work with me?"

Cai chuckled. "They're starting a specialist unit there. Haemophile crime. They want me to head it up. Besides, being together and working together? Wouldn't that be too much of a good thing?"

"No such thing."

Cai smiled and kissed him. Mason's entire body lit like sunlight breaking through the clouds. There were still a million questions. Would they live together? How would that work? How would he cope only seeing his partner after sunset? Knowing they would never sleep in the same bed, never share a meal and would never grow old together?

But Mason broke the kiss, knowing, right now, none of that mattered.

"We'll make it work," he said, meaning it.

"We will." Cai squeezed his hands then straightened his tie. "We should go out there or people will start talking."

The sound of a string quartet striking up the wedding march made Cai look over his shoulder.

"Everyone's focused on the happy couple," Mason said, drawing him close again. "They won't be paying any attention to us."

"Well, perhaps they should." Cai stepped back and held out his hand. "I want to attend this wedding with my boyfriend. I want to dance with him in front of everyone, on the same dance floor as Emory and Jesse, as Lucien and Tyler."

Mason took his hand, but he didn't move, somehow reluctant to step into the light, still half-afraid the spell would break.

"The whole point of all of this is showing the world that love is everything. Right?"

Mason smiled. "Right," he said. He moved toward the curtain, his hand in Cai's.

They stepped back into the light together.

Epilogue

Cai lay in Mason's arms. Mason was asleep, his soft breathing brushing the back of Cai's neck. Every breath sent warmth rolling through him. He knew he'd have to leave soon, that the sun would be rising in a couple of hours. He needed to get back to his sleeping cell at Oswald House, at least for the day. He would get one ordered to be delivered to Mason's house the very next night so they wouldn't have to spend any more time apart.

He had been so happy when Mason had suggested it at the wedding. He'd already started planning a basement conversion, so the space under his house could be a real space for Cai, with furnishings, a TV, a workspace, everything. He said he'd never been interested in doing anything to his house before, but now he couldn't wait.

Cai had been so dizzily happy as they'd danced together that he'd not even replied to any of Mason's excited propositions. Even now as he lay in his lover's arms, the sweet burn of another lovemaking session fresh in the most intimate parts of his body, he wasn't sure anything could make him happier.

But he couldn't help but wonder what Mason would think when the sleeping cell actually arrived. Or when Cai insisted on a double-locking mechanism on the basement door—and refused to share the code.

He had to keep Mason safe. He could never live with himself if he hurt him. That hadn't changed. Just because Mason could take, and even enjoyed, some rough sex didn't mean Cai was willing to put him at risk of accidentally opening his sleeping cell a minute before it was safe to do so.

He shivered, suddenly cold, despite Mason's warm body at his back. Mason had said he wasn't afraid. But Cai spread his hands and looked at them, at the sharp nails, like claws, at the tendons he knew were stronger than steel cable. He remembered how he'd tackled Soroka to the ground. How his haemophile Blood had burned in his veins, how it had taken over, bent on eliminating the danger, whether Cai wanted to or not.

He'd told Mason he was struggling to hold onto Soroka. The reality of it was he was struggling not to rip his head from his body, was trying very hard not to dismember him right there on Mason's floor. Even through the Blood-fueled haze, he knew if Mason had seen that, seen what he was capable of, he'd never want to go near him again.

The fear chilled in his veins. He closed his eyes. It frightened him…even now.

But then Mason's words came back to him.

"Stay with me. We'll figure it out together."

He remembered the sincerity in Mason's face, the strength of the feeling in the words.

All of it was real. And Cai knew he was right. Had been right. All along.

He turned with a sigh of contentment and burrowed into Mason's sleeping embrace, savoring this wonderful, safe feeling that was so new and so precious and so strong.

Mason mumbled in his sleep and drew him closer. Cai smiled. There was some time until sunrise. He could stay here a little longer. He knew, now, that he could always return, that Mason would always help him to feel safe. And was strong enough to take Cai on.

Whatever future awaited ahead.

* * * *

Lucien lay in Tyler's arms. Tyler wasn't quite asleep. Lucien could tell by his pulse. But he soon would be.

Lucien marveled again at this novel sensation. Lying with a human as he drifted off to sleep, his touch still burning on his body. The smell of Tyler's heated, living skin and the memory of his hot, fevered words as they'd made love were still fresh in his mind.

Lucien ran a finger over Tyler's arm where it was draped over his belly, watching the tiny hairs stand up with a sort of a dazed fascination.

He'd been alive for so long, he thought he'd seen and felt it all. Knew it all. But Tyler taught him something new every day.

He sighed, enjoying the sensation of just breathing. The ship rocked gently. The sea was smooth. They were making good time. The chug of the engine was a distant hum beyond the steel walls of the cabin.

Lucien knew he'd have to move into his sleeping cell soon. They were sailing directly into the rising sun, and soon it would be too dangerous for him to be out.

He was swamped with a desperate longing to stay with Tyler, to not have to separate from him to spend the day in a sealed box. It wasn't something he'd ever remembered thinking about before. His human life was long gone. Not even a ghost of a memory remained. And his life and purpose as a haemophile had sustained him and made sense for hundreds of years.

If the price for this gift was sleeping in a box, so be it.

But meeting Tyler had made him consider things differently for the first time in centuries, made him think about something that was only for him.

Tyler had fallen asleep. Lucien allowed himself a smile. He didn't often smile. Didn't often feel the need. But that was something Tyler had changed as well.

Tyler had really enjoyed seeing his sister again, Lucien knew. And other humans. Even Emory and Jesse, despite the complex history between them. Seeing the animation in his lover's face as he'd drunk and laughed and danced with his friends had made Lucien feel shades of the same sorts of feelings, even if he'd hung back on the outskirts and just watched.

His smile fell. Was he right, taking Tyler away from all that again? True, if he'd stayed he'd've been arrested. He was still facing aiding-a-fugitive charges among a number of other ridiculous human constraints. Such things didn't matter to Lucien. He could always move on. Always escape. But Tyler couldn't. He was still bound by some of those human rules...and morals.

Lucien found he was pleased Tyler had prompted him to think about such things again. To consider them in the light of a human perspective. He didn't remember what it was like, to have to obey social norms. But being with Tyler helped him think about it. Helped bring him closer to modern times, modern people.

Emory had always told him it was important to stay in touch with the world. To stay connected. Stay present or go mad.

He'd never really understood or believed his ex-lover before.

Now he knew.

He kissed Tyler softly. Tyler twitched in his sleep but didn't wake. Lucien pulled himself from his arms and went over to his open sleeping cell. He looked inside the silky, padded interior then back at Tyler, lying peaceful and tousled on the bunk.

He'd started off resenting all the things Tyler had made him feel again. Now he was grateful he was actually still capable of feeling them.

Tyler wouldn't be around forever. Whether by choice or by death, one day they would part. Lucien had thought about it a lot and found he dreaded it, more than he'd dreaded anything else in his long, long life.

But every time he reminded himself that it would be worth it. To live one lifetime with Tyler would be better than never having met him, than never having the chance to really live again.

He watched Tyler stretch in his sleep and felt a wave of something that was still new, but deep and so intense it almost frightened him.

Lucien was in love. Different to any other time before. Different...and better.

And that was always going to be worth it.

* * * *

Emory lay in Jesse's arms. His husband was drifting, not quite asleep, still stubbornly trying to keep his beautiful, thick-lashed eyes open, even though the exhaustion of the day was catching up to him.

It had been a long, crazy road. First, their meeting, what felt like a lifetime ago, when Jesse had deliberately botched the break-in to Emory's home to ensure no one got hurt. To coming to work for him, to dedicate his skills and time to helping make Emory's home safe, both for himself and Dimity, their daughter.

There'd been the instant connection, whether Jesse had been wanting to admit it or not. Emory hadn't wanted to deny it, not even once. But he'd been down this road before. He knew where it led. And he wasn't sure, as much as he wanted it, whether it was fair to expect it of Jesse.

But once they'd taken the first step, Jesse had plunged in, feet-first, risking arrest and his safety for Emory and their family. Now, he was married to him, and he'd changed his surname to Magnusson. He was Dimity's dad, just as much as Emory was. They had been through hell together and come out the other side and, he hoped, had dragged the world into that better place with them.

Emory looked at the wedding band on Jesse's finger with a surge of joy unlike anything he'd ever known before. He was constantly thrilled and surprised by the depths of emotion his husband could conjure in him. Even now, as he lay, sprawled, naked on his back, the fading marks of the rope burns on his wrists evident from the sort of love play he enjoyed so much. The tattoos that covered his body, moving as he breathed, were tempting and fascinating. Emory knew what every single one tasted like, how the black ink tasted different to the red and the blue—and how delicious the blank, empty skin was between the designs.

Jesse was endlessly enthralled, endlessly passionate and endlessly patient. He was never phased by Emory's intensity and sometimes stubborn unwillingness to compromise on anything as far as the welfare of his family was concerned.

Emory had wanted the big wedding. He was the one who had wanted the press there, the one who had wanted it to happen on October thirty-first—not because of any ancient pagan rites, but because that was the first day marriage between a haemophile and a human became legal. He wanted to send a message. For Kelly. For everyone.

Jesse had wanted a small, private ceremony, just them and Dimity and his nephew, Oliver, with Tom and his brother Anton as witnesses. He said it was no one else's business. That it was their lives, and they weren't responsible for whether the world sorted itself out or not.

But Emory had been insistent. He loved Jesse. He loved their daughter. He wanted the world to know about their family and about how proud he was to be part of it. He wanted the voices of joy, inclusion and encouragement to be louder than those that railed against them, that judged them or who thought anyone had a right to be happier than anyone else.

Dragomir Soroka was going to prison for a long, long time. His enemy was old and strong and, like Lucien, more than capable of breaking out of any human prison.

But Emory had been working with the International Assembly for Haemophile Affairs to help strengthen the security of the specialist facility in Russia, the one that had held Terje Kristiansen's old Magister, Evgeniya Morak—the first haemophile that had tried to trigger a revolution against humans by haemophiles and lost her life, and took several others, in the process.

Soroka was *not* going to escape.

Emory hadn't told Jesse yet, but he'd agreed to see Soroka in prison. It had been his idea. Knowing him as Emory did, he thought he'd be able to reach him in a way no one else could. Emory was convinced Soroka would listen to him.

You often had more in common with an old enemy than an old friend.

And whatever his misguided ways of achieving it, Soroka's main aim was to bring about a change that would mean an end to judgment and violence. He just thought the only way was the hard way.

But Emory knew you reached humans with love. That's how they sided with you. That's how they became your allies. Your champions, even. That's how they came to believe in you.

As Jesse believed in him, from before they'd even met. From the day he'd brought Oliver to his Christmas light switch-on, to show his nephew that Emory was not a monster.

Emory didn't think he'd ever be able to show Jesse just how much that meant to him. But he was filled with joy at the thought of being able to try, every day, for the rest of Jesse's life.

Jesse mumbled and turned over, blinking his eyes open.

"Em?" he mumbled. "You okay?"

"Never better, my love," he whispered and kissed his husband, happy beyond words that their day was finally dawning.

Want to see more from this author? Here's a taster for you to enjoy!

Blood Winter
S. J. Coles

Excerpt

Sparks waterfalled to the concrete floor, spattered, guttered and died into nothing around my boots. The air was filled with the firework smell of welding and my face was sweaty and itching under my mask. The radio twittered away on the shelf but I hardly registered the newsreader's dull, professional catastrophizing. I rarely did. The real world didn't intrude here and that was just the way I liked it.

"You'll need to grind that back."

I straightened and accepted the mug Clem held out without replying. I knew it needed grinding. He knew I knew. I'd stopped being Clement Dalgleish's apprentice and become his partner more than a year before, but the old man hadn't changed much more than a pair of socks in all the time I'd known him.

I sipped the coffee, grimacing at the slightly oily taste, and checked over the rust repairs on the 1969 Morris Oxford, my sweat rapidly cooling in the chill air. When further commentary wasn't forthcoming, I looked up to see Clem staring at the radio, his heavy white brows drawn together

"What's wrong?"

"Nothing," he grumbled, glaring into his own mug. "Just this shit."

"The coffee?"

He grunted and jerked his head at the radio. I made myself focus on the flat, English voice.

"Whereas there has been no direct link established between the disappearance of what are now being called 'Blood dealers' and any registered haemophiles, anti-haemo protest groups are labeling them 'revenge kidnappings', executed in retaliation for the capture and abuse of haemophiles at human hands. Haemophile Blood-dealing is still a highly controversial topic, sparking heated debate on both sides with no satisfactory resolution in sight. The public is now demanding a review of the investigation into Shelly Morris' murder, which is still popularly believed to be an act of haemophile violence.

"Haemophile spokesperson Ivor Novák has assured the government that all haemophiles registered in the UK abide by their registration laws and would never take matters into their own hands, but the human public remains far from reassured."

I switched the channel. A jaunty pop tune rattled out of the tinny speaker. It set my teeth on edge, but the round lines of Clem's large frame eased. He ambled back to the open bonnet of the 1964 Austin Healey and bent into the cavity. I stared at the radio a moment longer, something unwelcome ghosting under my belly, then shook my head and strode across the workshop to turn the bar-heater on.

"Any idea what that'll do to the electric bill?" Clem grumbled from the depths of the Austin's engine.

"It'll be snowing before the end of the month," I replied, taking the air filer from the tool rack. "Personally, I'd struggle to work if my fingers dropped off."

"Wear gloves," he retorted, but he was staring into the Austin's engine and I knew he wasn't even aware he was arguing with me.

I started to file back the weld on the Morris, relieved that whatever had been unsettled in the air had gone.

"Alec. *Alec.*" Clem had to bark my name twice before I heard him over the grind of the filer.

"What now?"

Clem nodded toward the front door. A dark, heart-shaped face framed by black curls was pressed against the glass, frowning into the dim interior. She waved as I approached the door, a smile warming her face.

"We're closed."

"Very funny," came her muffled reply. "Let me in, will you? It's bloody perishing out here."

I unbolted and opened the door, shuddering in the gust of winter air that rushed in with her. "What are you doing here, Meg?"

"I'm on my way back to Glasgow," she said, smiling that wide, brilliant smile of hers. "Been up to Inverness for a meeting."

"You're a long way off the A9."

"So even social calls aren't allowed anymore?"

My gaze slid over her shoulder to where Clem stood chewing on something and watching our exchange with interest. I nodded to an interior door and led her through to the cluttered kitchen.

"Uh, drink?"

"I'd kill for a coffee."

I fired up the coffee machine. It rattled and shuddered as Meg shed her powder-blue coat and cashmere scarf.

"You're looking thin, Alec," she said. "Is everything okay?"

"Of course it is."

"You've not been ill? The damp in that old place—"

"Meg"—I cut her off—"I'm fine. Was there something you needed?"

She pressed her lips together, her sloe-black eyes full of concern. "It's just been a while. That's all."

"I've been busy," I said, pouring coffee into our least filthy mug.

She wrapped her hands around it but didn't drink. "So business is picking up?"

"It's steady."

"Well, that's good news." She raised the mug, sipped and her face twisted.

"Yeah, I know. It's all the Aviemore Co-op stocks. But it's strong."

She took another careful sip. "I'll need it if I'm gonna stay awake long enough to get home."

"How's everything with you?" I said, because all I could hear in the silence that followed was her waiting for me to ask.

Her smile broadened. "Good, thanks. Really good. I got the division leader position and we're expanding. I get to hire an assistant."

"That's great."

She narrowed her eyes. "You don't even remember me telling you about the division leader job, do you?"

I raised my eyebrows. "'Course I do. You mentioned it the last time you rang."

"Which was?"

"I don't know. A few weeks ago?"

She raised her eyebrows. "Try three months, Alec."

I fought a sigh. "I'm sorry. This place… It keeps me busy."

"It keeps you isolated. Well, that and your nonexistent broadband."

I clamped my mouth shut on the immediate reply. "Okay, Meg, you've checked in on me and I'm clearly alive. Is there anything else?"

She set the mug aside. "I just can't get my head around why you barely come down anymore. It's been forever since you and David—"

I scowled. "Meg—"

"Let me finish," she said, firmly. "It was painful, sure. He hurt you. I know that. But cutting yourself off from all human interaction isn't healthy."

"What about Clem?"

"He barely qualifies as human."

"And what if I've decided I don't like humans?"

She sighed. "Believe me... I know how much my brother can screw people up. But when I think of you out here..." She cast her eyes around the messy kitchen then out of the window to the rolling hillside and the gray sky hanging low over the black mountains.

I took another long moment to marshal my response. "I like it here."

"You never used to."

"It's different now."

She nodded, but I could tell it was more in acknowledgement than agreement. "So long as you're happy."

I schooled my face. "I'm happy."

"All right. I believe you. Just do me one favor?"

I eyed her warily. "What sort of favor?"

She flashed her smile again. "Get your best suit dry-cleaned. You're coming to a club opening with me at the end of the month."

I blinked at her. "I'm *what*?"

"A new nightclub. Lure. It's opening right in the middle of Glasgow, a super-exclusive, members-only deal. It's the Ogdell-Paiges' newest project. The likes of Angus Mackie and Mayor Frederick are going."

"Who?"

She tilted her chin. "Don't be obtuse. This is a big deal, Alec."

I pinched the bridge of my nose. "Don't you think we're a bit old for nightclubs?"

"Speak for yourself."

"We're the same age."

"Uh, excuse me. I'm a full six months and four days younger."

I sighed. "I don't know—"

"Seriously"—she cut me off—"some of the top legal firms in the country are sending people, not to mention the politicians and business executives going for the social kudos. And *I* was the one who got the invite. Me. Not Bryce, not Sofia, but *me*, Megan Carlisle from Nowhere, Newtonmore." Her face grew serious. "This is my chance to bring in some big-name clients of my own. It's important, Alec."

"Why do you need me?"

"For moral support. Because you know how to talk to these sorts of people. And, well"—she gave an awkward shrug—"because they want to meet you."

Heat rose to my face. "They *what*?"

She held up her hands. "Don't bite my head off, okay? Word got around that we were at primary school together. I met Olivia Ogdell-Paige at a conference and you came up in conversation…"

"The only reason anyone like that would want to meet me—"

She made an impatient gesture. "No one's going to make a move on Glenroe, Alec. We've already established that legally no one can, though you still haven't convinced me that it wouldn't be a bad thing."

I made an indignant noise.

"It's not about the estate," she said in a gentler voice. "They're just interested in you."

"I'm not interesting."

"You're coming with me, Alec," she said firmly. "I want you to spend time with people. Real people. And, well" — her eyes softened — "I miss you."

I chewed on that for a moment whilst glaring at the wall.

"Please?"

I let out a breath and nodded.

She beamed. "That's the spirit. Here." She produced a fountain pen and marked the *Autospares* calendar with a large X on the last Saturday of the month. "It's official. And no hotels. Stay with me. Come for the whole weekend. We'll make a proper thing of it. Okay?"

"Okay."

She screwed the lid back on her pen in a deliberate manner. "Try not to jump too high in excitement, Lord Aviemore. You'll pull a muscle."

I fetched her coat but paused before opening the workshop door.

"What is it?"

I took a breath. "Have you heard from David?"

A pause. "Why?"

"Have you?"

"Please don't put me in this position, Alec."

"I just want to know he's safe."

"Safe?"

I ran my hand through my hair. "I heard on the radio that dealers are going missing in London."

"*Blood* dealers. David was never into Blood. Was he?" she added, eyes widening slightly.

"No. But he was headed down a bad road."

"He's many things, but he's never been a dealer, Alec...of any sort."

"I know that," I said, hearing the lie.

She chewed on the inside of her cheek for a long moment, her dark eyes haunted. "He's fine," she eventually said, "as far as I know. But we don't talk much these days."

I nodded and opened the door. Meg strode across the workshop floor, her neat heels clicking on the concrete. She turned at the front door, eyed Clem warily then leaned in and said in a low voice, "Look after yourself, you hear?"

"I will," I said, trying for a smile of my own. She examined me for another long moment then kissed me on the cheek, briefly surrounding me with the delicate scents of cinnamon and coconut before returning to her sporty electric-blue Mazda. She waved again, then the car was zooming down the twisting lane, its roar gradually fading to nothing in the cold air.

"Sweet on you, that one is."

"What?"

"She likes you," Clem said. "Always has, by my reckoning."

I tried to figure out if there was anything more than the usual truculence behind Clem's words, but his face was as readable as bearded granite. I went back to smoothing down the body work on the Morris, refusing to think about what I'd gotten myself into.

Clem left when it started to get dark, repeating unnecessary reminders to lock up properly. I heard the cranky growl of his ancient Land Rover coughing to life, then the rumble as it drove away. I took a second to enjoy the utter silence that enveloped me — the silence that only ever came from being truly alone —

then locked the workshop and made for the path leading up the hillside.

I bent my head against the wind. It smelled like snow. The winter-brittle grass hissed against my overalls. I startled a deer in a patch of scrubby heather. It bounded up the path and was gone.

Glenroe was little more than a darker patch of gray against the slate-colored slope of mountain. The boarded windows watched me like dead eyes. I reached the overgrown track that passed for the driveway and spotted a wooden plank splintered on the weedy gravel. Craning my neck, I spotted where it had fallen from — one of the windows in the turret on the west wing — and cursed.

Mentally logging the job for another day, I followed the track through the sprawling bushes around the side of the house. I was shivering by the time I got the key into the side door. I shut it on the swirling wind and stood for a second in the enclosed quiet. The passage was dark and the silence complete. I couldn't even hear the scuff of rats in the walls. It was too cold even for vermin.

My footsteps echoed on the stone flags. I didn't look into the faces of the dead people who smiled at me from photo frames on the walls whilst I strode through the dust-shrouded rooms to the kitchen. I hurriedly shut the door on the rest of the house and flicked on the light, the strip bulb humming as it came to life. The rickety table was covered with engine parts. The counters were piled with mismatched crockery, books and old copies of *Classic Motor*. There was a three-year-old calendar on the wall that I'd kept because I'd liked the photo of Buachaille Etive Mor that they'd used for July. Hiking up that mountain with David during our good summer was still one of my fondest memories, though I rarely admitted it, even to myself. I lit the wood-burning stove, switched on the kettle then the radio, clicking the channel over from another report of the London disappearances. I went through to my bedroom next door—what had been some of the old staff quarters—to change whilst the stove warmed water for a shower.

The wind was hammering at the windows when I emerged. By the time I was dumping my dirty dinner plates into the sink, I'd almost managed to forget about Meg. Then I caught my reflection in the darkened window. No wonder the sight of me had concerned her. My cheeks were hollow, my blue eyes lackluster and dull, the skin under them smudged gray. I scratched at a week's worth of stubble and pushed back my over-long hair, scowled and turned away.

About the Author

S. J. Coles is a Romance writer originally from Shropshire, UK. She has been writing stories for as long as she has been able to read them. Her biggest passion is exploring narratives through character relationships.

She finds writing LGBT/paranormal romance provides many unique and fulfilling opportunities to explore many (often neglected or under-represented) aspects of human experience, expectation, emotion and sexuality.

Among her biggest influences are LGBT Romance authors K J Charles and Josh Lanyon and Vampire Chronicles author Anne Rice.

S. J. Coles loves to hear from readers. You can find her contact information, website details and author profile page at https://www.firstforromance.com/

PUBLISHING

Sign up for our newsletter and find out about all our romance book releases, eBook sales and promotions, sneak peeks and FREE romance books!